DEDICATION

This book would not have been possible without my husband – my partner in life and close collaborator in the writing of the *Krinar Chronicles*. His guidance in all aspects of plot development, scientific elements, and general editing has been invaluable.

I would also like to give special thanks to my friends T and L (you know who you are!) for being my beta readers and proofreaders. Your sharp eye for detail has been extremely helpful in the editing process.

PROLOGUE

Five Years Earlier

"Mr. President, they're all waiting for you."

The President of the United States of America looked up wearily and shut the folder lying on his desk. He had slept poorly for the past week, his mind occupied by the deteriorating situation in the Middle East and the continued weakness in the economy. While no president had it easy, it seemed like his term had been marked by one impossible task after another, and the daily stress was beginning to affect his health. He made a mental note to get himself checked out by the doctor later this week. The country didn't need a sick and exhausted president on top of all of its other woes.

Getting up, the President exited the Oval Office and headed toward the Situation Room. He had been briefed earlier that NASA had detected something unusual. He'd hoped that it might be nothing more than a stray satellite, but that didn't appear to be the case, given the urgency with which the National Security Advisor requested his presence.

Entering the room, he greeted his advisors and sat down, waiting to hear what necessitated this meeting.

The Secretary of Defense spoke first. "Mr. President, we have discovered something in Earth's orbit that doesn't belong there. We don't know what it is, but we have reason to believe that it may be a threat." He motioned toward the images displayed on one of the six flat screens lining the walls of the room. "As you can see, the object is large, bigger than any of our satellites, but it seems to have come out of nowhere. We didn't see anything launching from any point on the globe, and we haven't detected anything approaching Earth. It's as though the object simply appeared here a few hours ago."

The screen showed several pictures of a dark blur set against a dark, starry background.

"What does NASA think it could be?" the President asked calmly, trying to analyze the possibilities. If the Chinese had come up with some new satellite technology, they would have already known about it, and the Russian space program was no longer what it used to be. The presence of the object simply didn't make any sense.

"They don't know," the National Security Advisor said. "It doesn't look like anything they've ever seen before."

"NASA couldn't even venture an educated guess?"

"They know it's not any kind of an astronomical body."

So it had to be man-made. Puzzled, the President stared at the images, refusing to even contemplate the outlandish idea that had just occurred to him. Turning to the Advisor, he asked, "Have we reached out to the

Chinese? Do they know anything about this?"

The Advisor opened his mouth, about to reply, when there was a sudden flash of bright light. Momentarily blinded, the President blinked to clear his vision—and froze in shock.

In front of the screen that the President had just been looking at, there was now a man. Tall and muscular, he had black hair and dark eyes, and his olive skin contrasted with the white color of his outfit. He stood there calmly, relaxed, as though he had not just invaded the inner sanctum of the United States government.

The Secret Service agents reacted first, shouting and firing at the intruder in panic. Before the President could think, he found himself pushed against the wall, with two agents forming a human shield in front of him.

"There's no need for that," the intruder said, his voice deep and sonorous. "I don't intend to hurt your president—and if I did, there's nothing you can do about it." He spoke in perfect American English, without even a hint of an accent. Despite the gunfire that had just been directed at him, he appeared to be completely uninjured, and the President could now see the bullets lying harmlessly on the floor in front of the man.

Only years of handling one major crisis after another enabled the President to do what he did next. "Who are you?" he asked in a steady voice, ignoring the effects of terror and adrenaline rushing through his veins.

The intruder smiled. "My name is Arus. We've decided that it's time for our species to meet."

CHAPTER ONE

The air was crisp and clear as Mia walked briskly down a winding path in Central Park. Signs of spring were everywhere, from tiny buds on still-bare trees to the proliferation of nannies out to enjoy the first warm day with their rambunctious charges.

It was strange how much everything had changed in the last few years, and yet how much remained the same. If anyone had asked Mia ten years ago how she thought life might be after an alien invasion, this would have been nowhere near her imaginings. *Independence Day*, *The War of the Worlds*—none of these were even close to the reality of encountering a more advanced civilization. There had been no fight, no resistance of any kind on government level—because *they* had not allowed it. In hindsight, it was clear how silly those movies had been. Nuclear weapons, satellites, fighter jets—these were little more than rocks and sticks to an ancient civilization that could cross the universe faster than the speed of light.

Spotting an empty bench near the lake, Mia gratefully headed for it, her shoulders feeling the strain of the backpack filled with her chunky twelve-year-old laptop and old-fashioned paper books. At twenty-one, she sometimes felt old, out of step with the fast-paced new world of razor-slim tablets and cell phones embedded in wristwatches. The pace of technological progress had not slowed since K-Day; if anything, many of the new gadgets had been influenced by what the Krinar had. Not that the Ks had shared any of their precious technology; as far as they were concerned, their little experiment had to continue uninterrupted.

Unzipping her bag, Mia took out her old Mac. The thing was heavy and slow, but it worked—and as a starving college student, Mia could not afford anything better. Logging on, she opened a blank Word document and prepared to start the torturous process of writing her Sociology paper.

Ten minutes and exactly zero words later, she stopped. Who was she kidding? If she really wanted to write the damn thing, she would've never come to the park. As tempting as it was to pretend that she could enjoy the fresh air and be productive at the same time, those two had never been compatible in her experience. A musty old library was a much better setting for anything requiring that kind of brainpower exertion.

Mentally kicking herself for her own laziness, Mia let out a sigh and started looking around instead. People-watching in New York never failed to amuse her.

The tableau was a familiar one, with the requisite homeless person occupying a nearby bench—thank God it wasn't the closest one to her, since he looked like he might smell very ripe—and two nannies chatting with each other in Spanish as they pushed their Bugaboos at a leisurely pace. A girl jogged on a path a little further ahead, her bright pink Reeboks contrasting nicely with her blue leggings. Mia's gaze followed the jogger as she rounded the corner, envying her athleticism. Her own hectic schedule allowed her little time to exercise, and she doubted she could keep up with the girl for even a mile at this point.

To the right, she could see the Bow Bridge over the lake. A man was leaning on the railing, looking out over the water. His face was turned away from Mia, so she could only see part of his profile. Nevertheless, something about him caught her attention.

She wasn't sure what it was. He was definitely tall and seemed well-built under the expensive-looking trench coat he was wearing, but that was only part of the story. Tall, good-looking men were common in model-infested New York City. No, it was something else. Perhaps it was the way he stood—very still, with no extra movements. His hair was dark and glossy under the bright afternoon sun, just long enough in the front to move slightly in the warm spring breeze.

He also stood alone.

That's it, Mia realized. The normally popular and picturesque bridge was completely deserted, except for the man who was standing on it. Everyone appeared to be giving it a wide berth for some unknown reason. In fact, with the exception of herself and her potentially aromatic homeless neighbor, the entire row of benches in the highly desirable waterfront location was empty.

As though sensing her gaze on him, the object of her attention slowly turned his head and looked directly at Mia. Before her conscious brain could even make the connection, she felt her blood turn to ice, leaving her paralyzed in place and helpless to do anything but stare at the predator who now seemed to be examining her with interest.

* * *

Breathe, Mia, breathe. Somewhere in the back of her mind, a small rational voice kept repeating those words. That same oddly objective part of her noted his symmetrical face structure, with golden skin stretched tightly over high cheekbones and a firm jaw. Pictures and videos of Ks that she'd seen had hardly done them justice. Standing no more than thirty feet away, the creature was simply stunning.

As she continued staring at him, still frozen in place, he straightened and began walking toward her. Or rather stalking toward her, she thought stupidly, as his every movement reminded her of a jungle cat sinuously approaching a gazelle. All the while, his eyes never left hers. As he approached, she could make out individual yellow flecks in his light golden eyes and the thick long lashes surrounding them.

She watched in horrified disbelief as he sat down on her bench, less than two feet away from her, and smiled, showing white even teeth. No fangs, she noted with some functioning part of her brain. Not even a hint of them. That used to be another myth about them, like their supposed abhorrence of the sun.

"What's your name?" The creature practically purred the question at her. His voice was low and smooth, completely unaccented. His nostrils flared slightly, as though inhaling her scent.

"Um . . ." Mia swallowed nervously. "M-Mia."

"Mia," he repeated slowly, seemingly savoring her name. "Mia what?"

"Mia Stalis." Oh crap, why did he want to know her name? Why was he here, talking to her? In general, what was he doing in Central Park, so far away from any of the K Centers? *Breathe, Mia, breathe.*

"Relax, Mia Stalis." His smile got wider, exposing a dimple in his left cheek. A dimple? Ks had dimples? "Have you never encountered one of us before?"

"No, I haven't." Mia exhaled sharply, realizing that she was holding her breath. She was proud that her voice didn't sound as shaky as she felt. Should she ask? Did she want to know?

She gathered her courage. "What, um—" Another swallow. "What do you want from me?"

"For now, conversation." He looked like he was about to laugh at her, those gold eyes crinkling slightly at the corners.

Strangely, that pissed her off enough to take the edge off her fear. If there was anything Mia hated, it was being laughed at. With her short, skinny stature and a general lack of social skills that came from an awkward teenage phase involving every girl's nightmare of braces, frizzy hair, and glasses, Mia had more than enough experience being the butt of someone's joke.

She lifted her chin belligerently. "Okay, then, what is *your* name?"

"It's Korum."

"Just Korum?"

"We don't really have last names, not the way you do. My full name is much longer, but you wouldn't be able to pronounce it if I told you."

Okay, that was interesting. She now remembered reading something like that in *The New York Times*. So far, so good. Her legs had nearly stopped shaking, and her breathing was returning to normal. Maybe, just maybe, she would get out of this alive. This conversation business seemed safe enough, although the way he kept staring at her with those unblinking yellowish eyes was unnerving. She decided to keep him talking.

"What are you doing here, Korum?"

"I just told you, making conversation with you, Mia." His voice again held a hint of laughter.

Frustrated, Mia blew out her breath. "I meant, what are you doing here in Central Park? In New York City in general?"

He smiled again, cocking his head slightly to the side. "Maybe I'm hoping to meet a pretty curly-haired girl."

Okay, enough was enough. He was clearly toying with her. Now that she could think a little again, she realized that they were in the middle of Central Park, in full view of about a gazillion spectators. She surreptitiously glanced around to confirm that. Yep, sure enough, although people were obviously steering clear of her bench and its otherworldly occupant, there were a number of brave souls staring their way from further up the path. A couple were even cautiously filming them with their wristwatch cameras. If the K tried anything with her, it would be on YouTube in the blink of an eye, and he had to know it. Of course, he may or may not care about that.

Still, going on the assumption that since she'd never come across any videos of K assaults on college students in the middle of Central Park, she was relatively safe, Mia cautiously reached for her laptop and lifted it to stuff it back into her backpack.

"Let me help you with that, Mia—"

And before she could blink, she felt him take her heavy laptop from her suddenly boneless fingers, gently brushing against her knuckles in the process. A sensation similar to a mild electric shock shot through Mia at his touch, leaving her nerve endings tingling in its wake.

Reaching for her backpack, he carefully put away the laptop in a smooth, sinuous motion. "There you go, all better now."

Oh God, he had touched her. Maybe her theory about the safety of public locations was bogus. She felt her breathing speeding up again, and her heart rate was probably well into the anaerobic zone at this point.

"I have to go now . . . Bye!"

How she managed to squeeze out those words without hyperventilating, she would never know. Grabbing the strap of the backpack he'd just put down, she jumped to her feet, noting somewhere in the back of her mind that her earlier paralysis seemed to be gone.

"Bye, Mia. I will see you later." His softly mocking voice carried in the clear spring air as she took off, nearly running in her haste to get away.

CHAPTER TWO

"Holy shit! Get out of here! Seriously? Tell me what happened, and don't leave out any details!" Her roommate was nearly jumping up and down in excitement.

"I just told you . . . I met a K in the park." Mia rubbed her temples, feeling the band of tension around her head left over from her earlier adrenaline overdose. "He sat down on the bench next to me and talked to me for a couple of minutes. Then I told him that I had to go and left."

"Just like that? What did he want?"

"I don't know. I asked him that, but he just said he wanted to talk."

"Yeah, right, and pigs can fly." Jessie was as dismissive of that possibility as Mia herself had been. "No, seriously, he didn't try to drink your blood or anything?"

"No, he didn't do anything." Except briefly touch her hand. "He just asked me my name and told me his."

Jessie's eyes now resembled big brown saucers. "He told you his name? What is it?"

"Korum."

"Of course, Korum the K, makes perfect sense." Jessie's sense of humor often kicked in at the strangest times. They both snickered at the ridiculousness of that statement.

"Did you know immediately that he was a K? How did he look?" Recovering, Jessie continued with her questions.

"I did." Mia thought back to that first moment she saw him. How did she know? Was it his eyes? Or something instinctual in her that knew a predator when she saw one? "I think it maybe had to do with the way he moved. It's difficult to describe. It's definitely inhuman. He looked a lot like the Ks you'd see on TV—he was tall, good-looking in that particular way that they have, and had strange-looking eyes—they looked almost yellow."

"Wow, I can't believe it." Jessie was pacing the room in circles. "How did he talk to you? What did he sound like?"

Mia let out a sigh. "Next time I get ambushed in the park by an extraterrestrial, I will be sure to have a recording device handy."

"Oh come on, like you wouldn't be curious if you were in my shoes."

True, Jessie did have a point. Sighing again, Mia relayed the whole encounter to her roommate in full detail, leaving out only that brief moment when his hand brushed against hers. For some odd reason, that touch—and her reaction to it—seemed private.

"So you told him 'bye,' and he said he will see you later? Oh my God, do you know what that means?" Far from satisfying Jessie, the detailed story seemed to send her into excitement overdrive. She was now almost bouncing off the walls.

"No, what?" Mia felt weary and drained. It reminded her of the feeling after an interview or an exam, when all she wanted was to give her poor overworked brain a chance to unwind. Maybe she shouldn't have told Jessie about the encounter until tomorrow, when she'd had a chance to relax a bit.

"He wants to see you again!"

"What? Why?" Mia's tiredness suddenly vanished as adrenaline surged through her again. "It's just a figure of speech! I'm sure he meant nothing by that—English is not even his first language! Why would he want to see me again?"

"Well, you did say he thought you were pretty—"

"No, I said that *he* said he was there to meet 'a pretty curly-haired girl.' He was just mocking me. I'm sure that was just his way of toying with me . . . He was probably just bored standing there, so he decided to come by and talk to me. Why would a K be interested in me?" Mia cast a disparaging glance in the mirror at her two-year-old Uggs, worn jeans, and a too-big sweater she got on sale at Century 21.

"Mia, I told you, you're constantly underestimating your appeal." Jessie sounded earnest, the way she always did when trying to boost Mia's self-confidence. "You look very cute, with that big mass of curly hair. Plus, you have really pretty eyes—very unusual, to have blue eyes with hair as dark as yours—"

"Oh, please, Jessie." Mia rolled said eyes. "I'm sure *cute* doesn't cut it if you're a gorgeous K. Besides, you're my friend—you have to say nice stuff to me."

As far as Mia was concerned, Jessie was the pretty one in the room. With her curvy athletic build, long black hair, and smooth golden skin, Jessie was every guy's fantasy—particularly if they happened to like Asian girls.

A former high school cheerleader, her roommate of the last three years also had the outgoing personality to match her looks. How the two of them had become such good friends will always remain a mystery to Mia, as her own social skills at the age of eighteen had been all but nonexistent.

Thinking back to that time, Mia remembered how lost and overwhelmed she'd felt arriving in the big city after spending all her life in a small town in Florida. New York University was the best school she'd been accepted to, and her financial aid package ended up being generous, making her parents very happy. However, Mia herself had been far from excited about going to a big-city school with no real campus. Getting caught up in the competitive college application process, she'd applied to most of the top fifteen schools, only to face numerous rejections and inadequate financial aid offers. NYU had seemed like the best alternative all around. Local Florida schools had not even been considered by Mia's parents at the time, as the rumor had been that the Ks might set up a Center in Florida and her parents wanted her far away from there if that happened. It hadn't happened— Arizona and New Mexico ended up being the preferred K locales in the United States. However, by then it was too late. Mia had started her second semester at NYU, met Jessie, and slowly began to fall in love with New York City and everything it had to offer.

It was funny how everything turned out. Only five years ago, most people thought they were the only intelligent beings in the universe. Sure, there had always been crackpots claiming UFO sightings, and there had even been things like SETI—serious, government-funded efforts to explore the possibility of extraterrestrial life. But people had no way of knowing whether any kind of life—

even single-celled organisms—actually existed on other planets. As a result, most had believed that humans were special and unique, that homo sapiens were the pinnacle of evolutionary development. Now it all seemed so silly, like when people in the Middle Ages thought that the Earth was flat and that the moon and the stars revolved around it. When the Krinar arrived early in the second decade of the twenty-first century, they upended everything that scientists thought they knew about life and its origins.

"I'm telling you, Mia, I think he must've liked you!" Jessie's insistent voice interrupted her musings.

Sighing, Mia turned her attention back to her roommate. "I highly doubt it. Besides, what would he want from me even if he did? We're two different species. The thought of him liking me is just plain scary . . . What would he want from me, my blood?"

"Well, we don't know that for a fact. That's just a rumor. Officially, it's never been announced that the Ks drink blood." Jessie sounded hopeful for some weird reason. Maybe Mia's social life was so bad in her roommate's eyes that she was eager to have Mia date someone, anyone—same species optional.

"It's a rumor that many people believe. I'm sure there's a reason for that. They're vampires, Jessie. Perhaps not the Draculas of legend, but everyone knows they're predators. That's why they've set up their Centers in isolated areas . . . so they can do whatever they want there with none the wiser."

"All right, all right." Her excitement waning, Jessie sat down on her bed. "You're right, it would be very scary if he actually did intend to see you again. It's just fun to pretend sometimes that they're simply gorgeous humans from outer space, and not a completely different mystery species."

"I know. He was unbelievably good-looking." The two girls exchanged understanding glances. "If only he were human . . ."

"You're too picky, Mia. I've always told you that." Shaking her head in mock reproach, Jessie used her most serious tone of voice. Mia looked at her in disbelief, and they both burst out laughing.

* * *

That night, Mia slept restlessly, her mind replaying the encounter over and over. As soon as she would drift off to sleep, she would see those mocking amber eyes and feel that electrifying touch on her skin. To her embarrassment, her unconscious mind took things even further, and Mia dreamed of him touching her hand. In her dream, his touch would send shivers through her entire body, warming her from within—then he would slide his hand up her arm, cupping her shoulder, and bring her toward him, mesmerizing her with his gaze as he leaned in for the kiss. Her heart racing, Mia would close her eyes and lean toward him, feeling his soft lips touch hers, sending waves of warm sensations throughout her body.

Waking up, Mia felt her heart pounding in her chest and heat pooling slowly between her legs. It was 5 a.m. and she'd barely slept for the last five hours. Dammit, why was a brief encounter with an alien having such an effect on her? Maybe Jessie was right, and she needed to get out more, meet some more guys. Over the past three years, under Jessie's tutelage, Mia had shed a lot of her former shyness and awkwardness. For her high school graduation, her parents got her laser eye surgery, and her post-braces smile was nice and even. She now felt comfortable going to a party where she knew at least a few people, and she could even go out dancing after having a sufficient number of shots. But for some reason, the dating world still eluded her. The few dates she'd been on in recent months had been disappointing, and she couldn't remember the last time she had actually kissed a guy. Maybe it was that nice kid from biology last year? For some reason, Mia had never clicked with any of the men she'd met, and it was becoming embarrassing to admit that she was still a virgin at twenty-one years of age.

Thankfully, she and Jessie no longer shared a room, having found a flex one-bedroom that could be converted into a two-bedroom apartment for a reasonable (for NYC) rate of only $2,380. Having her own room meant a degree of freedom and privacy that was very nice in situations like this.

Turning on her bedside lamp, Mia looked around the room, making sure that the door to her bedroom was fully closed. Reaching into her bedside drawer, she took out a small package that was normally hidden all the way in the back of the drawer behind her face cream, hand lotion, and a bottle of Advil. Carefully unwrapping the bundle, she took out the tiny rabbit-ears vibrator that had been a gag gift from her older sister. Marisa had given it to her for high school graduation with the joking admonition to use it whenever she "felt the urge" and "to stay away from those horny college boys in the big city." Mia had blushed and laughed at the time, but the thing had actually proven handy. At certain times in the dark of the night, when her loneliness became more acute, Mia played with the device, gradually exploring her body and learning what a real orgasm felt like.

Pressing the small object to the sensitive nub between

her legs, Mia closed her eyes and relived the sensations brought on by her dream. Gradually increasing the speed of vibration on the toy, she let her imagination soar, picturing the K's hands on her body and his lips kissing her, stroking her, touching her in sensitive and forbidden places, until the ball of tension deep within her belly got even tighter and exploded, sending tingly warmth all the way to her toes.

* * *

The next morning, Mia woke up to a grey and overcast sky. Reaching for the phone to check the weather, she groaned. Ninety percent chance of rain with temperature in the mid-forties. Just what she needed when her Sociology paper awaited. Oh well, maybe she would make it to the library before the rain started.

Jumping out of bed, she pulled on her comfiest pair of sweats, a long-sleeved T-shirt, and a big hooded sweater she got on a high-school trip to Europe. It was her studying/paper-writing outfit, and it looked just as ugly today as it had the first time she'd worn it while cramming for her algebra test in tenth grade. The clothes fit her about the same now too, as she seemed to have developed a disgusting inability to gain inches either in girth or height since the age of fourteen.

Hastily brushing her teeth and washing her face, Mia stared critically in the mirror. A pale, slightly freckled face looked back at her. Her eyes were probably her best feature, an unusual shade of blue-grey that contrasted nicely with her dark hair. Her hair, on the other hand, was a whole different animal. If she spent an hour carefully blowdrying it with a diffuser, then she could maybe get her corkscrew curls to resemble something civilized. Her normal routine of going to sleep with it wet, however, was not conducive to anything but the frizzy mess she had on her head right now. Letting out a deep sigh, she ruthlessly pulled it back into a thick ponytail. Some day soon, when she had a real job, she might go to one of those expensive salons and try to get a straightening treatment. For now, since she didn't have an hour each morning to waste on her hair, Mia figured she just had to live with it.

Library time. Grabbing her backpack and her laptop, Mia pulled on her Uggs and headed out of the apartment. Five flights of stairs later, she exited her building, paying little attention to the peeling paint on the walls and the occasional cockroach that liked to live near the garbage chute. Such was student life in NYC, and Mia was one of the lucky ones to have a semi-affordable apartment so close to campus.

Real estate prices in Manhattan were as high as they'd ever been. In the first couple of years after the invasion, apartment prices in New York had cratered, just as they had in all the major cities around the world. With the hokey invasion movies still ruling the public's imagination, most people figured that cities would be unsafe and departed for rural areas if they could. Families with children—already a rare commodity in Manhattan—left the city in droves, heading for the most remote areas they could find. The Ks had encouraged the migration, as it relieved the worst of the pollution in and around urban areas. Of course, people soon realized their folly, since the Ks wanted nothing to do with the major human cities and instead chose to build their Centers in warm, sparsely populated areas around the globe. Manhattan prices skyrocketed again, with a few lucky people making fortunes on the real estate bargains they'd picked up in the crash. Now, more than five years after K-Day—as the first day of the Krinar invasion came to be called—New York City rents were again testing record highs.

Lucky me, Mia thought with mild irritation. If she had been a couple of years older, she could've rented her current apartment for less than half the price. Of course, there was something to be said for graduating next year, instead of in the depths of the Great Panic—the dark months after Earth first faced the invaders.

Stopping by the local deli, Mia ordered a lightly toasted bagel (whole-grain, of course, the only kind available) with an avocado-tomato spread. Sighing, she remembered the delicious omelets her mom used to make, with crumbled bacon, mushrooms, and cheese. Nowadays, mushroom was the only ingredient on that list that was in any way affordable for a college student. Meat, fish, eggs, and dairy were premium products, available only as an occasional treat—the way foie gras and caviar used to be. That was one of the main changes that the Krinar had implemented. Having decided that the typical developed-world diet of the early twenty-first century was harmful both to humans and their environment, they shut down the major industrial farms, forcing meat and dairy producers to switch to growing fruits and vegetables. Only small farmers were left in peace and allowed to grow a few farm animals for special occasions. Environmental and animal-rights organizations had been ecstatic, and obesity rates in America were quickly approaching Vietnam's. Of course, the fallout had been huge, with numerous companies going out of business and food shortages during the Great Panic. And later on, when the Krinar's vampiric tendencies were discovered (though still not officially proven), the Far Right activists had claimed that the real reason for the forced change in diet was that it made the human blood taste sweeter to the Ks. Be that as it may, the majority of the food that was available and affordable now was disgustingly healthy.

"Umbrella, umbrella, umbrella!" A scruffy-looking man stood on the corner, hawking his wares in a strong Middle Eastern accent. "Five-dollar umbrella!"

Sure enough, less than a minute later, a light drizzle began. For the umpteenth time, Mia wondered if the street umbrella vendors had some kind of sixth sense about rain. They always seemed to appear right before the first drop fell, even if there was no rain in the forecast. As tempting as it was to buy an umbrella to stay dry, Mia only had a few blocks left to go and the rain was too light to justify an unnecessary expenditure of five dollars. She could've brought her old umbrella from home, but carrying an extra object was never high on her list of priorities.

Walking as fast as she could while lugging her heavy bag, Mia turned the corner on West 4th Street, with the Bobst Library already in sight, when the downpour began. Crap, she should've bought that umbrella! Mentally kicking herself, Mia broke into a run—or rather a jog, given the backpack weighing her down—as raindrops pelted her face with the force of water bullets. Her hair somehow managed to escape from the ponytail, and was in her face, blocking her vision. A bunch of people rushed past her, hurrying to get out of the rain, and Mia was pushed a few times by pedestrians blinded by the combination of heavy rain and umbrellas held by more fortunate souls. At times like this, being 5'3" and barely a hundred pounds was a severe disadvantage. A big man brushed past her, his elbow bumping into her shoulder, and Mia stumbled, her foot catching on a crack in the sidewalk. Pitching forward, she managed to catch herself with her hands on wet pavement, sliding a few inches on the rough surface.

All of a sudden, strong hands lifted her from the ground, as though she weighed nothing, standing her upright under a large umbrella that the man held over both of their heads.

Feeling like a dirty, drowned rat, Mia tried to brush her sodden hair off her face with the back of one scraped hand, while blinking the remnants of rain out of her eyes. Her nose decided to add to her humiliation, choosing that particular moment to let loose with an uncontrollable sneeze all over her rescuer.

"Oh my God, I'm so sorry!" Mia frantically apologized in utter mortification. Her vision still blurry from the water running down her face, she desperately tried to wipe her nose with a wet sleeve to prevent another sneeze. "So sorry, I didn't mean to sneeze on you like that!"

"No apologies necessary, Mia. Obviously, you got cold and wet. And injured. Let me see your hands."

This could not be happening. Her discomfort forgotten, all Mia could do was stare in disbelief as Korum carefully lifted her wrists palms-up and examined her scrapes. His large hands were unbelievably gentle on her skin, even as they held her in an inescapable grip. Although she was soaked to the skin in chilly mid-April weather, Mia felt like she was about to burst into flames, his touch sending a wave of heat rushing through her body.

"You should get those injuries treated immediately. They could scar if you're not careful. Here, come with me, and we'll get them taken care of." Releasing her wrists, Korum put a proprietary arm around her waist and began shepherding her back toward Broadway.

"Wait, what——" Mia tried to recover her wits. "What are you doing here? Where are you leading me?" The full danger of the situation was just now beginning to hit home, and she began to shiver from a combination of cold and fear.

"You're obviously freezing. I'm getting you out of this rain, and then we'll talk." His tone brooked no disagreement.

Desperately looking around, all Mia saw were people rushing to get out of the pouring rain, not paying any attention to their surroundings. In weather like this, a murder in the middle of the street was likely to go unnoticed, much less the struggles of one small girl. Korum's arm was like a steel band around her waist, completely unmovable, and Mia found herself helplessly going along in whichever direction he was leading her.

"Wait, please, I really can't go with you," Mia protested shakily. Grasping at straws, she blurted out, "I have a paper to write!"

"Oh really? And you're going to write it in this condition?" His tone dripping with sarcasm, Korum gave her a disparaging once-over, lingering on her dripping hair and scraped hands. "You're hurt, and you're probably going to catch pneumonia—with that puny immune system you've got."

As before, he somehow managed to get a rise out of her. How dare he call her puny! Mia saw red. "Excuse me, my immune system is just fine! Nobody catches pneumonia from getting stuck in the rain these days! Besides, what concern is it of yours? What are you doing here, stalking me?"

"That's right." His reply was smooth and completely nonchalant.

Her temper immediately cooling, Mia felt tendrils of

fear snaking through her again. Swallowing to moisten her suddenly dry throat, she could only croak out one word. "W-Why?"

"Ah, here we are." A black limo was sitting at the intersection of West 4th and Broadway. At their approach, the automatic doors slid open, revealing a plush cream-colored interior. Mia's heart jumped into her throat. No way was she getting into a strange car with a K who admitted to stalking her.

She dug in her heels and prepared to scream.

"Mia. Get. In. The. Car." His words lashed at her like a whip. He looked angry, his eyes getting more yellow by the second. His normally sensuous-looking mouth appeared cruel all of a sudden, set in an uncompromising line. "Do NOT make me repeat myself."

Shaking like a leaf, Mia obeyed. Oh God, she just wanted to survive this, whatever the K had in store for her. Every horror story she'd ever heard about the invaders was suddenly fresh in her mind, every image from the gruesome fights during the Great Panic. She stifled a sob, watching as Korum got in the limo and closed the umbrella. The car doors slid shut.

Korum pressed the intercom button. "Roger, please take us to my place." He looked much calmer now, eyes back to the original golden brown.

"Yes, sir." The driver's reply came from behind the partition that fully blocked him from view.

Roger? That was a human name, Mia thought in desperation. Maybe he could help her, call the police on her behalf or something. Then again, what could the police do? It's not like they could arrest a K. As far as Mia knew, they were above the reach of human law. He could pretty much do anything he wanted with her, and there was no one to stop him. Mia felt tears running down her rain-wet face as she thought about her parents' grief when they found out that their daughter was missing.

"What? Are you crying?" Korum's voice held a note of incredulity. "What are you, five?" He reached for her, his fingers locking around her upper arms, and pulled her closer to stare into her face. At his touch, Mia started shaking even harder, gasping sobs breaking out of her throat.

"Hush, now. There's no need for that. Shhh . . ." Mia suddenly found herself cradled fully on his lap, her face pressed against a broad chest. Still sobbing, she vaguely registered a pleasant scent of freshly laundered clothing and warm male skin, as his hand moved in soothing circles on her back. He really was treating her like a five-year-old crying over a boo-boo, she thought semi-hysterically. Strangely enough, the treatment was working. Mia felt her fear ebbing as he held her gently in those powerful arms, only to be replaced by a growing sense of awareness and a warm sensation somewhere deep inside. Adrenaline amplified attraction, she realized with a peculiar detachment, remembering a study on the subject from one of her psychology classes.

Still ensconced on his lap, she managed to pull away enough to look up at his face. Up close, his appearance was even more striking. His skin, a warm golden hue that was a couple of shades darker than her roommate's, was flawless and seemed to glow with perfect health. Thick black lashes surrounded those incredible light-colored eyes—which were framed by the straight dark slashes of his eyebrows.

"Are you going to hurt me?" The question escaped her before she could think any better of it.

Her kidnapper let out a surprisingly human-like sigh, sounding exasperated. "Mia, listen to me, I mean you no harm . . . Okay?" He looked straight into her eyes, and Mia couldn't look away, mesmerized by the yellow flecks in his irises. "All I wanted was to get you out of the rain and to treat your injuries. I'm taking you to my place because it's nearby, and I can provide you with both medical assistance and a change of clothes there. I really didn't mean to scare you, much less get you into this kind of state."

"But you said . . . you said you were stalking me!" Mia stared at him in confusion.

"Yes. Because I found you interesting at the park and wanted to see you again. Not because I want to hurt you." He was now rubbing her upper arms with a gentle up-and-down motion, as though soothing a skittish horse.

At his admission, a wave of heat surged through her body. Did that mean he was attracted to her? Her heart rate picked up again, this time for a different reason.

There was something else she needed to understand. "You forced me to get into the car . . ."

"Only because you were being stubborn and refusing to listen to common sense. You were wet and cold. I didn't want to waste time arguing in the rain when a warm car was standing right there." Put like that, his actions sounded downright humanitarian.

"Here." Pulling a tissue from somewhere, he carefully blotted the remaining tears on her face and gave her another tissue to wipe her nose, watching with some amusement as she tried to blow into it as delicately as possible. "Feeling better now?"

Strangely enough, she was. He could be lying to her, but what would be the point? He could do anything he wanted with her anyway, so why waste time trying to soothe her fears? Her earlier terror gone, Mia suddenly felt exhausted from her emotional roller coaster. As though sensing her state, Korum gathered her closer to him, pressing her face gently against his chest again. Mia did not object. Somehow, sitting there on his lap, inhaling his warm scent and feeling the heat of his body surrounding her, Mia felt better than she had in a long time.

CHAPTER THREE

"Here we are. Welcome to my humble abode."

Mia stared around in amazement, her gaze lingering on floor-to-ceiling windows looking out over the Hudson, gleaming wooden floors, and luxurious cream-colored furnishings. A few pieces of modern art on the walls and luscious-looking plants near the windows provided tasteful touches of color. It was the most beautiful apartment she had ever seen. And it looked completely human.

"You live here?" she asked in astonishment.

"Only when I come to New York."

Korum was hanging his trench coat in the closet by the door. It was such a simple, mundane action, but somehow his movements were just too fluid to be fully human. He was now clad only in a blue T-shirt and a pair of jeans. The clothes hugged his lean, powerful body to perfection. Mia swallowed, realizing that her incredible surroundings paled next to the gorgeous creature who was apparently occupying them.

How could he afford this place? Were all the Ks rich?

When the limo had pulled into the parking garage at the newest luxury high-rise in TriBeCa, Mia had been shocked to find herself escorted to a private elevator that took them directly to the penthouse floor. The apartment looked huge, particularly by Manhattan standards. Did it occupy the entire top floor of the building?

"Yes, the apartment is the whole floor."

Mia blushed, just realizing that she had asked the question out loud. "Umm . . . it's a beautiful place you've got here."

"Thank you. Here, sit down." He led her to a plush leather couch—cream-colored, of course. "Let me see your hands."

Mia hesitantly extended her palms, wondering what he intended to do. Use his blood to heal them, the way vampires from popular fiction used to do?

Instead of cutting his palm or doing anything vampiric, Korum brought a thin silvery object toward her right palm. The size and thickness of an old-fashioned plastic credit card, the thing looked completely innocuous. That is, until it began to emit a soft red light directly over her hand. There was no pain, just a pleasant, warm sensation where the light touched her damaged skin. As Mia watched, her scrapes began to fade and disappear, like pencil marks getting erased. Within a span of two minutes, her palm was completely healed, as though there had been nothing there to begin with. Mia tentatively touched the area with her fingers. No pain whatsoever.

"Wow. That is amazing." Mia exhaled sharply, releasing a breath she hadn't even realized she was holding. Of course, she had known that the Ks were far more technologically advanced, but seeing what amounted to a miracle with her own eyes was still shocking.

Korum repeated the process on her other hand. Both of her palms were now completely healed, with no trace of an injury.

"Uh . . . thank you for that." Mia didn't really know what to say. Was this a K version of offering a Band-Aid, or did he just perform some kind of a complicated medical procedure on her? Should she offer to pay him? And if he said yes, would he accept student health insurance? *Snap out of it, Mia! You're being ridiculous!*

"You're welcome," he said softly, still lightly holding her left hand. "Now let's get you changed out of your wet clothes."

Mia's head jerked up in horrified disbelief. Surely he couldn't mean to—

Before she even had a chance to say anything, Korum blew out an exasperated breath. "Mia, when I said that I don't intend to harm you, I meant it. My definition of harm includes rape, in case you think we have some cultural differences there. So you can relax, and stop jumping at every word I say."

"I'm sorry, I didn't mean to imply . . ." Mia wished the ground would open up and simply swallow her. Of course, he wouldn't rape her. He probably wasn't even interested in her that way. Why would he want some skinny, pale little human when he could have any of the gorgeous K females she'd seen on TV? He'd never said he was attracted to her—just that he found her "interesting." For all she knew, he could be a K scientist studying the New York breed of humans—and he had just found a curly-haired lab rat.

Letting out another sigh, Korum rose gracefully from the couch, his every move imbued with inhuman athleticism. "Here, come with me."

Still feeling embarrassed, Mia barely paid attention to her surroundings as he led her down the hall. However, she couldn't help but gasp at the first sight of the enormous bathroom that lay before her.

The glass shower enclosure was bigger than her entire bathroom back home, and a large elevated jacuzzi occupied the center of the room. The entire bathroom was done in shades of ivory and grey, an unusual combination that nonetheless paired well in this luxurious environment. Two of the walls were floor-to-ceiling mirrors, further adding to the spacious feel. There were plants here too, she noticed with bemusement. Two exotic-looking plants with dark red leaves seemed to be thriving in the corners, apparently getting enough sunlight from the large skylight in the ceiling.

"This is for you." Korum slid open part of the glass wall and took out a large ivory towel and a soft-looking thick grey robe. "You can take a hot shower and change into this, and then I will throw your clothes in the dryer."

With a nod and a murmured thank-you, Mia accepted the two items, watching as Korum exited the room and closed the door behind him.

A sense of unreality gripped her as she stared at the cutting-edge luxury all around her. This could not be happening to her. Could this be a really vivid dream? Surely Mia Stalis, from Ormond Beach, Florida, was not standing here in a bathroom fit for a king, having been told to take a hot shower by a K who had practically kidnapped her in order to heal her insignificant scratches with an alien magic device. Maybe if she blinked a few times, she would wake up back in her cramped room at the apartment she shared with Jessie.

To test that theory, Mia shut her eyes tightly and opened them again. Nope, she was still standing there, feeling the plush towel and robe heavy in her arms. If this was a dream, then it was the most realistic dream she'd ever had. She might as well take that shower—now that the excitement was starting to wear off a bit, she felt the chill from her damp clothes sinking deep into her bones.

Putting down her burden on the edge of the tall jacuzzi tub, Mia walked to the door and locked it. Of course, if Korum really wanted to get in, it was doubtful that the flimsy lock would keep him out. The incredible strength of the Krinar was discovered in the first few weeks after the invasion, when some guerrilla fighters in the Middle East ambushed a small group of Ks in violation of the recently signed Coexistence Treaty. Video footage of the event, recorded by some bystander on his iPhone, showed scenes straight out of a horror science fiction movie. The band of thirty-plus Saudis, armed with grenades and automatic assault rifles, had stood no chance against the six unarmed Ks. Even wounded, the aliens moved at a speed exceeding that of all known living creatures on Earth, literally tearing apart their attackers with bare hands. One particularly dramatic scene showed a K throwing two screaming men—each with one hand— high up into the air. The exact height of the throw was later determined to be about sixty feet. Needless to say, the men had not survived their descent. The sheer savagery of that fight—and some subsequent encounters during the days of the Great Panic—stunned the human population, lending credence to the rumors of vampirism that emerged some months later. For all their advances in technology and seeming eco-consciousness, the Ks could be as brutal and violent as any vampire of legend.

And here she was stuck with one. Who wanted to heal her negligible scratches and have her take a hot shower in his fancy penthouse. And put her clothes in his dryer.

A hysterical giggle escaped Mia at the thought.

Of course, he might like his snacks clean and sweet-smelling, but somehow Mia believed him when he said he didn't want to hurt her. Besides, there was very little she could do about her current situation—she might as well stop freaking out and take advantage of the most luxurious shower of her life.

Peeling off her wet clothes, Mia caught sight of herself in the mirror. Why was he interested in her? Sure, she was skinny, which was still in vogue, but he probably had the most beautiful women of both species fawning over him. Standing there naked, Mia tried to look at herself objectively and not through the eyes of a self-conscious teenager. The mirror reflected a thin young woman, with small, but nicely rounded breasts, slim hips, and a narrow waist. Her butt was reasonably curvy, considering the rest of her frame. Naked, she didn't look like the shapeless stick figure she always felt like in her baggy clothes. If she were taller, she might even think she had a nice figure. However, her skin was way too pale and the dark mess of curls framing her face was much too frizzy for her to ever be considered more than moderately cute or passably pretty.

Sighing, Mia stepped into the shower. After a brief battle with the touchscreen controls, she figured out how to work them and was soon enjoying warm water coming at her from five different directions. She even used his soap, which had a very faint but pleasing scent of something tropical.

Ten minutes later, Mia regretfully turned off the water and stepped out onto a thick ivory bath rug. She dried herself with the towel Korum had so graciously provided, wrapped it around her wet hair, and put on the robe—which was, to her surprise, only a little big on her. It had to be a woman's robe, she realized with an unpleasant pang of something that felt oddly like jealousy. *Don't be silly, Mia, of course he has female guests!* A creature that gorgeous would hardly be celibate. He might even have a girlfriend or a wife.

Mia swallowed to get rid of an obstruction in her throat that seemed to rise up at that thought. *Stop it, Mia!* She had no idea what he wanted from her, and she had absolutely no reason to feel like this about an alien from outer space who may or may not drink human blood.

Padding to the door in her bare feet, Mia picked up her discarded clothes from the floor. They felt wet and yucky in her hands, and she was glad she was no longer wearing them. Carefully opening the door, she peeked out into the hallway, spotting a soft-looking pair of grey house slippers that Korum apparently left for her.

No sign of Korum himself.

Putting on the slippers, Mia left the bathroom and headed to the left, hoping that she was going back toward the living room. The last thing she wanted was to stumble into his bedroom, even though that thought made her feel warm and flushed all over.

He was sitting on the couch, looking at something in his palm. Sensing her presence, he lifted his head, and a luminous smile slowly lit his face at the sight of her standing there in the too-big robe and turban-like towel on her head.

"You look adorable in that." His voice was low and somehow intimate, even from across the room, making her insides clench in a strangely sexual way. Oh God, what did he mean by that? Was he actually interested in her? Mia was sure she had just turned beet-red as her heart rate suddenly picked up.

"Ah, thanks," she mumbled, unable to think of a better

response. Was it her imagination, or did his eyes turn an even deeper shade of gold?

"Here, let me have those." Before she had a chance to recover her composure, he was next to her, taking her wet clothes from her slightly shaky arms. "Have a seat, and I'll drop these in the dryer."

With that, he disappeared down the hall. Mia stared after him, wondering if she should be worried. He said he wasn't going to hurt her, but would he take no for an answer if he really was interested in her sexually? More importantly, would she be able to say no, given her response to him thus far?

She'd heard of humans having sex with Ks, so their species were definitely compatible in that way. In fact, there were even websites where people who wanted to have sex with Ks posted ads designed to attract them. Some of the ads must have garnered responses, since the websites stayed in business. Mia always used to think that these xenos—short for xenophiles, a derogatory term for K addicts—were crazy. Sure, most of the invaders tended to be very good-looking, but they were so far from being human that one might as well have sex with a gorilla; there were fewer differences between gorilla and human DNA than between human and Krinar.

Yet here she was, apparently very attracted to one particular K.

A minute later, Korum returned empty-handed, interrupting Mia's chain of thought. "The clothes are drying," he announced. "Are you hungry? I can make us something to eat in the meanwhile."

Ks could cook? Mia suddenly realized that she was, in fact, famished. With all the excitement of the past hour, her bagel breakfast seemed like a very long time ago. Cooking and eating also seemed like a very innocuous way to pass the time.

"Sure, that sounds great. Thank you."

"Okay, come with me to the kitchen, and I'll make something."

With that promise, he walked over to a door she hadn't noticed before and slid it open, revealing a large kitchen. Like the rest of the penthouse, it was striking. Gleaming stainless steel appliances, black and ivory marble floors, and black enameled lava countertops populated the space, for an almost futuristic look. Some kind of big-leafed plants in silvery pots hung from the ceiling near the windows, seeming very much at home in an otherwise sterile-looking environment.

"How do you feel about a salad and a roasted veggie sandwich?" Korum was already opening the refrigerator, which looked like the latest version of the iZero—a smart fridge jointly created by Apple and Sub-Zero a couple of years ago.

"That sounds great, thanks," Mia answered absentmindedly, still studying her surroundings. Something was nagging at her, some obvious question that begged an answer.

Suddenly, it hit her.

"Your home only has our technology in it," Mia blurted out. "Well, except for the little healing tool you used on me. All of these appliances, all of our technology—it must seem so primitive to you. Why do you use it instead of whatever you guys have instead?"

Korum grinned, revealing the dimple in his left cheek again, and walked over to the sink to rinse the lettuce. "I enjoy experiencing different things. A lot of your technology is really so ingenious, considering your limitations. And, to use one of your sayings, when in Rome..."

"So you're basically slumming," Mia concluded. "Living with the primitives, using their basic tools—"

"If you want to think of it that way."

He started chopping the veggies, his hands moving faster than any professional chef's. Mia stared at him in fascination, struck by the incongruity of a creature from outer space making a salad. All of his movements were fluid and elegant—and somehow very inhuman.

"What do you normally eat on Krina?" she asked, suddenly very curious. "Is your diet very different from ours?"

He looked up from the chopping and smiled at her. "It's different in some ways, but very similar in other ways. We're omnivorous like you, but lean even more toward plant foods in our diet. There's a huge variety of edible plants on Krina—more so than here on Earth. Some of our plants are very dense in calories and rich in flavor, so we never quite developed the taste for meat that humans seem to have acquired recently."

Mia blinked, surprised. There was something predatory in the way he moved—the way all Ks moved. Their speed and strength, as well as the violent streak they'd displayed, did not make sense for a primarily herbivorous species. So there must be something to the vampire rumors after all. If they didn't hunt animals for their meat, then how had they evolved all these hunter-like traits?

She wanted to ask him that, but had a feeling that she might not want to know the answer. If his species really did view humans as prey, it was probably best not to remind him about it when she was alone with him in his lair.

Mia decided to stick with something safer instead. "So is that why you guys emphasize plant foods so much for us? Because you like it yourselves?"

He shook his head, continuing to chop. "Not really. Our main concern was the abuse of your planet's resources. Your unhealthy addiction to animal products was destroying the environment at a much faster rate than anything else you were doing, and that was not something we wanted to see."

Mia shrugged, not being particularly environmentally conscious herself. Since he was being so accommodating, though, she decided to resume her earlier line of questioning. "Is that why you're here in New York, to experience something different?"

"Among other reasons." He turned on the oven and placed sliced zucchini, eggplant, peppers, and tomatoes on a tray inside.

How frustrating. He was being evasive, and Mia didn't like it one bit. She decided to change her approach. "What brings you to Earth in general? Are you one of the soldiers, or the scientists, or do you do something else . . ." Her voice trailed off suggestively.

"Why, Mia, are you asking me about my occupation?" He sounded like he was again laughing at her.

Predictably, Mia felt her hackles rising. "Why, yes, I am. Is that classified information?"

He threw back his head and burst out laughing. "Only for curious little girls." Mia stared back at him with a stony expression on her face. Still chuckling, he revealed, "I'm an engineer by profession. My company designed the ships that brought us here."

"The ships that brought you here? But I thought the Krinar had been visiting Earth for thousands of years before you formally came here?" That had been one of the most striking revelations about the invaders—the fact that they'd been observing humans and living among them long before K-Day.

He nodded, still smiling. "That's true. We've been able to visit you for a long time. However, traveling to Earth had always been a dangerous task—as was space travel in general—so only a few intrepid individuals would attempt it at any given time. It's only in the past few hundred years that we fully perfected the technology for faster-than-light travel, and my company succeeded in building ships that could safely transport thousands of civilians to this part of the universe."

That was interesting. She'd never heard this before. Was he telling her something that wasn't public knowledge? Encouraged and unbearably curious, Mia continued with her questions. "So have *you* been to Earth before K-Day?" she asked, staring at him in wide-eyed fascination.

He shrugged—a human gesture that was apparently used by the Ks as well. "A couple of times."

"Is it true that all our UFO sightings are based on actual interactions with the Krinar?"

He grinned. "No, that was mostly weather balloons and your own governments testing classified aircraft. Less than one percent of those sightings could actually be attributed to us."

"And the Greek and Roman myths?" Mia had read recent speculation that the Krinar may have been worshipped as deities in antiquity, giving rise to the Greek and Roman polytheistic religions. Of course, even today, some religious groups had embraced the Ks as the true creators of humankind, spawning an entirely new movement dedicated to venerating and emulating the invaders. The Krinarians, as these K-worshippers were known, sought every opportunity to interact with the beings they viewed as real-life gods, believing it increased their odds of reincarnating as a K. The Big Three—Christianity, Islam, and Judaism—had reacted very differently, refusing to accept that Ks were in any way responsible for the origin of life on Earth. Some more extreme religious factions had even declared the Krinar to be demons and claimed that their arrival was part of the end-of-days prophecy. Most people, however, had accepted the aliens for what they were—an ancient, highly advanced species that had sent DNA from Krina to Earth, thus starting life on this planet.

"Those *were* based on the Krinar," confirmed Korum. "A few thousand years ago, a small group of our scientists, sent here to study and observe, became overly involved in human affairs—to the point that they overstayed their mission by a few hundred years. They ultimately had to be forcibly returned to Krina when it became obvious that they were purposefully preying on human ignorance."

Before Mia had a chance to digest that information, the oven let out a little beep signifying the food's readiness.

"Ah, here we go." He took out the roasted veggies and dropped them into a marinade he'd managed to whip up during their conversation. Placing a large salad in the middle of the table, he picked up a sizable portion and deposited it on Mia's plate. "We can start with this while the veggies are marinating."

Mia dug into her salad, holding back an inappropriate giggle at the thought that she was literally eating food of the gods —or at least food that had been prepared by someone who would've been worshipped as a god a couple of thousand years ago. The salad was delicious—crispy lettuce, creamy avocado, crunchy peppers, and sweet tomatoes were combined with some type of tangy lemony dressing that was mildly spicy. She was either super-hungry, or it was the best salad she'd had in a long time. In the past few years, she'd learned to tolerate salad out of necessity, but this kind of salad she could actually grow to like.

"Thank you, this is delicious," she mumbled around a mouthful of salad.

"You're welcome." He was digging in as well, with obvious enjoyment. For a little while, there was only the sound of them munching on the salad in companionable silence. After finishing his portion—he even ate faster than normal, Mia noticed—Korum got up to make the sandwiches.

Two minutes later, a beautifully made sandwich was sitting in front of Mia. The dark crusty bread appeared to be freshly baked, and the veggies looked tender and were seasoned with some kind of orange spices. Mia picked up her portion and bit into it, nearly stifling a moan of enjoyment. It tasted even better than it looked.

"This is great. Where did you learn to cook like this?" Mia inquired with curiosity after swallowing her fifth bite.

He shrugged, finishing up his own larger sandwich. "I enjoy making things. Cooking is just one manifestation of that. I also like to eat, so it's helpful to know how to make good food."

That made sense to her. Mia ate the last bite of her sandwich and licked her finger to get the remainder of the delicious marinade. Lifting her head, she suddenly froze at the look on Korum's face.

He was staring at her mouth with what looked like raw hunger, his eyes turning more golden by the second.

"Do that again," he ordered softly, his voice a dark purr from across the table.

Mia's heart skipped a beat.

The atmosphere had suddenly turned heavy and intensely sexual, and she had no idea how to deal with it. The full vulnerability of her situation dawned on her. She was completely naked underneath the thick robe. All he had to do was pull on the flimsy belt holding the robe together, and her body would be fully revealed to him. Not that clothes would provide any protection against a K—or a human male for that matter, given her size—but wearing only a robe made her feel much more exposed.

Slowly getting up, she took a step away from the table. Her heartbeat thundering in her ears, Mia nervously blurted out, "Thank you for the meal, but I should really get going now. Do you think my clothes might be dry?"

For a second, Korum did not respond, continuing to look at her with that disconcertingly hungry expression. Then, as if coming to some internal decision, he slowly smiled and got up himself. "They should be ready by now. Why don't you put the dishes in the dishwasher while I go check?"

Mia nodded in agreement, afraid that her voice would tremble if she spoke out loud. Her legs felt like cooked noodles, but she started gathering the dishes. Korum smiled approvingly and exited the room, leaving Mia alone to recover her composure.

By the time he came back, his arms loaded with her dry clothes, Mia had managed to convince herself that she had overreacted to a potentially harmless remark. Most likely, her imagination was working in overdrive, adding sexual overtones to where there were none. Given his apparent fascination with human technology and lifestyle, it wasn't all that surprising that he would find an actual human interesting as well—maybe even cute in something they did—the same way Mia felt about animals in the zoo.

Feeling slightly bad about her earlier awkwardness, Mia tentatively smiled at Korum as he handed her the clothes. "Thanks for drying these—I really appreciate it."

"No problem. It was my pleasure." He smiled back, but there was a hint of something mildly disturbing in the look he gave her.

"If you don't mind, I'll just go change." Still feeling inexplicably nervous, Mia turned toward the kitchen exit.

"Sure. Do you remember the way to the bathroom? You can go change there." He pointed down the hall, watching with a half-smile as she gratefully escaped.

Locking the bathroom door, Mia hurriedly changed into her comfortably ugly—and pleasantly warm from the dryer—clothes. He had somehow managed to dry her Uggs as well, Mia noticed with pleasure as she pulled them on. Feeling much more like herself, she unwrapped the towel from her hair, which was only slightly damp at this point, and left the curly mess down to finish drying. Then, thinking that she was as ready as she would ever be, Mia left the relative safety of the bathroom and ventured back out into the living room to face Korum and his confusing behavior.

He was again sitting on the couch, analyzing something in his palm. He seemed very absorbed in it, so Mia cautiously cleared her throat to notify him of her presence.

At the sound, he looked up with a mysterious smile. "There you are, all nice and dry."

"Ah, yeah, thanks for that." Mia self-consciously shifted from one foot to another. "And thanks again for your hospitality. I really should get going now, try to write that paper and finish up some other homework . . ."

"Sure, I'll take you wherever you want to go." He got up in one smooth motion, heading to the coat closet.

"Oh no, you don't have to do that," protested Mia. "Really, I have no problem taking the subway. The rain has stopped, so I'll be totally fine."

He just gave her an incredulous look. "I said I will take you there." His tone left no room for negotiation.

Mia decided not to argue. It's not as if she rode in a limo every day. Since Korum was so determined to give her a lift, she might as well enjoy the experience. So Mia kept quiet and meekly followed him as he entered a posh-looking elevator and pressed the button for the ground floor.

Roger and his limo were already waiting in front of the building. The doors slid open at their approach, and Korum courteously waited until Mia climbed inside before getting in himself. Mia wondered where he had learned all of these polite human gestures. Somehow she doubted that "ladies first" was a universal custom.

"Where would you like to go?" he inquired, sitting down next to her.

Mia thought about it for a second. As much as she'd love to run home and blab about the entire unbelievable encounter to Jessie, the deadline for her paper was looming. She needed to go to the library. She only hoped that she could put the day's events out of her mind for a few hours, or however long it took her to write the damn paper. "The Bobst Library, please, if it's not too much trouble," she requested tentatively.

"It's no trouble at all," he reassured her, pressing the intercom button and conveying the instructions to Roger.

Sitting in the closed quarters of the limo, Mia became increasingly aware of his large, warm body less than a foot away from her. Her body reacted to his nearness without reservations.

He really was an incredibly beautiful male specimen by anyone's standards, Mia thought with an almost analytical detachment. She guessed his height to be somewhere just over six feet, and he appeared to be quite muscular, judging by the way his T-shirt fit him earlier. With his striking coloring, he was easily the most handsome man she'd ever seen, in real life or on video. It was no wonder he was having such an effect on her, she told herself—any normal woman would feel the same. Understanding the rationale behind her attraction to him, however, did not lessen its power one bit.

"So, Mia, tell me about yourself." His softly spoken directive interrupted her thoughts.

"Um, okay." For some reason, the question flustered her. "What do you want to know?"

He shrugged and smiled. "Everything."

"Well, I'm a junior at NYU, majoring in psychology," Mia began, hoping she wasn't babbling. "I'm originally from a small town in Florida, and I came to New York to go to school."

He stopped her with a shake of his head. "I know all that. Tell me something more than basic facts."

Mia stared at him in shock, suddenly feeling like a hunted rabbit. With surprising calm, she asked, "How do you know all this?"

"The same way I knew where to find you today. It's very easy to find information on humans, especially those with nothing to hide." He smiled, as though he hadn't just shattered all of her illusions about privacy.

"But why?" Mia could no longer hold back a question that had been tormenting her for the last two days. "Why are you so interested in me? Why go to all these lengths?" She waved her hand, indicating the limo and everything he had done so far.

He looked at her steadily, his gaze nearly hypnotizing in its intensity. "Because I want to fuck you, Mia. Is that what you're afraid of hearing, why you've been acting so scared of me all along?" Without giving her a chance to catch her breath, he continued in the same gently mocking tone. "Well, it's true. I do. For some reason, you caught my attention yesterday, sitting there on that bench with your curly hair and big blue eyes, so frightened when I looked your way. You're not my type at all. I don't typically go for scared little girls, particularly of the human variety, but you—" he reached across with his right hand and slowly stroked her cheek, "—you made me want to strip you down right there in the middle of that park, and see what's hidden underneath these ugly clothes of yours. It took all my willpower to let you go then, and, when you licked your little finger so enticingly in my kitchen, I could barely stop myself from spreading open your robe and burying myself between your thighs right there on the kitchen table."

His touch felt like it was leaving burning streaks in its aftermath as he tucked a strand of hair behind her ear and gently brushed his knuckles across her lips. "But I'm not a rapist. And that's what it would be right now—rape—because you're so frightened of me, and of your own sexuality." Leaning closer, he murmured softly, "I know you want me, Mia. I can see the flush of arousal on your pretty cheeks, and I can smell it in your underwear. I know your little nipples are hard right now, and that you're getting wet even as we speak, your body lubricating itself for my penetration. If I were to take you right now, you would enjoy it once you got past the fear and the pain of losing your virginity—yes, I know about that too—but I will wait for you to get used to the idea of being mine. Just don't take too long—I only have so much patience left for you."

CHAPTER FOUR

Mia hardly remembered the remainder of the ride.

At some point in the next few minutes, the limo had pulled up to the Bobst Library, and Korum had courteously opened the door for her again and handed her the backpack. He then proceeded to gently brush his lips against her cheek, as though parting ways with his sister, and left her standing on the curb in front of the imposing library building.

Moving on autopilot, Mia somehow found herself inside, sitting in one of the plush armchairs that were her favorite place to study. Going through the motions, she took out her Mac and placed it on the side table, noting with some interest that her hand was shaking and her fingernails had a slight bluish tint to them. She also felt cold deep inside.

Shock, Mia realized. She had to be in a state of mild shock.

For some reason, that pissed her off. Yes, she felt like he had stripped her naked with his words in the car, leaving her feeling raw and vulnerable. Yes, if she thought too deeply about the meaning of his last words, she would probably start running and screaming. But she was hardly a Victorian maiden—her lack of experience notwithstanding—and she refused to let a few explicit phrases send her into vapors.

Resolutely getting up, Mia left her bag in the chair as a placeholder—nobody would steal a computer that old—and headed to the coffee shop to get something hot to drink. On the way there, she stopped by the bathroom. Splashing warm water on her face in an attempt to regain her equilibrium, Mia inadvertently caught a glimpse of herself in the mirror. The usual pale face staring back at her looked subtly different—somehow softer and prettier. Her lips appeared fuller, as though slightly swollen where he had touched them. Her eyes looked brighter, and there was a hint of color on her cheeks.

He was right, Mia thought. She had been extremely turned on in the car, his words alone bringing her nearly to the edge of orgasm—despite her shock and fear. What that said about her was not something she cared to analyze too deeply. Even now, she could feel the residual dampness in her underwear and a slight pulsing sensation deep within her sex whenever she thought back to that limo ride.

Taking a deep breath, Mia squared her shoulders and exited the restroom. Her sex life in all its extraterrestrial manifestations would have to wait until the paper was done and submitted.

Her priorities were two-fold right now—an extra-large coffee and a few hours of uninterrupted quality time with the Mac.

ᛉ ᛉ ᛉ

The ringing of the doorbell and an excited squeal by her roommate woke up Mia twelve minutes before her alarm.

Groaning, she rolled over and put her pillow over her head, hoping that the source of the noise would go away and let her get the remaining few minutes of precious sleep.

She had gotten home at three in the morning, after finally finishing the evil paper. Unfortunately, she had a 9 a.m. class on Mondays, which meant that she would get less than five hours of sleep that night. Even so, her overtired brain had refused to let go of the day's events, with dark, erotic dreams interrupting her sleep—dreams in which she would see his face, feel his touch burning her skin, hear his voice promising both pain and ecstasy.

And now she couldn't even enjoy a few moments of peaceful rest, as Jessie apparently couldn't contain her excitement over whatever it was that came to the door.

"Mia! Mia! Guess what?" Jessie was practically singing as she knocked on Mia's bedroom door.

"I'm sleeping!" Mia growled, wanting to smack Jessie for the first time in her life.

"Oh come on, I know your alarm is about to go off. Rise and shine, Sleeping Beauty, and see what you got from Prince Charming!"

Mia bolted upright in her bed, all trace of sleepiness forgotten. "What are you talking about?" Jumping out of bed, she flung open the door, confronting her disgustingly cheerful and bright-eyed roommate.

"This!" With a huge excited grin, Jessie gestured toward a large vase of exotic pink and white flowers that occupied the center of their kitchen table. "The delivery guy just came and brought this. Look, there's even a card and everything! Do you know who sent it? Is there some secret admirer that you haven't told me about?"

Mia felt a sudden inner chill even as her pulse speeded up. Approaching the table, she reached for the card and opened it with trepidation. The content of the note—written in neat, but clearly masculine handwriting—was simple:

Tonight, 7pm. I will pick you up. Wear something nice.

Her hand shaking slightly, Mia put down the note. For some reason, she hadn't thought he would want to see her again so soon, much less come to her apartment.

"Well? Don't keep me in suspense!" Unable to wait any longer, Jessie grabbed the note and read it herself. "Ooh, what's this? You have a date?"

Mia felt the beginnings of a throbbing headache. "Not exactly," she said wearily. "Let me get dressed for class, and we can talk on the way."

Ten minutes later, Mia grabbed a breakfast bar and headed out the door with Jessie, who was nearly bursting with curiosity at this point. Sighing, Mia relayed a shortened version of the story, leaving out a few details that she felt were too private to share—such as his exact words and her reaction to him.

"Oh my God." Jessie's face reflected horrified disbelief. "And now he wants to see you again? Mia—this is bad, really bad."

"I know."

"I can't believe he just openly told you he intends to have sex with you." Jessie was wringing her hands in distress. "What if you don't show up tonight—go to the library instead or something?"

"I'm pretty sure he'll be able to find me there. He's done that before. And I don't know what he'll do if he gets mad."

Jessie's eyes widened. "Do you think he would hurt you?" she asked in a hushed tone.

Mia thought about it for a few seconds. All his actions toward her thus far had been . . . solicitous, for lack of a better word. It could all be an act, of course, but somehow she doubted that he would physically abuse her.

"I don't think so," she said slowly. "But I don't know what else he might be capable of."

"Like what?"

"Well, that's the thing—I just don't know." Mia nervously tugged at one long curl. "He's definitely not playing by any kind of normal dating rules. I mean, he practically kidnapped me off the street yesterday . . ."

"What if you go home to Florida?" Jessie was obviously desperate to find a solution.

"That seems like an overreaction. Besides, it's the middle of the semester. I can't go anywhere until this summer."

"Crap." Jessie sounded stumped for a second. "Well, then just tell him no when he shows up tonight. Do you think he would force you to go with him anyway?"

"I have no idea," Mia said wryly, pausing in front of the building that was her destination. "I'm going to have to think about this some more. Maybe if I look particularly ugly tonight, he'll lose interest."

"That's a great idea!" Jessie clapped her hands in excitement. "He wants you to wear something nice tonight? Well, you show him! Put on your ugliest clothes, eat some fresh garlic and onion, put some oil in your hair so it looks all greasy, and maybe do something that makes you sweaty—like a run—and don't shower or use deodorant afterwards!"

Mia stared at her roommate in fascination. "You're scary. How did you come up with all of this? It's not like you try to un-attract guys on a regular basis."

"Oh, it's easy. Just think of all the things you'd do to

get ready for a date—and do just the opposite." Jessie breezily waved one hand with such a know-it-all expression that Mia couldn't help but burst out laughing.

* * *

At six o'clock, Mia began implementing Jessie's plan. Her roommate had been dying to see her first K and lend Mia moral support for the confrontation, but she had a biology lab that couldn't be missed. Mia was glad about that. The last thing she wanted was to put Jessie in harm's way.

She started out by doing jumping jacks, lunges, squats, and sit-ups. Within fifteen minutes, her leg and stomach muscles—unused to so much exertion—were burning, and Mia was covered with a fine layer of sweat. Without bothering to shower, she put on her oldest, rattiest underwear, thick brown tights that her sister absolutely despised, and a long-sleeved black dress that Jessie had once claimed made her look completely washed out and shapeless. A pair of old black Mary-Janes with medium-height heels, worn out and scuffed, completed the look. No makeup, except for a slight dusting of dark blue shadow directly under her eyes—to imitate under-eye circles. Her hair already looked like a frizzy mess, but Mia brushed it for good measure and added hair conditioner only to the roots, leaving the ends to poof out in every direction. And for the grand finale, she cut up an entire clove of garlic, mixed it with green onion, and thoroughly chewed it, making sure that the smelly mixture got into every nook and corner of her mouth before she spit it out. Satisfied, she took one last look in the mirror. As expected, she looked ghastly—like somebody's crazy spinster aunt—and probably smelled even worse. If Korum remained interested in her after tonight, she would be very surprised.

When the doorbell rang promptly at seven, Mia put on her scruffy wool peacoat and opened the door with a mixture of trepidation and barely contained glee.

The sight that greeted her was breathtaking.

Somehow, in the short span of a day, Mia had managed to forget just how beautiful he was. Dressed in a pair of dark designer jeans and a light grey button-down shirt that fit his tall, muscular body to perfection, he fairly gleamed with health and vitality, his bronzed skin and glossy black hair providing a stark contrast for those incredible amber-colored eyes. Mia suddenly felt irrationally embarrassed about her own grungy appearance.

At the sight of her, his lips parted in a slow smile. "Ah, Mia. Somehow I suspected that you would be difficult."

"I don't know what you're talking about," Mia said defiantly, lifting her chin.

"I'm glad you decided to play this game." He reached out and stroked her cheek, sending an unwanted shiver of pleasure down her spine. "It will make your eventual surrender that much sweeter."

Still smiling, he politely offered her his arm. "Ready to go?"

Fuming, Mia ignored his offer, stomping down the stairs on her own. *Idiot!* She should've realized he would see her deliberately ugly appearance as a challenge. With his looks and apparent wealth, he probably had women fawning all over him. It must be refreshing to meet someone who didn't immediately fall into his bed. Maybe she should just sleep with him and get it over with. If the pursuit was what he enjoyed, then he would lose interest very quickly if he got what he wanted.

The limo was waiting as they exited the building. "Where are we going?" Mia asked, wondering about it for the first time.

"Percival," Korum answered, opening the door for her. The place he named was a popular restaurant in the Meatpacking District that was notoriously difficult to get into, even on a Monday night.

Mia mentally kicked herself again. It was one thing to look repellent for Korum—a wasted effort, as it turned out—but it was a whole different level of embarrassing to show up in the fanciest, trendiest district of New York City looking and smelling like a homeless person. Still, she'd rather die of embarrassment than give Korum the satisfaction of knowing how discomfited she felt.

He climbed into the car and sat down next to her. Reaching out, he took one of her hands and brought it to his lap, studying her palm and fingers with some apparent fascination. Her hand looked tiny in his large grasp, his golden skin appearing much darker next to her own whiteness, creating a surprisingly erotic contrast. Mia attempted to yank her hand away, trying to ignore the sensations his touch was provoking in her nether regions. He held her hand just long enough to let her feel the futility of her struggles, and then let go with a small smile.

It was strange, Mia thought, somewhere along the way she had stopped being so afraid of him. For some reason, knowing his intentions toward her—as crude and base as they were—gave her a peace of mind. The scared girl who sat in this car yesterday would not have dared to oppose him in any way for fear of unknown retaliation. Mia no longer had such qualms, and it was oddly liberating.

A minute later, the limo pulled up to the door of the restaurant. Korum exited first and Mia followed, noticing with mortification the double-takes they got from the well-dressed men and women on the street. A gorgeous K in his limo was bound to attract attention, and Mia was sure they wondered about his dowdy companion.

A tall, rail-thin hostess greeted them at the door. Without even asking for their reservations, she led them to a private booth in the back of the restaurant. "Welcome back to Percival," she purred, leaning suggestively over Korum while handing them the menus. "Should I start you off with sparkling or flat?"

"Sparkling would be fine, Ashley, thanks," he said absentmindedly, studying the menu.

Mia felt a sudden, shocking urge to tear out every straight blond hair from Ashley's model-like head. A strange nausea-like sensation roiled her stomach as she pictured the two of them together in bed, his muscular body wrapped around the blonde's. *Stop it, Mia! Of course, he slept with other women!* Undoubtedly, the creature left a trail of Ashleys anywhere he went.

"Have you decided what you'd like?" he inquired, looking up from his menu, seemingly oblivious to the murderous expression on Mia's face.

"No, not yet." Taking a deep breath, she forced herself to concentrate on the menu. This was undoubtedly the nicest restaurant she'd ever been to, and the menu—which lacked prices for some reason—listed some dishes and ingredients that she'd never heard of. Her eyes widened as she noticed goat cheese and caviar in the appetizer section and eggs in one of the noodle dishes. Her mouth watered. "I think I'll get the roasted beets and goat cheese salad, followed by the pesto-artichoke Pad Thai."

Korum smiled at her indulgently. "Of course." He motioned to the waiter and relayed her order. "And I will have the watercress jicama salad and the shiitake parsnip ravioli in cashew cream. We'll also get a bottle of Dom Perignon."

Mia looked at him in fascination. She hadn't known that Ks consumed alcohol. In fact, there was so much that she—and the public in general—didn't know about the invaders who now lived alongside them. It dawned on Mia that she had the perfect opportunity to learn sitting across her at the table.

Feeling slightly reckless, she decided to start with the question that had been bothering her ever since their first meeting. "Is it true that you drink human blood?"

Korum's eyebrows shot up on his forehead, and he nearly choked on his drink. "You don't pull any punches, do you?" A big grin breaking out on his face, he asked, "Are you asking if we have to drink human blood, or if we do it anyway?"

Mia swallowed. She was suddenly far from sure this was the best line of questioning. "I guess both."

"Well, let me set your mind at ease . . . We no longer require blood for survival."

"But you did before?" Mia's eyes widened in shock.

"Originally, when we first evolved into our current form, we needed to consume significant amounts of blood from a group of primates that had certain genetic similarities to us. It was a deficiency in our DNA that made us vulnerable and tied our existence to another species. We have since corrected this defect."

"So it's true? There were humans on your planet?" Mia was staring at him open-mouthed.

"They weren't exactly human. Their blood, however, had the same hemoglobin characteristics as yours."

"What happened to them? Are they still around?"

"No, they are now extinct."

"I don't understand," Mia said slowly, trying to make

sense of what she'd learned thus far. "If you needed them to survive, how and when did they go extinct? Was that before or after you ... um ... fixed your defect?"

"It happened long before then. We succeeded in developing a synthetic substance before the last of their kind disappeared, and it enabled us to survive their demise. They were an endangered species for millions of years. It was partially our fault for hunting them, but a lot of it had to do with their own low birth rate and short lifespan. Just like you, they had a weak immune system, and a plague nearly wiped them out. That's when we began to work on alternative routes of survival for our species—synthetic hemoglobin substitutes, experimentation with our own DNA, and attempting to develop a comparable species both on Krina and on other planets."

A lightbulb went off in Mia's brain. "Is that why you planted life here on Earth? Is that how humans came to be—you needed a comparable species?"

"More or less. It was a shot in the dark, with minuscule odds of success. We disseminated our DNA as far as our then-primitive technology could reach. We didn't know which planets and where would be hospitable to life, much less bear any similarities to Krina, so we blindly sent billions of drones to planets that are located in what you now call the Goldilocks Zones."

"Goldilocks Zones?"

"Yes, these are also called the habitable zones— regions in the universe around various stars that potentially have the right atmospheric pressure to maintain liquid water on the surface. Based on our knowledge, those are the only places where life similar to Krina's could arise."

Mia nodded, now remembering learning about that in

high school.

Satisfied that she was following along, he continued his explanation. "One of the drones reached Earth, and the first simple organisms succeeded in surviving here. Of course, we didn't know that at the time. It wasn't until some six hundred million years ago that we reached this part of the galaxy and found Earth."

"Right before the Cambrian explosion began?" asked Mia, goosebumps breaking out on her arms. It was public knowledge now that the Ks had influenced evolution on Earth to a fairly significant degree, the timing of their initial arrival coinciding with the previously puzzling appearance of many new and complex life forms during the early Cambrian period. But their motives for planting life on Earth and later manipulating it had remained a mystery, and it was incredible to hear him speak about it so nonchalantly, revealing so much to her over dinner.

"Exactly. We have occasionally stepped in to guide your evolution, particularly when it threatened to drastically diverge from ours—such as when the dinosaurs had become a dominant life form—"

"But I thought the dinosaurs had been killed by an asteroid?"

"They were. But we could have easily deflected that strike. Instead, we simply ensured that the necessary life forms, such as the early versions of mammals, survived."

Mia stared at him open-mouthed as he continued the story.

"When the first primate appeared here, it was a tremendous achievement for us because its blood carried the hemoglobin. However, we no longer needed it by then because we'd recently had the breakthrough that allowed us to manipulate our own DNA without adverse consequences."

He paused when the salads were served, and continued speaking between bites of his watercress. "At that point, Earth and its primate species had become the grandest scientific experiment in the history of the known universe. The challenge for us became to see whether we could nudge along evolution just enough to see another intelligent species emerge."

Mia felt chills going down her spine as she listened to the story of human origins told by an alien from the gazillion-year-old civilization that had essentially played God. An alien who was munching on his salad at the same time, as though discussing nothing more important than the weather.

"You see," he continued, "the primates on Krina were of the same intelligence level as your chimpanzees, and few of us thought that a species as short-lived as yours could develop a truly sophisticated intellect. But we persisted, occasionally stepping in with genetic modifications to make you look more like us, and the result has surpassed all our expectations. While you share a lot of the characteristics of the Krinian primates— presence of the hemoglobin, a relatively weak immune system, and a short lifespan—you have a much higher birth rate and an intelligence that's nearly comparable to ours. Your evolution rate is also much faster than ours— mostly due to that higher birth rate. The transition from primitive primates to intelligent beings took you only a couple of million years, while it took us nearly a billion."

Dozens of questions were running through Mia's mind. She latched onto the first one. "Why did you care if we looked like you? Is that somehow a requirement for intelligence?"

"No, not really. It just made the most sense to the scientists who were overseeing the project at the time.

They wanted to create a sister species, intelligent beings that looked like us, so that it would be easier for us to relate to them, easier to communicate with them. Of course," he said with a wicked smile, twirling his empty fork, "there was an unexpected side benefit."

Mia looked at him warily. "What benefit?"

"Well, you see, when the first Earth primates appeared, some of the Krinar tried drinking their blood out of curiosity. And they quickly discovered that, in the absence of the biological need for the hemoglobin, drinking blood gave them a very pleasurable high—an almost sexual buzz. It was better than any drug, although synthetic versions of your blood have since become quite popular in our bars and nightclubs."

Mia nearly choked on her salad. Coughing, she drank some water to clear the obstruction in her throat while he watched with an amused look on his face.

"But the best thing of all was our more recent discovery." He leaned closer to her, his eyes turning a now-familiar shade of deeper gold. "You see, it turns out that there's nothing quite as pleasurable as drinking blood from a living source during sex. The experience is simply indescribable."

Mia reflexively swallowed, feeling horrified and oddly aroused at the same time. "So you want to drink my blood while . . . fucking?"

The corners of his mouth turned upward in a sensuous smile. "That would be the ultimate goal, yes."

She had to know, even if the answer made her sick to her stomach. "Would I die?"

He laughed. "Die? No, taking a few sips of your blood won't kill you any more than giving blood at a doctor's office. In fact, our saliva contains a chemical that makes the whole process quite pleasurable for humans. It was originally intended for our prey, to make them drugged and docile when we fed on them—but now it merely serves the purpose of enhancing your experience."

Mia's head felt like it was exploding with everything she'd just learned, but there was something else she needed to find out. "How exactly do you do it?" she asked cautiously. "Drink blood, I mean? Do you have fangs?"

He shook his head. "No, that's an invention of your literary fiction. We don't need fangs—the edges of our top teeth are sharp enough that they can penetrate the skin with relative ease, usually by just slicing through the top layer."

Their main course arrived, giving Mia a few precious moments to regain her composure.

It was too much, all of it.

Her thoughts spun around, all jumbled and chaotic. Somehow, in the past twenty-four hours, she'd gotten used to the idea that an extraterrestrial wanted to have sex with her, for whatever reason. But now he also wanted her to serve as a blood donor during sex. His species had basically created her kind, and they now used human blood as some sort of an aphrodisiac. The idea was disturbing and sickening on many levels, and all Mia wanted to do was crawl into her bed, pulling covers over her head, and pretend that none of this was happening.

Something of her inner turmoil must have shown on her face because Korum reached out, gently covering her hand with his, and said softly, "Mia, I know this is all a huge shock to you. I know that you need time to understand and get to know me better. Why don't you relax and enjoy your meal, and we can discuss something else in the meantime?" He added with a teasing smile, "I promise not to bite."

Mia nodded and obediently dug into her food as soon

as he released her hand. It was either that or run out of the restaurant screaming, and she wasn't sure how he would react to that. After everything she'd learned today, the last thing she wanted was to provoke whatever predatory instincts his species still possessed.

The Pad Thai was delicious, she realized, tasting the rich flavors complemented by bits of real egg. For some reason, despite her delicate build, nothing ever interfered with her appetite. Her family often joked that Mia must really be a lumberjack in disguise, given the large quantities of food she liked to consume on a regular basis. "How is your ravioli?" she asked between bites of her noodles, searching for the most innocuous subject.

"It's great," he answered, enjoying his dish with similar gusto. "I often come to this restaurant because they have one of the best chefs in New York."

"I don't know," Mia teased, trying to keep the conversation light. "The salad and sandwich you made yesterday was pretty tasty."

He grinned at her, exposing the dimple that made him seem so much more approachable. It was only on his left cheek, not the right—a slight imperfection in his otherwise flawless features that only added to his appeal. "Why, thank you. That's the best compliment I got all year."

"Do you cook a lot for yourself or mostly go out to restaurants?" Food seemed like a nice safe topic.

"I do both quite a bit. I like to eat, as you apparently do too—" he motioned to her rapidly disappearing portion with a smile, "—so that necessitates a lot of both. What about you? I imagine it's tough to go out too much in New York on a student's budget."

"That would be an understatement," Mia agreed. "But there are some really nice cheap places near NYU and in

Chinatown, if I want to venture out that far."

"What made you decide to come to New York for school? Your home state has a number of good universities, and the weather is so much better there." He seemed genuinely perplexed.

Mia laughed as the irony of her school choice only now occurred to her. "When I was applying to colleges, my parents were afraid that you—the Krinar, I mean— might establish a Center in Florida, so they wanted me to go to an out-of-state school."

Korum smiled in response. "We did actually think about settling there, but it was too densely populated for our taste." He took a sip of his champagne. "So I'm guessing they wouldn't be particularly happy that you're here with me today?"

"God, no." Mia shuddered. "My mom would probably be hysterical, and my dad would get one of his stress migraines."

"And your sister?"

"Um, she wouldn't be particularly happy either." For a moment, she had almost forgotten how much he knew about her.

"She's older than you, right?"

"By nearly eight years. She got married last year."

"I wonder what it would be like to have a sibling," he mused. "It's not a very common occurrence for us, having more than one child."

Mia shrugged. "I'm not sure if my experience was particularly authentic, given our age difference. By the time I was old enough to be anything more than a brat, she had already left for college." Her curiosity kicking in again, she asked, "So you don't have any siblings? What about your parents?"

"I'm an only child. My parents are back on Krina, so I

haven't seen them in a while. We do communicate remotely, though, on a regular basis."

Their waiter returned to clear the table and give them their dessert menus. Mia chose tiramisu—made with real cheese and eggs—and Korum went with the apple pecan tart. Somehow, in the course of their conversation, she'd managed to down two glasses of champagne, and was beginning to feel buzzed. The evening took on a slightly surreal tint in her mind, from the restaurant filled with Manhattan's most beautiful people to the gorgeous predator who sat across the table from her, blithely chatting about their families.

Mia wondered how old he was. She knew the Ks were very long-lived, so there was really no way to tell his age from appearance. Had he been human, she would have guessed late twenties. Her curiosity got the best of her again, and she blurted out, "How old are you?"

"About two thousand of your Earth years."

Mia stared at him in shock. That would put him somewhere in the very ancient category by human standards. Two thousand years ago, the Roman Empire still ruled the Western world, and the Christian religion was just getting its start. And he had been alive since that time?

She drank some more champagne to help with the dryness in her throat. "Does that make you old or young in your society?"

He shrugged his broad shoulders. "I guess on the younger side. My parents are much older. It doesn't matter, though. Once we reach full maturity, age literally becomes just a number."

"We must all seem like infants to you then, huh?" Mia took a big gulp from her glass and felt the room tilt slightly. She hoped she wasn't slurring her words. She probably should stop with the champagne. He could easily take advantage of her if she got drunk. But, then again, he could easily take advantage of her sober too. She was completely at the mercy of an alien who wanted to fuck her and drink her blood, so she might as well enjoy this undoubtedly excellent vintage.

"Not infants. Just naive in certain ways. More like teenagers, if anything."

Mia rubbed an itchy spot on her nose with the back of her hand, wondering if she wanted to know the answer to her next question. She decided to go for it. "So are you immortal, like the vampires of our legends?"

"We don't think of it that way. Everybody can die. Our species has always enjoyed negligible senescence, but we can still be killed or die in a bad accident."

"Negligible senescence?"

"Basically, we don't have the symptoms of aging. Before we were sufficiently advanced with our science and medicine, we could still die from a variety of natural causes, but we've now succeeded in achieving a very low—almost negligible—mortality rate."

"How is this possible?" asked Mia. "How can a living creature not age? Is that something peculiar to Krina?"

"Not really. There are actually a number of species right here on Earth that have that same characteristic. For instance, have you ever heard of the four-hundred-year-old clam?"

"What? No!" He had to be making fun of her ignorance; surely such a thing didn't exist.

He nodded. "It's true—look it up if you don't believe me. There are a number of creatures that don't lose their reproductive or functional capabilities with age—some species of mussels and clams, lobsters, sea anemones, giant tortoises, hydras . . . In fact, hydras are pretty much biologically immortal; they die from injury or disease, but not from old age."

Trying to process this incredible information, Mia rubbed her nose again. That's it, she realized, no more alcohol for her. For some reason, her nose had a tendency to get itchy after a few drinks, and Mia had learned to respect it as a sign of when to stop. The few times she'd ignored this warning, the consequences hadn't been pretty.

Seeing her weaving slightly in her seat, Korum motioned the waiter for the check. Mia hazily wondered if she should offer to split it, the way she always did when she went out with college guys. Nah, she decided. He had practically forced her to come out today, so she might as well get a free meal out of it. Besides, she wasn't sure she could afford this place, given the priceless menu. So instead, she just observed when Korum waived his wristwatch phone-wallet over the waiter's tiny digital receptor, and added what seemed to be a generous tip, judging by the grateful expression on the waiter's face.

"Ready to go?" He helped her put on her coat and again offered her his arm. Mia accepted this time, as she felt somewhat woozy and didn't have a high degree of confidence in her own ability to make it out of the restaurant without tripping at some point.

"Are you drunk?" he asked with amusement, observing her slightly unsteady gait as they exited onto the street. "I only saw you drink a couple of glasses."

Mia raised her chin and lied, "I'm perfectly fine." She hated it when people pointed out what a lightweight she was.

"If you say so." He looked like he was about to laugh, and Mia wanted to smack him.

Roger and the limo were waiting at the curb, of course.

Mia hesitated, her heart rate accelerating at the realization that she would be alone with an extraterrestrial predator who wanted her blood.

She turned to him. "You know, I really feel like getting some fresh air. I can just walk from here—my apartment is only about a dozen blocks away, and the weather is really quite nice and refreshing." The last bit was a lie. It was actually quite chilly, and Mia was already shivering in her thin coat.

His expression darkened. "Mia. Get in. I will take you home." It was his scary tone of voice, and it worked just as well on her the second time around. Shaking slightly from a combination of nerves and the cold air, she climbed into the car.

The ride to her apartment was oddly uneventful, taking only a few minutes in the absence of traffic. He again held her hand, gently rubbing her palm in a soothing manner. Despite her initial nervousness, Mia closed her eyes, leaned back against the comfortable seat, and was just starting to drift off when they arrived at their destination.

He walked her up the five flights of stairs to her apartment, holding her arm as an apparent precaution against any alcohol-induced unsteadiness. She felt tired and sleepy, wanting nothing more than to collapse into her bed at home. At one point, she managed to stumble and nearly fall anyway, missing a step with her high-heeled shoe. Korum sighed and lifted her into his arms, carrying her up the remaining two flights despite her mumbled protestations.

Upon reaching her apartment, he carefully set her back on her feet, briefly keeping her pressed against his hard body before letting her pull away. His hands remained on her waist, holding her at a short distance. Mia stared at him, mesmerized. Her breathing picked up, and warm moisture pooled between her legs as she realized what the large bulge she'd felt in his jeans meant. His breathing was a little fast too, and she doubted that it had anything to do with carrying a hundred-pound human girl up two flights of stairs. He leaned toward her, eyes nearly yellow at this point, and Mia froze as he cupped the back of her head and pressed his lips to hers.

He kissed her leisurely, his tongue exploring her mouth with exquisite gentleness, even as he held her against him in an unbreakable grip. Mia moaned, a wave of heat surging through her body and leaving an oddly pleasurable sense of lethargy in its wake. Somewhere in the back of her mind, a warning bell was going off, but all she could concentrate on was his mouth and the sensations spreading throughout her body. He brought her closer, pressing his groin against her belly, and she felt his hardness again, her sex clenching in response. He lightly sucked on her lower lip, pulling it into his mouth, and his hand slid down her back to cup her buttocks, lifting her off the ground so he could grind his erection directly against her clitoris through their layers of clothing.

The pressure building inside her was different and stronger than anything she'd ever experienced, and Mia groaned with frustration, wanting more. Her hands somehow found their way to his shoulders, kneading the heavy muscles through his shirt, and it was not enough. She wanted, needed the feel of his naked skin against her own, the slide of his heavy cock into her sex, quenching the empty pulsing sensation she felt there. She wrapped her legs around his waist, grinding against him, and the sensations built to a fever pitch. She hovered on the edge for a few delicious seconds, and then went over, climaxing with a muffled scream against lips. He groaned as well, his other hand reaching under her skirt and tearing at her tights as he let go of her mouth to press burning kisses on her neck and collarbone.

"Mia? Is that you?" A familiar voice reached through her daze, and Mia realized with mortification that Jessie had opened the apartment door and was staring at them in shock. "Are you okay? Do you want me to call the police?" Her roommate clearly wasn't sure how to interpret what she was seeing.

Still wrapped around Korum, Mia felt a shudder go through his body as he visibly fought to regain control. Suddenly fearing for Jessie, Mia barked at her, "Yes, I'm fine! Go back inside and leave us alone!" A hurt look appeared on her roommate's face, and she vanished inside the apartment, slamming the door behind her.

Mia pushed at Korum, trying to put some distance between them. "Please let me go," she said quietly, wanting nothing more than to curl up into a little ball in her room and cry. He hesitated for a second, and then lowered her to her feet, still keeping her pressed against his body. His golden skin appeared flushed from within, and his eyes still had a strong yellow undertone. The bulge against her stomach showed no signs of abating, and Mia shivered, realizing that he was holding onto his self-control by a hair. "Please," she repeated, knowing that there was nothing she could do to make him release her until he was ready.

"You want me to let you go? After all that?" His voice was harsh and guttural, and the arms locked around her back tightened until she could barely breathe.

Mia nodded, trembling, the white-hot desire she'd felt earlier giving way to a confusing jumble of fear and acute embarrassment. He looked at her, his expression dark and unreadable, and then very deliberately removed his arms from around her waist and stepped away.

"All right," he said softly. "Have it your way. Go to your little room, and tell your roommate all about it. Have yourself a good cry about what a little slut you are, coming like that from a kiss right out in the hallway." His eyes glittered at the stricken expression on her face. "And then you better get used to the idea that you'll come a lot more, from everything I do to you—and I will literally do everything."

With that promise, he turned away and walked toward the stairs. Pausing before entering the stairwell, he looked back and said, "I will pick you up after class tomorrow. No more games, Mia."

CHAPTER FIVE

Her legs shaking, Mia made her way into the apartment with as much dignity as she could muster considering that her underwear was soaking wet and her tights were hanging in shreds around her knees. Jessie sat on the couch in the living room, waiting for her to come in. She didn't look mad anymore, just extremely concerned.

"Oh my God, Mia," she said slowly. "What the hell was that out in the hallway?"

Mia shook her head, barely holding back tears. "Jessie, I'm sorry. I really can't talk now," she said, going directly to her room and closing the door.

Collapsing on the bed, she wrapped the coverlet around herself and pulled her knees up to her chest. Her body seemed like it didn't belong to her, with her sex still pulsating in the aftermath of her orgasm. Her lips were swollen from his kisses, and her nipples felt so sensitive that the bra was too abrasive against her skin. She also felt raw and devastated inside, exposed in a way that she'd never before experienced in her life.

She didn't want this—any of this. The complete loss of

control over her own body was overwhelming, and the fact that Korum was the one to solicit such a powerful response made her feel even more vulnerable.

He frightened her.

She was completely out of her league with him, and she knew it. As scary as it was to think about what the sexual act with an extraterrestrial vampire was likely to entail, the thing that Mia dreaded most was the effect he had on her emotions. He would take everything from her—her body and her soul—and when he was done, he would move on, leaving her broken and scarred for life, unable to ever forget her dark alien lover.

This was not how her life was supposed to turn out. Coming from a family of second-generation Polish immigrants, Mia had always followed the right path. She studied hard in school, both to please her parents and out of her own desire for achievement. Once she finished grad school, she intended to use her degree to counsel high school or college students on their own career path. She was close to her parents and sister, and she hoped to be a good mother to her own children one day. At some point, she was supposed to fall in love with a nice man from a good family and have a long happy marriage, the way her own parents did. While other girls dreamed of adventures and chased after bad boys, Mia just wanted a regular life, done the right way.

She had always known that she was a sexual creature. Despite her lack of experience, she had no doubt that she would enjoy sex once she found the right person. She loved reading racy novels and watching R-rated movies, and she considered herself far from a prude. In fact, she liked the idea of trying out new things and having several relationships before ultimately settling down. When she went out clubbing with Jessie, Mia frequently found herself turned on from dancing with some attractive guy, particularly after having a couple of shots. For some reason, it had never gone beyond a few kisses, perhaps because Mia was too cautious and rational to pick up a guy at a club for a one-night stand. Still, she had looked forward to her first time, preferably with a special someone that she cared about and who cared about her. An alien predator who wanted to fuck her and drink her blood was as far removed from that ideal as anything that Mia could imagine.

She wanted a shower.

Slowly getting up, Mia took off her clothes. The tights were beyond salvation, so she threw them in the trash. Her black dress was also slightly ripped in the front—Mia could not even remember when that happened—and she discarded it also. Feeling reckless, she chucked the Mary-Janes and her underwear into the bin as well, wanting nothing to remind her of this night. Wrapping herself in her robe, Mia left the safety of her room and headed into the shower, hoping that Jessie had gone to sleep.

* * *

The next morning, Mia woke up with a headache.

As soon as she opened her eyes, the events of the last evening rushed back into her mind, accompanied by a scalding feeling of humiliation. He had mockingly called her a slut, and she very much felt like one, particularly given what Jessie had been privy to. She also remembered what he'd said about picking her up today, and she suddenly felt nauseous from a combination of fear and some kind of sick excitement.

She only had one class today, and it didn't start until eleven. It was just as well, since she didn't even know if she wanted to get out of bed at all.

There was a timid knock on her door.

"Yes, come in," Mia said in resignation, knowing that Jessie must've been anxiously waiting for her to wake up and listening for any movements in her room.

Her roommate entered sheepishly and sat down on Mia's bed. "So I guess my patented guy-repellent strategy was a total fail, huh?"

Mia rubbed her eyes and gave Jessie a bitter smile. "It's pretty fair to say, yes." Taking a deep breath, she said, "Look, I'm sorry about yesterday. I didn't mean to yell at you—I just really didn't want you out there, seeing what I guess you saw."

Jessie nodded, clearly having figured it out on her own. "No worries. I would've done the same. I was just worried that he was forcing you or something. So, are you, like, really into him now?"

Mia groaned and buried her head in her pillow. "I don't know. Every sane part of me says to run as far away as I can, but every time he touches me, I just can't help myself. It's like I don't have any control over this thing. I hate it."

Jessie's eyes widened. "Oh, wow. That's *so* hot. It's like the kind of thing you read about in romance novels— he kisses her and she swoons!"

An elusive something kept nagging at Mia this morning, and Jessie's words suddenly put the puzzle pieces together.

Of course! He did kiss her, and he had explicitly told her that K saliva contained some chemical that kept their prey docile and drugged. It all made sense now—the pleasant lethargy that had spread through her veins and the way her brain had simply turned off the second his lips touched hers, leaving her to operate on pure animal instinct. The chemical was probably even more potent directly in the bloodstream, but she had undoubtedly gotten a nice dose of it last night.

No wonder she had acted like such a slut—not only was she drunk from champagne, but she was also literally high from his kiss.

A burning fury slowly built in her stomach, replacing the sense of humiliation she'd felt earlier. The bastard. He had basically drugged her and very nearly took advantage, and then he had the nerve to accuse *her* of playing games. Well, screw him! If he thought she would meekly go with him today after class, he had another thing coming.

Her brain whirled, searching for alternatives.

"Jessie," she said slowly. "Didn't you once tell me that a cousin of yours had some kind of connections in the Resistance?"

"Uh—" Jessie was clearly surprised. "Are you talking about that thing I once told you about Jason? That was a long time ago, when we were still freshmen. I'm pretty sure he doesn't have anything to do with that anymore, not that I've kept in touch with him." She stared at Mia with a concerned look on her face. "Why are you even asking? What, you want to join the freedom fighters now?"

Mia shrugged, not sure where she was going with this. All she knew was that she refused to meekly become Korum's sex toy, to be used and discarded at whim.

She had never believed in the anti-K movement and thought that the Resistance fighters were crazy. The Krinar were here to stay. Human weapons and technology were hopelessly primitive in comparison to theirs, and Mia had always thought that trying to fight them was the equivalent of banging your head against the wall—futile and likely dangerous. Besides, it didn't seem all that bad, once the days of the Great Panic were over. The Ks had mostly left them alone, choosing to live in their own settlements, and life went on with a few minor differences—cleaner air, a healthier diet, and a lot of shattered illusions about humanity's place in the universe. However, now that she'd had some personal interactions with one particular K, she felt a bit more sympathetic to the fighters' cause—not that it made the Resistance movement any less futile.

She sighed. "Never mind, it was just a stupid idea. I think I just need to clear my head." Hopping out of bed, Mia pulled on her jeans, an old T-shirt, and a comfy sweater.

"Wait, Mia. What's going on?" Jessie was confused by her actions. "Are you upset about what happened last night?"

Mia pulled on her socks and a pair of sneakers. "I guess," she muttered. Telling her roommate the whole story would just make her worry, and a worried Jessie sometimes did drastic things—such as calling the police once to report Mia missing, when she had simply fallen asleep in the library with a dead phone battery. Not that Jessie could do anything in this case, but she still preferred not to cause her unnecessary distress. "Look, I'm fine," Mia lied. "I just really need to take a walk and get some air. You know I haven't exactly had a lot of experience with this type of thing, and this is a little like being thrown in the deep end of the pool. I just want to try to figure out how I feel about all this before I can even begin to talk about it."

Jessie looked at her with a faintly hurt expression. "Okay, well, sure. Whatever you need to do." Then she brightened. "Are you going to be home for dinner tonight? I was thinking of cooking some pasta, and we could just have a girls' night in, watch some old movies . . ."

Mia shook her head with regret. "That sounds amazing, but I really don't know. I think I'll be seeing him again today."

Seeing the worried look on Jessie's face, she quickly added with a sly smile, "And it might be quite fun." Before Jessie had a chance to reply, Mia grabbed her backpack and ran out the door with a quick "see you later."

She walked briskly down the street with no particular destination in mind. Stopping by a deli, she bought a pack of chewing gum—since she hadn't even brushed her teeth this morning—and a wrap loaded with hummus, avocado, and fresh veggies. Her brain seemed to have gone into hibernation, and she simply walked without thinking about anything in particular, enjoying the feel of her feet striking the pavement and the mid-morning sun warming her face. She must've walked like that for a long time because, by the time she started paying attention to street signs, she was already in TriBeCa, a block away from the luxury high-rise that she'd been in less than forty-eight hours ago.

And just like that, she knew what she was going to do—what her subconscious must've known even earlier because it had brought her here.

It was really quite simple.

Running was futile. He could track her down anywhere she went, and he had already proven that he could manipulate her body into responding to his with the aid of various chemical substances. No, running wasn't the answer. He was a hunter. The chase was what he loved, and there was really only one thing she could do to thwart him. She could deny him the chase, take away the enjoyment of pursuing a reluctant prey.

She could come to him herself.

* * *

Having reached the decision, Mia lost no time in putting it into action.

Entering the lobby of his building, she calmly told the concierge that she was there to see Korum. The man's eyes widened a little—he clearly knew what the occupant of the top floor was—and he notified the unit of her presence. Ten seconds later, he motioned toward the elevator that was positioned a little to the left of the main one. "Please go ahead, miss. Just enter in 1159 when prompted for a code, and it will take you to the penthouse floor."

Korum was waiting when the elevator doors opened.

Despite her intention to remain unmoved, her breath caught in her throat and her pulse jacked up at the sight. He wore a soft-looking pair of grey pajama pants and nothing else. His upper body was completely bare, with bronze skin covering chiseled muscle and a light smattering of dark hair visible around small, masculine nipples. Broad shoulders, thick with ropy muscles, tapered down to a slim waist, and an actual six pack covered his flat abdomen. There wasn't an ounce of fat anywhere on his powerful body.

Mia swallowed to help the dryness in her throat, suddenly far less sure of the wisdom of her plan.

"Mia," he purred, leaning on the doorway and looking for all the world like a big jungle cat about to pounce. "To what do I owe this pleasure? I was not expecting to see you so early." Something in her expression must've betrayed her because he let out a short laugh. "Ah, I see. It was *because* I wasn't expecting you. Well, come on in."

Padding to the kitchen in his bare feet, he asked, "Have you had breakfast?"

Mia nodded, feeling like a mute but afraid that her voice might betray her nervousness. This was definitely not the best plan. Why had she thought that bearding the lion in his den was somehow better than trying to avoid him altogether?

But there was no turning back now.

"Okay, then, perhaps I might interest you in some coffee or tea?" His tone was overly courteous, making a mockery of the normally polite question.

Her chin went up at the realization that he found the whole situation amusing. "No, thanks," she said coolly, taking pride in the level tone of her voice. "You know why I'm here. Why don't *you* stop playing games, so we can just get on with it?"

He stopped and looked at her. There was no trace of laughter on his face. "All right, Mia," he said slowly. "If that's how you wish it."

"One more thing," she said, wanting to needle him and no longer caring about the consequences. "No drugs of any kind. No alcohol and no saliva anywhere in my body. If you want my blood, you can just cut my vein and drink it that way. And no mouth-to-mouth kissing. I don't want to be drunk *or* high today."

His face darkened, and his eyes seemed to turn into pools of liquid gold. "You think you were high yesterday? Is that what you're telling yourself to explain what happened? That a couple of glasses of champagne and my magic kisses turned you into a nymphomaniac?" He laughed sardonically. "Well, sorry to disappoint you, darling, but the chemical in our saliva only works if it gets directly into your blood. Maybe if I kissed you all day long, after a few hours you might feel a tiny buzz—if you're lucky. Of course, if I kissed you all day long, you would probably come dozens of times and be long past noticing any kind of saliva-induced effects." Still smiling, he said pleasantly, "But have it your way. No kissing and no biting. All else is fair game."

Coming up to her, he took her hand and led her down the hall. Her heart pounding, Mia went without protest, knowing that the time for changing her mind was long past. She didn't know whether to believe him and, more importantly, she didn't want to believe him. If he was telling the truth, then she had made a huge mistake in coming here today. Some foolish part of her had thought that she could do this—let him have sex with her unwilling, unresponsive body, reduce him to being the rapist he'd claimed he was not—and walk away with her emotions untouched, maintaining some kind of moral high ground. If he wasn't lying, then she was, quite literally, screwed.

He led her into what had to be his bedroom. Like the rest of his penthouse, the room was both modern and opulent at the same time. A large circular bed dominated the center of the room. It was unmade and had obviously been recently slept in. The sheets were a soft ivory color, and the thick blankets and pillows strewn around the bed were a pale shade of blue. Mia's heart climbed into her throat as she fully realized what she'd just agreed to do.

He released her hand and stepped back, leaving her standing in the middle of the room. "All right," he said softly, "now take off your clothes."

Mia stood there frozen, a hot wave of embarrassment rolling through her. He wanted her to remove her clothes, right there in the middle of the sunlit room?

"You heard me," he repeated, his voice cold despite the yellow heat in his eyes. "Take them off." Seeing her hesitation, he added, "I can guarantee your clothes will not survive it if I lay my hands on them."

Mia's hands shook as she slowly raised them to pull the sweater over her head. He merely watched her, his face inscrutable despite the hunger in his eyes. She took off her sneakers, and her jeans were next, leaving her clad in pink boy-short panties and a T-shirt. She had forgotten to wear a bra and now acutely felt that lack, with her nipples hard and visible against the thin fabric of the T-shirt.

"Now take off your shirt," he instructed, seeing her pause. The front of his pants was tented, she noticed, and somehow that was oddly reassuring—to know that she had that kind of effect on him, that he wasn't turned off by her awkwardness or her skinny body. Trembling slightly, she pulled the shirt over her head, revealing her breasts to male eyes for the first time. It took all her willpower not to cross her arms over her chest in a silly virginal gesture; instead, she stood there with her hands fisted at her sides, letting him look his fill.

He came toward her then and touched her, slowly stroking one palm down her back while another hand cupped her left breast, gently kneading it as though to test its weight and texture. "You're very pretty," he murmured, looking down at her as his hands deliberately explored her body, every stroke sending ripples of heat down to her nether regions. Standing there in her bare feet, Mia was acutely aware of how much larger his body was compared to hers, with her head barely reaching his shoulder and each of his arms thicker than half of her torso. His hands appeared dark against her pale skin, and she shivered when he moved his palm down to her belly, the width of his open hand nearly spanning the distance between her hip bones. His erection prodded her side, the thin material of his pajama pants doing little to conceal its heat and hardness.

Without the blurring effect from the alcohol or the shield of darkness, there was no retreat from his brutally intimate actions, no merciful escape into a sensual fog. Instead, Mia stood there in broad daylight, exposed and vulnerable, intensely aware of each stroke of his large hands over her body and the warm moisture lubricating her sex in response.

Hooking his thumbs into her underwear, he pushed her panties down her legs, removing her last defense. "Step out of them," he hoarsely ordered, and Mia obeyed, standing completely naked in his arms. The fact that he was still wearing his pants somehow made the whole thing worse, adding to her sense of complete powerlessness.

He touched her buttocks, his hands curving around the small pale globes of her ass and lightly squeezing them. "Very nice," he whispered, and Mia blushed for some inexplicable reason. The dark curls between her legs attracted his attention next, and Mia flinched when his fingers slowly stroked her pussy hair, looking for the tender flesh underneath. Feeling her wetness, he smiled with purely masculine satisfaction, and Mia's embarrassment grew tenfold. This was the worst part—knowing that her own body betrayed her, that a creature who was not even human could provoke this kind of response from her under the circumstances.

"No mouth-to-mouth, right?" he murmured, picking her up and carrying her over to the bed. Mia nodded, squeezing her eyes shut in the hopes that it would be over with quickly. Instead, he placed her in the middle of the circular bed, like some virginal sacrifice, and crawled down her body until his head was above the juncture of her legs. Mia tried to rear up then, realizing his intentions, but he had no intention of letting her go. Instead, he easily held down her flailing legs with his elbows while his fingers leisurely parted her folds, exposing her most sensitive place to his burning gaze. Lowering his head, he gently pressed his tongue, soft and flat, against her clitoris—just holding it there and letting her struggle until she could bear it no longer, her entire body arching with the most powerful climax of her life.

While she lay there, still shuddering with little aftershocks, he rose up on his knees, deftly stripping off the pants to reveal a large jutting penis. Mia's eyes widened as she realized that her first time would likely involve more than a minor discomfort, given the size of the cock in front of her.

Seeing her fear, he paused. "Mia," he said quietly, "we don't have to do this if you're not ready. I can wait—"

She shook her head, unable to think past the fog of desire clouding her brain. It had taken all her courage to get this far, to allow him so much intimacy. To retreat now seemed cowardly, and Mia felt a sudden, irrational dread that this was it—that if she gave up a chance to experience such passion now, she would never feel it again.

He didn't need much encouragement. Before her logical side could reassert itself, he was already over her, parting her legs with one powerfully muscled thigh and settling in between them. Looking steadily into her eyes, he began to push his cock into her opening, slowly working it in inch by slow inch.

Regretting her decision almost immediately, Mia

writhed under him, feeling like a heated baseball bat was attempting to enter her channel. Despite the wetness from her orgasm, her inner muscles did not want to let him in, desperately clenching to repel the invasion. "Shhh," he whispered soothingly as tears rolled down her face at the burning discomfort that threatened to morph into pain. Beads of sweat appeared on his own face at the obvious strain of holding back, his arms flexing as he held himself steady, trying to let the delicate muscles stretch around his shaft before proceeding. But Mia could not hold still, every instinct leading her to fight the penetration, little cries escaping from her throat as he pressed further, pausing briefly at the internal barrier. "I'm sorry," he said hoarsely, and Mia screamed as he pushed forward in one smooth motion, tearing through the membrane that was blocking his entrance and sheathing his cock to the hilt, his pubic hair pressing against her own.

Mia's vision went dark for a second, and hot nausea boiled up her throat as a knife-like pain tore through her insides. She had never expected to feel such agony, and she dug her nails into his shoulders, raw, guttural cries breaking out from her throat, desperately wanting to escape the object tearing her body apart. All earlier pleasure forgotten, she writhed under him like a fish on a hook, barely registering the soothing platitudes he was murmuring in her ear and the gentle kisses he was raining on her cheeks and forehead.

At some point, the agonizing pain began to abate, and she realized that he wasn't moving, just holding himself deep inside her, his muscles quivering from the effort it took to stay still. "I'm sorry," he was saying, apparently repeating it for the umpteenth time, "it will get better, I promise. Just let yourself relax, and it won't hurt like that anymore, I promise you . . . Shhh, my darling, just relax . . . there's a good girl . . . It will get better soon, I promise . . ."

Liar, Mia thought bitterly. How could it get better when he was still inside her, the organ that had caused her so much pain lodged deeply within? She felt violated and betrayed, pinned under his much larger body with no hope of escape until he was done. "Just finish it," she told him harshly, willing to tolerate anything to have this be over.

A small smile curved his lips despite the strain on his face. "Ah Mia, my sweet brave girl, your wish is my command." He pulled out slowly, and Mia squeezed her eyes shut, unable to hold back tears as the motion brought more pain at first. He kept moving, however, slowly retreating from her body and penetrating her again, and the ancient rhythm somehow ignited a small spark inside her again. Sensing it, he gradually picked up the pace and changed his angle slightly, so that the broad head of his shaft nudged some sensitive spot deep inside. His arm reached between them, knowing fingers unerringly finding her clitoris, and he pressed lightly, keeping the pressure steady and letting his strokes move her against his hand. Mia's body tensed again, this time for a different reason, and liquid heat began to gather in her core. She found herself starting to pant, echoing his heavy breathing, and the tension inside her became nearly unbearable, every thrust of his cock bringing her closer and closer to the edge without sending her over. The pain didn't go away—it was still there—but somehow it didn't matter as every nerve in Mia's body focused on her desperate need for the release. He groaned, his hips now hammering at her, and she screamed in frustration, small fists beating uselessly against his chest, her body vibrating like a guitar string from the intolerable tension deep inside. And suddenly it was too much. She felt him swell up even more, and then he was coming with one final deep thrust that sent her over the edge, his pelvis grinding against her sex as her entire body seemed to explode with an orgasm so powerful that she literally saw stars, her brain almost short-circuiting from the intensity of the climax.

She lay there afterwards, feeling his cock still twitching inside her even as it became softer and smaller. His shoulders and back were slick with sweat, and his breathing sounded like he had just run a marathon, his body lying heavily on top of hers. Her own limbs were shaking slightly, she noticed with a curiously detached interest, and her heart was pounding as though from a physical exertion.

He pulled out then, and Mia felt the loss of heat from his body, a strange inner coldness taking its place. He left the room, and she brought her knees up to her chest in a slow, painful motion, her body feeling foreign as she curled into a fetal position on her side, her mind oddly blank. There were streaks of blood on her thighs, much more blood than the spotting she'd always thought was the norm.

He came back a minute later, a small white tube in his hands. Squeezing out some clear substance, he coated his finger in it and reached between her legs, entering her sore opening despite her faint protest. Almost immediately, Mia felt the burning pain beginning to abate as the mystery gel worked its magic.

"It's an analgesic, and it will speed your recovery," he explained, wiping his hand on the sheets to get rid of the excess. "Unfortunately, I can't heal you completely because the last thing I want is for your membrane to regrow itself."

Mia responded by curling up into an even smaller ball. More than anything, she wanted to shrink and disappear, to pretend that none of this was real. He didn't let her though, gathering her closer to him in a spooning position, his large warm body curling around her own. "I hate you," she told him, wanting to lash out and hurt him somehow. She felt his sigh against her back. "I know," he said, gently stroking her tangled curls.

They must have lain like that for a few minutes. The sheets smelled like sex, Mia noticed, and like him. There was also a metallic odor that Mia realized had to be the remnants of her virginity.

"You never drank my blood," she said, finding it easier to communicate like that, with her back turned toward him.

"No, I didn't," he agreed, adding, "I think you've had enough new experiences for one day."

How considerate of him, Mia thought bitterly. Such a gentleman, sparing the poor virgin additional trauma. Never mind that he was the cause of that trauma in the first place.

As though sensing the direction of her thoughts, he said, continuing to stroke her hair, "I'm sorry it was so painful for you. I know you won't believe me right now, but I never wanted to hurt you like that and I never will again. Had I known how narrow you were inside and how thick your membrane would be, I would have made sure to remove it before we got anywhere near this bedroom. Once I was inside you, it was too late—I just couldn't stop. It won't be like this next time, I promise."

Mia listened to his little speech with a growing dread in her stomach. "Just to be clear," she said slowly, "I don't ever want to do this with you again. Ever. If you touch me again, it will be rape in the very real sense of the word."

Korum didn't answer, and Mia realized with a sinking feeling that he very much intended for there to be a next time. "You're a monster," she told him, trying to pull away. He let her go, getting up himself. Before she realized what he wanted, he bent over the bed and lifted her in his arms, carrying her naked out of the room.

He brought her to the same bathroom Mia had showered in before. At some point, he must have filled the jacuzzi because it was ready for them. He carefully set her on her feet in the wonderfully hot water that came up to her waist. Her legs still felt shaky, so Mia lowered herself into the bubbles, finding a step on which she could sit. Powerful jets pleasantly massaged her tired muscles, washing off dried blood and semen on her thighs, and Mia leaned back against the edge and closed her eyes, trying to ignore Korum's naked presence.

A scary thought suddenly entered her mind, causing her eyes to pop open. "You didn't use any protection," she hissed at him, horrified at the realization. "Am I going to catch some kind of a weird STD or worse—get pregnant?"

He laughed, throwing his head back. "No, my sweet—both would be an impossibility. You're far safer having sex with me than with any human male, regardless of how many condoms he wears."

Mia exhaled in relief. The gel he'd used earlier and the hot water were doing wonders for her physical state, and she felt nearly back to her old self. She was also hungry, she realized.

"I should get going," she said, looking around the bathroom for a towel or a robe to wrap herself in. She still didn't feel comfortable being naked in front of him.

"Why?" he asked lazily, moving his muscular back to take better advantage of the jets. "You already missed your class and you don't have anything on Wednesdays."

Apparently, he knew her class schedule by heart.

Mia shrugged, no longer surprised by anything. "I'm hungry, and I want to go home," she said, telling the truth.

He grinned at her, looking happy for some reason. "I'll make you something to eat. Why don't you relax here some more, and I'll come get you when the food is ready."

She nodded, deciding not to argue at the memory of the delicious meal he'd made before.

Still smiling, Korum rose and stepped out of the tub, water streaming down his golden skin and well-defined muscles. Despite everything that happened, Mia felt a spark of arousal at the sight of him fully naked. His back was broad and muscular, and his hips were narrow. His ass was the best she'd ever seen on a man, tight with muscle, and his legs looked powerful. She wondered if Ks needed to work out to maintain their looks and resolved to ask him at some point later.

"Like what you see?" he asked with a sly smile, obviously noticing her scrutiny.

Mia blushed a little and then told herself not to be a ninny. "Sure," she said with a straight face. "You're very pretty, like a male Barbie doll."

Far from offended, he laughed with genuine amusement. "Not like Ken, I hope. Isn't he missing the requisite equipment?"

Mia just shrugged in response, not wanting to get into this kind of banter with him right now. Grinning, he exited the room, leaving her alone to enjoy the jacuzzi for the next twenty minutes.

By the time he came back, Mia was already showered and wrapped in the familiar robe she'd discovered in the bathroom closet. She even found the slippers she'd worn before and gladly put them on. Showering here was becoming a habit.

She accompanied Korum to the kitchen, her mouth watering at the delicious smells emanating from there. He had made another one of his signature salads and a dish of roasted buckwheat with stir-fried carrots and mushrooms. Feeling like she was starving, Mia attacked her food with appreciation, and so did he. For a while, the kitchen was silent, except for chewing noises and the clattering of their silverware. Finally feeling replete, Mia leaned back in her chair. He was done with his portion, as usual, and was observing her with a half-smile.

"What?" asked Mia self-consciously, wondering if she had a bit of lettuce stuck between her teeth.

"Nothing," he said, and his smile got wider. "I just love watching you eat. You do it with such enthusiasm—it's very endearing."

Mia flushed a little. He obviously thought she was a glutton. Shrugging her shoulders, she said, "Yeah, what can I say? I really like food."

He grinned. "I know. I really like that about you. Very unexpected in a girl your size."

Mia smiled back tentatively and got up from her chair. Now was as good a time as any. "Okay, well, thank you for the meal. I'll just change and get out of your hair."

The smile left his face. He clearly didn't like hearing that. "Why don't you stay?" he suggested softly. "I promise not to touch you again today, if that's what worries you."

Mia swallowed, suddenly feeling on edge. "I really have to get going," she said, hoping that she was misreading his body language—that he didn't really have the intention of keeping her there against her will.

He looked directly into her eyes. Whatever he had seen there seemed to make up his mind. "Okay," he said slowly. "You can go home." Mia's breath escaped in relief—prematurely, as it turned out. Because he added next, "But I want you to come back here tonight. Gather whatever you need for the next day or two—or I can buy you new things if you prefer—and come back here by 7 p.m. I'll make us dinner."

Mia stared at him. "And if I don't?" she asked defiantly.

"Then I will come and get you," he answered, the look in his eyes leaving no doubt of his seriousness.

"But why?" Mia burst out in frustration. "Why do you want to be with someone who doesn't want you? Who hates you, in fact? Surely, there can't be a shortage of willing women for you. You've already gotten what you wanted from me. Can't you move on to another victim?"

His eyes narrowed in anger. "Well, Mia, you're right. There is no shortage of women who would love to be in your shoes, and I could easily get myself another 'victim,' as you so nicely put it." He took a step toward her. "The reason why I want you—as unwilling as you pretend to be—is because chemistry like ours is very rare. You're very young, even for a human, so you don't realize what we have. Do you honestly think that sex would be like that for you with another man? Or that just any woman could have that kind of effect on me?" He paused and continued in a softer tone, "This kind of attraction happens once in a blue moon, and I know better than to give up on it even if you're running scared right now." Staring into her shocked face, he added with a familiar golden gleam in his eyes, "I know this is all very new to you, and that you probably felt more pain than enjoyment today. It won't be like that again. The next time you're in my bed, I promise that your only screams will be those of pleasure."

CHAPTER SIX

Mia left his apartment and walked home, her thoughts whirling in chaos. She was no longer a virgin, and she had the residual soreness between her thighs to prove it. His gel thingy had helped with the majority of the pain, but she could still feel echoes of his fullness inside her. Her sex clenched slightly at the memory of the orgasms he'd given her, and she shivered with the intensity of her recollection. And he wanted to see her again, tonight. In fact, it sounded like he had no intention of dropping his pursuit—in complete disregard of her wishes.

At that thought, Mia got angry again. He had no right to do this to her. His species may have guided human evolution, but that didn't mean he owned her. Whatever special chemistry he thought they had did not excuse his behavior, and Mia hated the idea that he thought he could have her whenever he wanted. She wished there was something she could do to thwart him, but her own response to him had made a mockery of any resistance.

It was a long walk back to her apartment, but Mia wanted to stretch her legs and clear her head before potentially seeing her roommate. By the time she got to her building, she was sufficiently tired that going up five flights of stairs seemed like a chore. She was looking forward to plopping down on the couch and doing something totally brainless—like watching a show on her laptop.

This was not her day, however. Jessie had guests, Mia realized as she opened the door and heard masculine voices in the living room. Walking in, she was surprised to see two men she'd never met before.

One of them—an Asian guy—looked to be somewhere in his mid-twenties, while the other had to be at least thirty. The older guy caught her attention immediately. There was something about the way he sat on the couch that gave her the impression of a coiled spring. His hair was blond, and his ice-blue eyes were extraordinarily watchful. He looked to be of medium height and lean, maybe even a bit on the skinny side.

At Mia's entrance, they both got up. Jessie remained sitting, looking pale and strangely guilty. "Hi, Mia," she said with some hesitation. "This is my cousin Jason and his friend John."

Mia's eyebrows rose. "The Jason we mentioned this morning?" she asked in confusion.

The Asian guy nodded. "The one and only."

"Oh, hi . . . nice to meet you," Mia said politely, trying to connect the dots.

"They're here to talk to you," Jessie said, and Mia realized why she looked so guilty.

"Are you guys, like, the Resistance or something?" she asked incredulously. At their non-response, she drew her own conclusion. "Look, I don't know what Jessie told you, but we really don't have anything to talk about—"

"On the contrary, Miss Stalis," John said, speaking for

the first time in a slightly raspy voice, "we have a lot to discuss. Jason—why don't you catch up with your cousin while Miss Stalis and I conclude our discussion?"

Seeing Mia's response in the stormy expression gathering on her face, Jessie gave her a pleading look. "Please, Mia, I know you're mad at me, but I really think they can help you. Just hear them out, okay? Jason said they can give you some good tips on how to handle this situation—that's why they're here."

Mia sighed heavily and bit out, "Fine." Apparently, her relaxing afternoon at home was not to be.

"When does he want to see you again?" John asked quietly.

Mia blinked in surprise. "Uh—tonight at seven."

"Okay," he said, "that gives us enough time to bring you up to speed. Tell me—have you been shined?"

"Shined?"

"Did he use any kind of alien device on you that shined a reddish light on any part of your body where the skin was broken?"

Mia stared at him in shock. "How do you know about that?"

Taking that as an affirmative, he said, "You can't leave the apartment then. Jason—why don't you take your cousin to see a movie while Miss Stalis and I talk here?"

Jason nodded and left with Jessie in tow, although Mia could see that her roommate was just dying with curiosity.

When they were alone, Mia asked angrily, "What do you mean, I can't leave the apartment?"

"You have been shined. He basically branded you— you now have little nano machines embedded in whatever part of your body has been shined on. They transmit your location to him at all times. If you were to do something he doesn't expect, such as leaving your apartment when he thinks you should be home, he would know immediately—and it could make him suspicious."

Mia looked at her palms in horror. "You mean, when he healed my scrapes, he was really putting a tracking device inside me? Why would he do this?" She raised her head with suspicion. "And how do you know all this?"

"Miss Stalis—" he said wearily.

"Please call me Mia," she interrupted.

"—okay, Mia," he agreeably repeated, "we have been fighting the Krinar for a very long time. Don't you think we would've learned a lot about our enemy in the process?"

"Okay," Mia said slowly, "let's say I believe you. Why would he do this? Brand me like that?"

"To know your whereabouts at all times, of course. It's standard operating procedure for them."

Mia stared at him with shock. "Well then, what can you do to help me?"

"We can't help you, Mia," John said bluntly. "But you can help us."

Mia inhaled sharply. She was afraid it might be something like this. "I think you've been misinformed. I don't want to get involved with your cause in any way, shape, or form. You can't win, and the last thing we need is to return to the days of the Great Panic. I just want to be left alone—by Korum, by you, and by everyone else—and if you can't help me with that, then you should just get out." She pointed at the door.

"You are already involved, Mia, whether you like it or not. Do you know who your K lover is?"

"He's not my lover!" Mia said sharply.

"You haven't slept with him?" Seeing the color flooding her face, he said, "That's what I thought. I'm sure he wasted no time taking exactly what he wanted from you, just like they took our planet."

Mia fought her embarrassment. "What do you mean, do I know who he is?"

"Did he tell you anything about himself? Do you know why he's here, in New York? How the Ks ended up coming to Earth in general?"

Mia nodded slowly. "He said that he's an engineer, that the company he works for made the ships that brought them here to Earth."

"An engineer? That's rich." John let out a humorless chuckle. "He's one of the most powerful Ks on this planet, Mia. He owns the ships that brought them here—his company, in fact, has been the driving force behind them settling on Earth."

Seeing the look of sheer disbelief on her face, he added, "He's part of their ruling council—some even say he runs the council. His company provides everything for their Centers. Without him, there would be no K Centers and no Krinar on Earth."

"I don't understand," Mia said in confusion. "If he's all that, then why is he here? And what does he want with me?"

"He's here because, for the first time since K-Day, we actually stand a chance against them." John's eyes glittered with excitement. "Because he knows that we're very close to being able to give them a fair fight. Because he wants to stamp out the Resistance before we go any further."

He took a deep breath. "As to what he wants with you, it's pretty obvious. Do you know what a charl is?"

Mia shook her head, feeling overwhelmed.

"The literal translation of charl is *one who pleases*. It's the term they use for the human slaves they keep in their settlements. The purpose of the charl is to provide Ks with pleasure. As you may or may not know yet, they enjoy drinking blood during sex. So they keep us as captives, locked up in their high-tech cages, and use us whichever way they want."

Mia felt hot bile rising in her throat. "You're lying. Why would they do this? We're intelligent beings."

"They don't necessarily think of us that way. Most of them regard us as pets that they bred explicitly for this purpose—little better than the primates they'd hunted into extinction on their planet."

"So what are you saying? That Korum wants to keep me as a slave?" Mia asked incredulously. "That's bullshit. If he wanted to keep me locked up, I wouldn't be here, now would I?"

He sighed. "Mia, I don't know exactly what game he's playing with you. Maybe he finds it fun to give you the illusion of freedom for now. It's not real—you understand that, right? If you tried to leave New York instead of staying here and going to him whenever he wants, I don't know what he would do, whether your family would ever see you again. You're a smart girl. You sensed that, right? That's why you haven't been exactly avoiding him. That's why your roommate was so scared for you, why she came running to Jason even though they haven't spoken in three years—because she said you were in way over your head."

Mia wanted to throw up. If John was telling the truth, then her situation was far worse than she'd imagined. He was right; her subconscious must have realized the danger of running from Korum because she had never seriously contemplated leaving town. Her brain buzzed with a million questions, even as a hopeless pit of despair grew in her stomach.

"So what do you want from me?" she asked bitterly. "Did you come all the way here to tell me that I'm screwed? That I'm going to end up as an alien's pet, locked up somewhere and used for sex? Is that what you're here to say?"

"Yes, Mia," John answered calmly, his expression oddly flat. "There are no good options for you. If he gets tired of you, then you might be able to resume your life—particularly if you're still in New York at that time. Of course, you might also catch the attention of some other K and never be seen again. That's what happened to my sister—that's why I'm doing what I'm doing, so that other innocent young women can have a normal life."

Mia looked at him in horror. "Your sister? What happened to her?"

His mouth twisted bitterly. "What happened is I gave her a trip to Mexico as a college graduation present. She went with her girlfriends and met a handsome stranger on the beach. Turns out, he wasn't exactly human . . . The night before they were supposed to return home, Dana disappeared from her room. For the longest time, we had no idea what happened—just suspicions that the K was somehow involved. That's why I started fighting the Ks, to avenge my sister. It wasn't until a year ago that I learned she's still alive and is being held as a charl in the Costa Rican K Center."

Mia's eyes welled up with tears as she pictured his family's suffering. "Oh my God, I'm so sorry," she said. "Is there any way you can get her back?"

"No." He shook his head with angry regret. "Even if we succeeded in rescuing her from there—an impossibility in and of itself—she's been shined, like all charl. They will always know her exact whereabouts—there's no way we can reverse that procedure."

"Shined," Mia said. "Like all charl—like me."

"Like you," John agreed.

She wanted to scream and cry and throw things. She settled for asking, "So why did you come here today?"

"Because, Mia, although we can't really help you, you are actually in a position to help us. If we succeed, not only will you get your life back, but you will also have saved countless other young women—and men—from my sister's fate."

"I don't understand... What are you asking me?" Mia said slowly, her pulse picking up.

"We want you to work with us. To notify us of Korum's whereabouts, what he likes to eat, how he sleeps, any weaknesses that he might have. And if you happen to come across any information that might be even remotely useful—any passwords, security measures, anything at all—to convey that information to us."

"You're asking me to spy for you?" Mia's voice rose incredulously.

"I'm asking you to make the best of your admittedly unfortunate situation. To help yourself and all of humanity. All you have to do is keep your eyes and ears open when you're with him and occasionally report your findings to us."

"And you think I will be able to pull this off? With no training of any kind and no acting skills? Somehow fool one of the most powerful Ks on this planet? What makes you think he's not already aware that you're here, particularly if his goal is to crush your movement?"

"This apartment is not bugged—we checked. He would have no reason to spy on you here if you don't do anything suspicious and continue to play along. He doesn't know that we're here—if he did, we'd already be dead. Look, we're not asking you to be James Bond or some kind of femme fatale. You don't need to try to get close to him or seduce him or anything like that—just continue your relationship with him, such as it is, and occasionally give us information."

"How? And what would that accomplish anyway? What makes you think you have a chance in hell when all the governments in the world with their nuclear weapons were completely helpless in the invasion?" The whole thing was insane, and Mia had no intention of becoming a martyr in the name of some hopeless cause.

"The how—leave that up to us. If he still gives you a similar degree of freedom, it will definitely be much easier. If not, then it gets more complicated, but we have our ways." He paused for a second, apparently debating the wisdom of his next words. "As to why we think we can win, let's just say that not all Ks are the same. They don't all share the same beliefs about human inferiority. I can't tell you more without putting you in danger, but rest assured—we have some powerful allies."

Human allies among the Ks? The implications of that were mind-boggling.

"I don't know," Mia said, trying to think it through. "What if he catches on? What will happen to me then?"

He said truthfully, "I don't know. He may choose to have you killed or punished in some other way. I honestly don't know."

Mia let out a short bitter laugh. "And you don't care, right?"

John sighed. "I do, Mia. More than anything, I wish that things were different. That I wasn't asking you to do this, that the only thing you had to worry about were your midterms. But we don't live in that kind of world anymore. If we are to regain our freedom, we have to risk everything. You are our best chance to get close to

Korum. You can really make a difference, Mia."

Mia walked over to the table and sat down, closing her eyes for a minute so she could think. She had no reason to trust John, and she had no idea if anything he had told her was the truth. Still, she was somehow inclined to believe him. There was too much pain in his voice when he talked about his sister; he was either the best actor in the world, or the Ks really were abducting and enslaving humans who caught their eye. The way she had inadvertently caught Korum's.

Another question occurred to her. Opening her eyes, she asked, "What if Korum knows that Jason is Jessie's cousin, and he is already suspicious of me?"

John shrugged. "It's a possibility, of course. But Jason is Jessie's third cousin, so the connection is very distant. Also, he's a nobody in our operation—he has barely been involved in the last two years. He only came to me today because Jessie had called him about you. We can't completely rule out this possibility, but the odds are in our favor. Also, don't forget—Korum is the one who has been pursuing you, not the other way around, so he really has no reason to suspect anything."

"All right," said Mia, "let's pretend for a second that I do decide to spy for you. How do you expect me to go to him tonight, knowing everything you've just told me, and act like nothing has changed? He's thousands of years old—he can read me like an open book. I don't stand a chance."

"I don't know, Mia. At this point, you know him far better than we do. I know you've never been tested like this, but I believe in you. Your biggest advantage may simply be the fact that he likely underestimates your intelligence. As long as you're just his charl, he may not see you as a threat."

Mia had finally had enough. She stood up, a feeling of exhaustion washing over her.

"John," she said wearily, "I understand what you're trying to do, and I do sympathize with your cause. I can't promise you anything. I will not put my life in danger to report to you on Korum's whereabouts and what he had for dinner. But if I do happen to come across any information that could be material, I will do my best to get it to you."

He nodded. "That's fair, Mia. If you need to get in touch with us, just talk to Jessie—or if that's not possible, send her an email with 'Hi' in the subject line—we'll be monitoring her account. That way, if he decides to keep tabs on your email—which he probably will—he won't get suspicious. You'll just be saying hi to your roommate."

Mia nodded in agreement, wanting nothing more than to be alone. Her head was pounding with a brutal headache, and she gladly locked the door behind John as soon as he left.

Making her way to her room, she collapsed on the bed.

She felt sick, her stomach churning from John's revelations. It just couldn't be true—she didn't want to believe it. Yes, Korum did seem to ride roughshod over her objections, and he really hadn't given her much choice in their relationship thus far. But to actually keep her as a very real sex slave? To take away all her freedom and keep her locked up somewhere within a K Center? If the existence of the charl was anything more than a figment of John's imagination—and Korum intended to make her one—then he was definitely the monster that she'd accused him of being.

Mia felt nauseous at the thought that she would see him tonight and feel his touch on her body. And probably respond to it, as though he were really her lover. That last part made her want to throw up again. How could her body want him when he didn't even regard her as a person with basic human—or rather, intelligent being's—rights?

She was also terrified about spying on him. If she got caught, she was sure that she would probably be killed—perhaps even tortured first, for information. Anyone who kept slaves likely wouldn't blink at torture.

She shuddered.

In fact, if he found out about her conversation with John today, she might be doomed.

She tried to imagine him intentionally inflicting pain on her. For some reason, it was difficult. For the most part, he had been very gentle with her. Even her loss of virginity this morning—as traumatic as that had been—could have been much worse if he hadn't tried to control himself. In fact, some of his actions were almost caring—feeding her, making sure she was warm and dry, healing her (well, maybe not that one, given what she'd just learned)—and that hardly jived with the villainous image John had painted for her. Then again, she wouldn't want to hurt a kitten either, but would have no problem keeping said kitten locked up in her house. If that was truly how he saw her—as a cute pet that he just happened to want to fuck—then his behavior made perfect sense.

Mia tried not to think about the implications of it all, but it was impossible. Her future had always seemed so bright, and she had enjoyed thinking about it, planning out the next few years of her life. And now she had no idea what the next few weeks would hold—whether she would even be alive, much less still attending NYU.

The thought that she might end up as Korum's charl in an alien settlement was devastating, especially if she started thinking of her family's reaction to her disappearance. Would he at least let her tell them that she was alive, or would she vanish without a trace?

A wave of self-pity washing over her, Mia felt the hot prickle of tears behind her eyelids. Unable to contain her battered emotions any longer, she buried her face in her pillow and sobbed at the bitter unfairness of it all—until her eyes were red and swollen and she couldn't squeeze out another tear.

Then she got up, washed her face, and began to pack her things for tonight as per Korum's suggestion.

* * *

At 6:45 p.m. she took the subway down to TriBeCa and entered Korum's building at 6:59. Mentally patting herself on the back, Mia thought that she made quite a punctual spy.

He greeted her with a slow sensuous smile, looking as gorgeous as ever in a pair of light blue jeans and a plain white T-shirt. Even after John's revelations, Mia's heart skipped a beat at the sight. Her inner muscles clenched, and she felt herself starting to get wet. His smile got wider, exposing that damnable dimple. He could obviously sense her arousal.

Mia cursed her body. It had gotten conditioned to respond to him, despite everything. Then again, if she was literally sleeping with the enemy, she figured she might as well enjoy it. Now that she knew the truth about his kind and his probable intentions toward her, she was fairly certain that she could keep her emotions in check, no matter how many screaming orgasms he gave her.

The dinner that he prepared was outstanding as usual. Tender roasted potatoes with wild mushrooms, dill, and caramelized onions were the main course, preceded by an appetizer of spinach salad with poached pears. The dessert was a platter of fresh fruit, cut in various unique shapes, with a sweet walnut dip. The entire meal was served by candlelight. If she didn't know better, she would have thought he was wooing her with a romantic dinner. The more likely explanation was that he simply enjoyed great food in a beautiful setting, and she was the beneficiary of that.

Still, this hardly fit with the evil overlord image John had painted.

Despite Mia's initial concern, she found it easy to act naturally with him—perhaps because she didn't have to pretend to like him or be calm in his presence. He knew her feelings toward him perfectly well from this morning, and he wouldn't expect her to be anything but nervous, snarky, and reluctantly turned on—all of which Mia genuinely was.

Dinner flew by, dominated by light banter—she learned that he really enjoyed American movies from the early twenty-first century—and delicious food. As the meal drew to a close, Mia's anxiety levels began to rise at the thought of what awaited her later in the evening. Despite the gel he'd used on her, she still felt a slight discomfort deep inside and was not looking forward to experiencing sex again any time soon—even if, theoretically, it would hurt less the second time. She doubted that it could ever be completely pain-free, given the size of his cock and her own supposedly unusual narrowness. Still, her body did not appear to care as warm moisture gathered between her legs in anticipation.

After dinner was over, Mia helped Korum clean up, stacking the dishes in the dishwasher and wiping the table. It was a disconcertingly domestic task—something that she might have done with a boyfriend or husband in the future—and it made her even more aware of the strange turn her life had taken. It was difficult to believe that just four days ago, she was dreading her Sociology paper and worrying that her dating life was in the dumps. And now she was trying not to get caught spying on a two-thousand-year-old extraterrestrial who likely wanted to keep her as a sex slave.

Once the clean-up was done, Korum led her to the bedroom.

At this point, Mia felt like a nervous wreck, fear and desire fighting with each other in her stomach. Noticing her obvious apprehension, he said, "No intercourse tonight, I promise. I know you're still sore."

Mia's anxiety ratcheted up another notch. What exactly did he intend to do if intercourse was out of the question?

They entered the bedroom, and he led her to the familiar circular bed, now covered with a fresh set of blue and ivory sheets. The room was lit with a soft yellow light, and some kind of sensuous music was playing in the background. Sitting down on the bed, he pulled her closer to him until she stood between his open legs. In this position, Mia was nearly at his eye level. Trembling slightly, she stood still and tried not to look at him as he pulled her shirt over her head, revealing a plain white bra that she had remembered to wear this time. "You're so beautiful," he murmured, holding her gently by her sides while studying the body revealed to him thus far. Inexplicably, Mia blushed, her insecure inner teenager absurdly pleased at the compliment.

Bending toward her, he pressed a warm kiss to the sensitive spot where her neck met her shoulder. Mia shivered from the sensation, goosebumps appearing all over her body. Apparently pleased with the reaction, he did it again, and then lightly blew cool air on the damp spot his mouth left behind. Mia gasped, her nipples hardening from the pleasurable chill. He smiled, eyes gleaming with gold. "Still no mouth-to-mouth?" he asked softly, and Mia shrugged, remembering what happened the last time she set that condition.

Interpreting that as consent, he brought her toward him, burying one hand in her hair and keeping the other on the small of her back. Putting her own hands on his clothed shoulders, Mia closed her eyes and felt him press small butterfly-light kisses on her cheeks, forehead, and closed lids. By the time his soft lips reached her mouth, she was nearly squirming with anticipation.

At first, he kissed her very lightly, just brushing her mouth with his. Then he began gently nibbling on her lips, carefully teasing the rim with his tongue. She moaned, her body pressing closer to his, and he pushed his tongue into her mouth, penetrating it in an obvious imitation of the sexual act. A rush of moisture inundated her already wet sex as he alternated fucking her mouth with his tongue and lightly sucking on her swollen and sensitive lips.

Lost in the sensations, Mia only vaguely registered his unfastening of her bra. Tearing his mouth away from hers, he kissed her ear, sucking carefully on her earlobe. She arched with pleasure, knees buckling and head falling back, and he took advantage, licking and sucking his way down the delicate column of her throat and the collarbone region until his hot mouth reached the small white globes of her breasts. "So pretty," he whispered, before pulling one pink nipple into his mouth and scraping it softly with his teeth. Mia cried out, her clit throbbing on the verge of orgasm, and he gave her other breast the same treatment, holding her tightly as she writhed in his arms, maddeningly close to finding relief. He held her like that, pausing for a few seconds until the sensation waned a bit, and then lifted her astride one of his bent legs, grinding her jean-clad pussy firmly against his knee and swallowing her scream with his mouth as the long-awaited climax rushed powerfully through her body.

Collapsing bonelessly against him, Mia felt her inner muscles pulsing with little aftershocks. Without waiting for her to recover, Korum got up, lifting her in his arms, and lowered her onto the bed. Stripping off his own clothes with a speed that made her blink, he climbed over her, unzipped her jeans, and pulled them off together with her panties.

Lying there completely naked, Mia was unpleasantly reminded of the pain that followed the last time she was in this position. However, despite the large cock jutting aggressively at her, all he did was gently kiss his way down her body, starting with the sensitive spot near her shoulder and ending near her lower belly. She tensed in anticipation, and he did not disappoint. Pulling open her legs with strong hands, he bent his head and gently licked her folds, avoiding direct contact with the clitoris. Mia was surprised to feel herself getting turned on again, just minutes after her last orgasm. One long finger slowly entered her opening, pressing carefully on some sensitive spot deep inside, while his tongue flicked over her nub in an accelerating rhythm. There was no slow build-up this time; instead, her body simply spasmed around his finger, releasing the tension that had managed to coil inside her in a matter of seconds.

Stunned, Mia lay there. At some point, she must have grabbed his head because her fingers were buried in his short glossy strands. Feeling irrationally embarrassed, she let go, pulling her hands away. He slowly took his finger out, making her sex clench with a residual tremor, and licked it while looking up at her. Mia nearly moaned again.

He sat up, still maintaining eye contact with her. Mia realized that he was still extremely hard, not having come yet. She licked her lips nervously, wondering what he intended. His eyes hungrily followed her tongue, and she suddenly knew what he wanted her to do.

Sitting up herself, Mia cautiously extended her hand and gently brushed against his shaft with her fingers, feeling its smooth hardness. To her surprise, it jumped in her hand, as though alive. Mia's eyes flew up to Korum's face, and what she saw there was reassuring. He looked like he was in pain, eyes tightly shut and sweat beading up near his temples. Feeling her pause, he opened his eyes and hoarsely whispered, "Go ahead."

Emboldened, Mia wrapped her fingers around his cock and slowly stroked it in an up-and-down motion, the way she'd seen it done in porn. Her hand looked white and small wrapped around his thickness, and she wondered how it had ever fit inside her. He groaned at her action, his whole body tensing, and Mia suddenly felt very empowered. To know that she had this effect on him, that this formidable creature was at the mercy of her touch—somehow that went a long way toward restoring the balance of power in a relationship that had been very one-sided thus far.

Deciding to take things further, she got on her knees and bent over him. Her dark curls brushing against his thighs, she tentatively licked the engorged head. He hissed, thrusting his hips toward her, and she smiled, reveling in her ability to control him like this. Holding his shaft with one hand, she cupped his heavy balls with the other hand and squeezed gently, exploring the unfamiliar part with curiosity. "Mia . . ." he groaned, and she smiled, pleased. She wanted to wring an even stronger response from his body, the way he had from hers. Still holding his balls, she carefully wrapped her lips around the tip of his cock and swirled her tongue around it inside her mouth while moving her other hand on his shaft in a rhythmic motion. He let out a hoarse cry, his hips bucking, and she felt a warm, slightly salty liquid spurting out into her mouth. Surprised and delighted, Mia let him go, watching as the rest of the thick cream-colored fluid landed on his bronzed stomach. There was a strange taste in her mouth—not unpleasant—and she wondered briefly if there were differences between K and human semen. His cock was still twitching slightly before her eyes, even as it began to diminish in size.

Looking up, Mia found him staring at her with a smile. "Have you ever done this before?" he asked, motioning toward his sex.

Mia shook her head in response. For some weird reason, she had never wanted to go past a few kisses with any of the guys she'd dated in the past.

"Well, then, you're a natural," he said, his smile getting even wider. Reaching somewhere under the bed, he pulled out a box of tissues and used one to wipe his stomach. Mia blinked, wondering what else he kept under there. After cleaning himself, he got up and walked to the door completely naked. "Shower?" he asked, and Mia gladly agreed, following him to the bathroom.

They got into the giant shower stall together, and Korum set the water controls to have warm water raining at them from all directions. Pouring shampoo into his hand, he massaged it into her hair, washing it with experienced movements. Eyes closed, Mia just stood there, enjoying the feel of his fingers on her scalp and the water pouring over her sensitized skin. Afterwards, he washed her entire body, making her blush with his thoroughness. Feeling slightly shy, Mia tentatively reciprocated, rubbing soap all over his golden skin and powerful muscles. He unashamedly took pleasure in her touch, arching into it like a big cat getting stroked.

When they were done, he dried her body with a thick towel and then toweled off himself. Relaxed from the warm water and the two orgasms, Mia felt a wave of drowsiness washing over her. Noticing her barely stifled yawn, Korum picked her up and carried her back to bed. Putting her in the middle, he pulled a soft blanket toward them and lay down next to her, hugging her from the back. Feeling oddly comforted by the feel of his large body curving around her own, Mia closed her eyes and fell asleep easily for the first time since her world got turned upside down by the extraterrestrial lying next to her.

CHAPTER SEVEN

Streaming sunlight woke up Mia the next morning.

Keeping her eyes closed against the brightness, Mia thought with a minor annoyance that she must've forgotten to close the blinds last night. It didn't matter, though; she felt well-rested and extremely comfortable. *Perhaps too comfortable?* At the sudden realization that the bed she was lying on was much too soft to be her own IKEA mattress, Mia jackknifed to a sitting position and stared in shock at her surroundings. Memories of yesterday rushed into her brain, and she recognized where she was.

She was also completely naked and alone.

Pulling the blanket up to her chest, Mia warily surveyed the room. She was sitting in the middle of the giant round bed—she guesstimated it had to be at least fifteen feet in diameter—in Korum's beautifully decorated bedroom. A few potted plants were thriving near the large window that looked out over the Hudson River.

Noticing the robe and slippers that Korum must have

left for her, she put them on and went in search of the restroom. Surprisingly, there wasn't one connected to the bedroom. Peeking out into the hallway, Mia spotted the bathroom door. She made a quick beeline for it, not wanting Korum to know that she was awake yet.

After taking care of business, Mia gratefully brushed her teeth with the toothbrush that he left for her and washed her face. Staring into the bedroom mirror, she was surprised to see that she actually looked quite well. Her pale skin was almost radiant, and her eyes looked unusually bright. Even her hair—the bane of her existence—seemed silkier, with dark brown curls glossy and nicely defined. Whatever shampoo he had used on her yesterday clearly worked miracles. As did orgasms, apparently.

Mia wondered where her clothes were. Her tummy rumbled, reminding her that the dinner last night was already in the distant past. Still wearing the robe, she decided to go in search of food.

Entering the living room, Mia heard voices coming from somewhere to her left.

Thinking that Korum might be watching TV, she headed in that direction. The voices got louder, and she realized that they were speaking in a foreign language she'd never heard before. Slightly guttural, it nonetheless flowed smoothly, unlike anything she was familiar with.

Mia's breath caught.

She had to be listening to the Krinar language—which meant that Korum likely had visitors, and there were other Ks in the house. This might be her chance to learn something useful, she realized even as her heart skipped a beat.

Quietly approaching the room, she was startled when the heavy doors abruptly slid open in front of her, revealing its occupants and exposing her to their eyes.

Korum and two other Ks stood around a large table that had some kind of a three-dimensional image displayed on it. At the sight of her, Korum waved his hand and the image vanished, leaving only a smooth wooden surface.

Mia froze as three pairs of alien eyes examined her.

The expression on Korum's face was cold and distant, unlike anything she'd seen before. The other male K, about Korum's height, had brown hair and hazel eyes, with a similarly golden skin tone. The female was a bit lighter-skinned, closer to Jessie's color, and the silky hair streaming down to her waist was an unusual shade of dark red. Her eyes were nearly black and looked enormous in her strikingly beautiful face. She was also tall, probably close to 5'9", and wore a dress that looked like it had been poured on her curves. She could have easily stepped off the pages of an old Victoria's Secret catalogue—if they had first air-brushed the image, of course.

Standing there in her bath robe, Mia felt like a naughty child getting caught stealing from a cookie jar.

There was no help for it. She cleared her throat, heart pounding in her chest. "Um, hi. I was just looking for the kitchen—"

A small smile appeared on Korum's face, warming up his features, and his distant look vanished. "Of course," he said, "you must be hungry."

He turned toward his visitors. "Mia, these are my . . . colleagues," he said, seeming to hesitate slightly at the last word, "Leeta and Rezav."

"It's nice to meet you," Mia said politely, eyeing them with caution.

She had a strong impression that those two were not

happy to see her. Leeta stared back, her beautiful mouth pinched with dislike. Rezav was a bit friendlier, curving his lips in a half-smile and inclining his head graciously toward her. Speaking to Korum, he asked him something in their language, to which Korum absently nodded in response.

"Okay, well, I didn't mean to intrude," Mia apologized, her pulse roaring in her ears. "I'll leave you to your work."

Korum gestured toward the kitchen. "Feel free to grab some fruit or whatever you wish. I'll join you soon."

With a muttered thanks, Mia escaped as fast as her shaking legs could carry her.

Entering the kitchen, she sank down on one of the chairs, hugging herself protectively. Her head spun in a sickening manner, and her stomach churned with nausea.

Because in Rezav's question, spoken entirely in Krinar, Mia had caught one familiar word: *charl.*

* * *

By the time Korum came to the kitchen, Mia had managed to compose herself.

At his entrance, she gave him a small smile and continued eating her blueberries as though she had not a care in the world—as though she had not just heard him confirm her worst fears.

He came toward her and bent down, thoroughly kissing her mouth. For the first time, Mia simply endured his touch, the bile in her stomach too strong to allow her normal sexual response.

She didn't know why she'd needed this confirmation. For the most part, she had believed John when he'd told her about the Ks and their atavistic approach to human rights. Yet some small part of her must have been clinging to the hope that John was mistaken—that Korum would feel differently about her, that she was somehow special in his eyes.

To hear him admit that she was his glorified sex slave—his human pet—was like being punched repeatedly in the stomach.

If he had treated her with cruelty from the very beginning, it would have been easy to hate him. Instead, his arrogance toward her was often tempered with tenderness—and that made the whole thing so much worse. Despite her better judgment and common sense, he had succeeded in getting under her skin, and today's revelation felt like the cruelest of betrayals.

Sensing her lack of response, he pulled away and frowned slightly. "What's the matter?" he asked, perplexed. "Are you feeling all right?"

Mia's brain worked quickly. It would be dangerous for her—and for the Resistance—if he knew she had understood Rezav's question. However, she couldn't hide the fact that she was upset—Korum was too astute for that. Suddenly, a risky but brilliant idea came to her.

"I'm fine," she said with quiet dignity, obviously lying.

"Uh-huh," Korum said sarcastically, "sure you are."

Sitting down next to her, he lifted her chin toward him so he could look into her eyes. "Now tell me again what's going on."

Mia felt a furious tear escape. "Nothing," she told him angrily.

"Mia," he said her name in that special tone he reserved for intimidating her. "Stop lying to me."

Staring directly into his beautiful eyes, Mia channeled all of her frustrated fury and irrational feelings of betrayal into her next words. "How often do you fuck her?" she threw at him, summoning up remembered feelings of jealousy at his familiarity with Ashley the hostess. "In general, how many women do you go through in any given day? Two, three, a dozen?"

At the surprised look on his face, she continued, injecting as much bitterness into her tone as possible, "Why are you even forcing me to be here if you have her? And Ashley, and God knows how many others?"

Still holding her chin with his fingers, Korum said slowly, "Are you talking about Leeta? You think we're somehow involved?"

Mia allowed another tear to slide down her face. "Aren't you?"

He shook his head. "No. In fact, we're actually distant cousins, so that would be an impossibility."

"Oh," Mia said, pretending to be embarrassed about her outburst. She tried to pull away, and he let her go, watching as she got up and walked over to the window, carelessly wiping her face with the robe sleeve.

Mia stood there, looking out over the Hudson. Some stupidly romantic part of her was foolishly glad to hear about Leeta, even though her little jealousy act had been designed to throw him off track. She didn't say anything when he came up to her, embracing her from behind. He didn't make any promises or offer any other clarifications, Mia noticed. Of course, why should he try to reassure her, to convince her that she meant something special to him when she clearly didn't? She wouldn't have been particularly concerned about her dog's feelings either.

"I'm thinking of going for a walk in the park," he murmured, still holding her close. "Would you like to come with me?"

She was to be given a choice? What would happen if

she said no? "I don't know," she said. "I have some studying that needs to get done, and I wanted to catch up with my parents. Wednesday is usually our day to Skype . . ."

She couldn't see his expression, and she was glad about that. Now he would show his true colors, she thought.

"Okay," he said, "that sounds good."

Mia blinked, surprised. Then he continued, "For tonight, I made us a reservation at Le Bernardin at 7 p.m. I'll pick you up at 6:30. Since you don't seem to have any nice clothes, I'll have something appropriate sent to your apartment."

Now that was the dictator she knew—and now truly hated.

"I don't need any clothes," Mia protested. "I have better dresses. I just didn't wear them that time."

Turning her around in his arms, he looked down and smiled. "Mia, no offense, but I haven't seen you wear a single piece of clothing that was in any way flattering. You're a very pretty girl, but your clothes make you look like a ten-year-old boy most of the time. I think it's safe to say that dressing nicely is not one of your strengths."

Mia flushed with anger and embarrassment, but decided to hold her tongue. If he wanted to dress her up like a doll, then let him. It was hardly the worst thing he would likely do to her, anyway.

At the mutinous expression on her face, his smile got wider and his eyes gleamed with gold. Lifting her by the waist, he brought her up toward him and kissed her again. His lips were softly searching on hers, and his tongue stroked the recesses of her mouth with such expertise that Mia felt a spark of desire kindling again. Relieved that she no longer had to act, she looped her arms around his neck, let her mind go blank, and focused on the sensations. Her body, already so used to his touch, reacted with animal instinct, and she kissed him back with all the passion she could muster.

At her response, he groaned and pressed her closer to him, grinding his hips against her and letting her feel the hard bulge that had developed in his pants. Mia's insides clenched, and she found herself rubbing against his body like a cat in heat. All of a sudden, he was no longer satisfied with just kissing. Mia felt the shift of gravity as he lay her down on the table, her butt near the edge and legs hanging over the side. Stepping between her open legs, Korum pulled apart her robe with impatient hands. Before she even realized his intentions, he already had his jeans unzipped and was pushing into her opening.

Mia was wet, but not enough, and he could only get the tip inside her before she cried out in pain. Pulling out, he lowered himself to a squatting position, his head between her spread thighs, and licked her folds with his tongue, spreading moisture around her entrance. She arched, blindsided by the sudden intensity, and he pushed his finger inside her, rubbing the sensitive spot until her inner muscles spasmed uncontrollably. Before the pulsations even stopped, he was already over her, pressing his thick cock to her opening and pushing it inside in a slow, agonizing slide.

Mia writhed beneath him, little cries escaping from her throat as her interior channel tried to expand around his width. Despite the orgasm, his penetration was far from easy, and she could see the strain on his face from the effort it took him to go slowly.

There was no pain this time—just an uncomfortable feeling of invasion and extreme fullness. He felt too big, his shaft like a heated pipe entering her body. Yet there was a promise of something more behind the discomfort. He continued his inexorable advance, and Mia gasped as her inner muscles gave way, allowing him to bury his full length inside her. He paused, letting her adjust to the unfamiliar sensation, and then pulled out slowly and pushed back in. A wave of heat rushed through her veins as his cock rubbed that same sensitive spot, and she cried out from the intense pleasure, digging her nails into his shoulders.

At the feel of her sharp nails on his skin, the last shred of his restraint seemed to dissolve. With a low growl, he began thrusting in a deep, driving rhythm, each stroke of his cock pushing her back and forth on the slick table. Somewhere in the distance, a woman's cries seemed to echo his thrusts, and Mia vaguely realized that she was that woman. Every cell in her body screamed for completion, for relief from the terrible tension that was gripping her every muscle and tendon, and then it was suddenly there—a climax so powerful that it seemed to tear her asunder, leaving her bucking uncontrollably in his arms even as he reached his own peak with a guttural roar.

CHAPTER EIGHT

Mia walked back to her apartment, desperately needing some alone time before she faced Jessie and her questions.

She felt raw and emotional, filled with self-loathing. Rationally, she knew that responding to him that way made her task easier and more tolerable. It would have been infinitely worse if she had found him repulsive or had to pretend to feel passion where there was none. However, the romantic teenager buried deep inside her was weeping at the perversion of her love story. There was no hero in her romance, and the villain made her feel things that she had never imagined she could experience.

After he had finished fucking her on the kitchen table, he carried her back to the bathroom and gently cleaned her off. He then allowed her to get dressed and go home, with a parting kiss and an admonition to be dressed and ready by 6:30 p.m. Mia had meekly agreed, wanting nothing more than to get away, her body still throbbing in the aftermath of the episode.

She debated how much to tell Jessie. The last thing she wanted was to drag her into this whole mess. Then again, Jessie was already involved through Jason, and one could argue that she'd made things worse for Mia by unintentionally bringing her into the anti-K movement.

Entering the apartment, she was surprised and relieved to find that no one was there. Jessie had to be out studying or running errands.

Sighing, Mia decided to use the quiet time to catch up with her family. The last time she'd spoken to them was last Saturday, which now seemed like a lifetime ago. Her parents likely thought that she was swamped with schoolwork, so they hadn't bothered her beyond sending a couple of text messages to which Mia had managed to respond with a generic "things r good - luv u."

She powered on her old computer and saw that her mom was already waiting for her on Skype. Her dad was in the back of the room, reading something. Seeing Mia log in, a big smile broke out on her mom's face.

"Sweetie! How are you? We haven't heard from you all week!"

If there was one thing that Mia was grateful to the Ks for, it was the impact they'd had on her parents and other middle-aged Americans across the nation. The new K-mandated diet had done wonders for her parents' health, reversing her father's diabetes and drastically lowering her mom's abnormally high cholesterol levels. Now in their mid-fifties, her parents were thinner, more energetic, and younger-looking than she remembered them ever being in the past.

Mia grinned at the camera with pleasure. The worst thing about being in New York was seeing her parents so infrequently. Although she went back home every chance she got—flying to Florida for spring break was hardly a chore—she still missed them. One day, she hoped to move closer to them, perhaps once she'd finished grad school.

"I'm good, mom. How are things with you guys?"

"Oh, you know, same old—all the news are with you youngsters these days. Have you spoken to your sister yet?"

"Not yet," said Mia, "why?'

Her mom's smile got really big. "Oh, I don't know if I should tell you. Just call her, okay?"

Mia nodded, dying of curiosity.

"How are things in school? Did you finish your paper?" her mom asked.

Mia barely remembered the paper at this point. "The paper? Oh, yeah, the Sociology paper. I finished it on Sunday."

"You've had more papers since then?" Her mom asked disapprovingly. Without waiting for a response, she continued, "Mia, honey, you study way too hard. You're twenty-one—you should be going out and having fun in the big city, not sitting holed up in that library. When is the last time you had a date?"

Mia flushed a little. This was an old argument that came up more and more frequently these days. For some reason, unlike every other parent out there who would love to have a studious and responsible daughter, her mom fretted about Mia's lack of a social life.

Mia tried to imagine her parents' reaction if she told them just how active her dating life had been in the past week. "Mom," she said with exasperation, "I go on dates. I just don't necessarily tell you all about it."

"Yeah, right," her mom said disbelievingly. "I remember perfectly well the last date you went on. It was with that boy from biology, right? What was his name? Ethan?"

Mia smiled ruefully in response. Her mom knew her too well. Or at least she knew the Mia she'd been prior to last Saturday, when her world had gone topsy-turvy.

"By the way," her mom said, "you look really nice. Did you do something to your hair?" Turning behind her, she said to Mia's dad, "Dan, come here and take a look at your daughter! Doesn't Mia look great these days?"

Her father approached the camera and smiled. "She always looks great. How are you doing, hon? You meet any nice boys yet?"

"Dad," Mia groaned, "not you too."

"Mia, I'm telling you, all the good ones get taken early." Once her mom got on this topic, it was difficult to get her to stop. "One more year for you, and you're going to be done with college, and then where are you going to meet a good boy?"

"In grad school, on the street, online, at a party, in a club, in a bar, or at work," Mia responded by listing the obvious. "Look, mom, just because Marisa met Connor in college does not mean that it's the only way to meet someone." One could also meet an alien in the park—she was proof of that.

Her mom shook her head in reproach, but wisely moved on to another topic. They chatted about some other inconsequential things, and Mia learned that her parents were contemplating going on vacation to Europe for their thirtieth wedding anniversary and that her mom's job search was going well. It was a wonderfully normal conversation, and Mia reveled in it, wanting to remember every moment in case this was the last time she would speak to her parents this way. Finally, she reluctantly said goodbye, promising to call Marisa right away.

Her acting skills must have drastically improved in the last few days, Mia thought. Despite her inner turmoil, her parents hadn't suspected a thing.

Trying to reach Marisa on Skype was always a little challenging, so she called her cell instead.

"Mia! Hey there, baby sis, how are you? Did you see any of my postings on Facebook?" Her sister sounded incredibly excited.

"Um, no," Mia said slowly. "Did something happen?"

"Oh my God, you're such a study-wort! I can't believe you never go on Facebook anymore! Well, something did happen. You're going to have a niece or nephew!"

"Oh my God!" Mia jumped up, nearly screaming in excitement. "You're pregnant?"

"I sure am! Oh, I know you're going to think I'm too young, and we just got married, and blah, blah, blah, but I'm really excited."

"No, I think it's great! I'm very happy for you," Mia said earnestly. "I can't believe my favorite sis is having a baby!"

At twenty-nine, Marisa had exactly the kind of life Mia had always hoped to have. She was happily married to a wonderful guy who adored her, lived an hour's drive away from their parents in Florida, and worked as an elementary school music teacher. And now she had a baby on the way. Her life could not have been more perfect, and Mia was truly glad for her. And if she felt a twinge—okay, more than a twinge—of envy, she would never let it intrude on Marisa's happiness. It was not her sister's fault that Mia's own life had become such a screw-up in the last week.

They caught up some more, with Mia learning all about the first-trimester nausea and cravings, and then Marisa had to run since her lunch break was over. Mia let her go, already missing her cheerful voice, and then decided to use the remaining time for studying.

An hour later, Mia had gone through the requisite

Statistics exercises and had just started reviewing her Child Psychology textbook when Jessie showed up.

"Mia!" she exclaimed with relief, spotting her curled up on the couch. "Oh, thank God! I was so worried when you didn't come home last night! I called Jason, but he said that you were probably fine and that I shouldn't worry. What happened? Did John tell you anything useful?"

Mia stared at her roommate, once more debating how much to share with the girl who had been her best friend for the last three years. "He did," she said slowly, trying to come up with something that would put Jessie at ease.

"Well, what did he say? And where were you last night? Was it with that K?"

Mia sighed, deciding on a plausible storyline. "Well, John basically said that the Ks occasionally get interested in humans this way. It's usually a passing fancy, and they get tired of the relationship and move on fairly quickly. It's nothing to worry about, and I should just play along and enjoy it for as long as it lasts."

"Enjoy what? Sleeping with the K?" Jessie's eyes widened in shock.

"Pretty much," Mia confirmed. "It's really not that bad. He also takes me out to nice places. We're going to Le Bernardin tonight."

"Wait, Mia, you're sleeping with him now?" Jessie's voice rose incredulously. "But you've never been with anyone before! Are you telling me you lost your virginity to him already?"

Mia blushed, feeling embarrassed. At this point, she was about as far from being a virgin as one could get. Seeing her answer in the color washing into Mia's face, Jessie softly said, "Oh my God. How was it? You weren't hurt, were you?"

Mia's blush deepened. "Jessie," she said desperately, "I really don't feel like discussing this in detail. We had sex, and it was good. Now can we please change the topic?"

Jessie hesitated and then reluctantly agreed. Mia could see that her roommate was dying with curiosity, but Mia knew she could not keep up her brave act for long. More than anything, Mia wanted to tell Jessie the whole messy story, to reveal the sickening fear she felt at the prospect of ending up as a sex slave or getting caught spying for the Resistance. But doing so would likely put Jessie in danger as well, and that was the last thing Mia wanted.

Lying was a small price to pay for keeping her loved ones safe.

Before Mia had a chance to do much more studying, she was interrupted by the ringing of the doorbell. Opening the door, she was surprised to see a sharply dressed middle-aged woman and a young flamboyantly trendy man standing at her doorstep. The man was holding a zippered clothing bag that was nearly as tall as he was. "Yes?" she said warily, fully expecting to hear them say that they've got the wrong apartment.

"Mia Stalis?" the woman asked with a faint British accent.

"Uh, yeah," Mia said, "that would be me."

"Great," the woman said. "I'm Bridget, and this is Claude. We're personal shoppers from Saks Fifth Avenue, and we're here to remake your wardrobe."

Light dawned.

Trying to hold on to her temper, Mia asked, "Did Korum sent you? I thought he was just getting me a dress for tonight."

"He did. This is your dress right here. We're going to

make sure it fits you properly, and then we'll take some additional measurements." Bridget sounded snooty, or maybe that was just the British accent.

Mia took a deep breath. "All right," she acquiesced, "come on in." By now, Jessie had come out of her room and was observing the proceedings with great interest, and Mia didn't want to throw a scene over something so inconsequential.

They came in, and Claude unzipped the bag with a flourish. "Wow," Jessie said in a reverent tone, "I think I've seen that dress on the runway . . ."

The dress was truly beautiful, made of a shimmery blue fabric that seemed to flow with every move. It had three-quarter-length sleeves—perfect for a chilly restaurant—and looked like it might end just above the knees. It also seemed tiny, and Mia doubted that even she would be able to fit in it.

Nonetheless, she went to her room and tried it on. Twirling in front of her mirror, she was shocked to see that it actually fit her like a glove. The dress was very modest in the front, but had a deep plunge in the back, so she couldn't wear a bra. However, it was so cleverly made, with the cups already sewn in, that no bra was necessary for someone of Mia's size. The young woman reflected in the mirror was more than merely pretty; she actually looked hot, with all her small curves highlighted and shown to their best advantage.

Feeling shy, Mia walked out of her bedroom and modeled the dress to her audience. Claude and Bridget made admiring noises, and Jessie wolf-whistled at the sight. "Wow, Mia, you look amazing!" she exclaimed, walking around Mia to look at her from all angles.

"Here," Bridget said, her tone less snooty now, "you can wear these tights and shoes with it." She was holding up a pair of silky black pantyhose and simple black pumps with red soles.

Trying on the shoes and tights, Mia discovered that they were a great fit as well. She wondered how Korum knew her size so precisely. If she had been the one choosing the clothes, she would have never gone for the dress, sure that it was too small to fit her. Still caught up in the beauty of the dress, Mia graciously allowed Bridget to take her full measurements.

Checking on the time, Mia was surprised to see that it was already six o'clock. She only had a half-hour to get ready—not that she needed all that time given that she was already dressed. Her hair was still magically behaving, so she only needed to worry about makeup. Two minutes later, she was done, having brushed on two coats of mascara, a light sprinkling of powder to hide the freckles, and a tinted lip balm. Satisfied, she settled on the couch to finish studying and wait for Korum to pick her up.

* * *

Greeting Korum at the door, she was pleased to see his eyes turn a brighter amber at the sight of her in the dress.

"Mia," he said quietly, "I always knew you were beautiful, but you look simply incredible tonight."

Mia blushed at the compliment and mumbled a thank-you.

The dinner was the most amazing affair of Mia's life. Le Bernardin was utterly posh, with the waiters anticipating their every wish with almost uncanny attentiveness and the food somewhere between heavenly and out-of-this-world. They got a special tasting menu, and Mia tried everything from the warm lobster carpaccio to the stuffed zucchini flower. The wine paired with their courses was delicious as well, although Korum kept a strict eye on her alcohol consumption this time, stopping the waiter when he tried to refill her glass too often.

Keeping the conversation neutral was surprisingly easy. Korum was a good listener, and he seemed genuinely interested in her life, as simple and boring as it must have seemed to him. Since he knew everything about her anyway and she wasn't trying to get him to like her, Mia found herself opening up to him in a way that she'd never had with her dates before. She told him about the first boy she'd ever kissed—an eight-year-old she'd had a crush on when she was six—and how jealous she'd felt of her perfect older sister when she was a young child. She spoke of her parents' high expectations and of her own desire to positively influence young lives by serving as a guidance counselor.

She also learned that he normally lived in Costa Rica. Supposedly, the climate there best mimicked the area of Krina where he was from. "Our Center in Guanacaste is the closest thing we have to a capital here on Earth. We call it Lenkarda," he explained. She remembered then that Costa Rica was where John had said his sister was being held. She wondered if Korum had ever seen her there. It was feasible—he'd said there were only about five thousand Ks living in each of their Centers.

As the dinner went on, she found herself straying more and more from the safe topics. Unable to contain her curiosity, she asked him about life on Krina and what the planet was like, in general.

"Krina is a beautiful place," Korum told her. "It's like a very lush green Earth. We have many more species of plants and animals, given our longer evolutionary history. We've also succeeded in preserving the majority of our biodiversity there, avoiding the mass extinctions that took place here in recent centuries." For which humans were responsible—that part he didn't have to say out loud.

"The majority, with the exception of your human-like primates, right?" Mia asked caustically, slightly chafing at his holier-than-thou attitude.

"With the exception of them, yes," Korum agreed. "And a few other species that were particularly ill-equipped to survive."

Mia sighed and decided to move on to something less controversial. "So what are your cities like? Since you're so long-lived, your planet must be very densely populated by now."

He shook his head. "It's actually not. We're not as fertile as your species, and few couples these days are interested in having more than one or two children. As a result, our birth rate in modern times has been very low, barely above replenishment levels, and our population hasn't grown significantly in millions of years." Pausing to take a sip of his drink, he continued, "Our cities are actually very different from yours. We don't enjoy living right on top of each other. We tend to be very territorial, so we like to have a lot of space to call our own. Our cities are more like your suburbs, where the Krinar live spread out on the edges and commute into the denser center, which is only for commercial activities. And everywhere you go, the air is clean and unpolluted. We like to have trees and plants all around us, so even the densest areas of our cities are nearly as green as your parks."

Mia listened with fascination. This explained the flora all over his penthouse. "It sounds really nice," she said. Then an obvious question occurred to her. "Why would you leave all that and come to Earth, with all of our pollution and overpopulation? It must be really unpleasant for you to be in New York, for instance."

He smiled and reached for her hand, stroking her palm. "Well, I've recently discovered some definite perks to this city."

"No, but seriously, why come to Earth?" she persisted. "I can't believe you'd give up your home planet just to come here and drink our blood." Which he still hadn't done with her for some reason, she realized.

He sighed and looked at her, apparently coming to some decision. "Well, Mia, it's like this. As beautiful as our planet is, it's not immortal. Our sun, which is a much older star than yours, will begin to die in another hundred million years. If we're still on Krina at that time, our entire race will perish. So we have no choice but to seek out some other alternatives."

"In a hundred million years?" That seemed like a very long time to Mia. "But that's so far away. Why come here now? Why not enjoy your beautiful planet for, say, another ninety million years?"

"Because, my darling, if we had left Earth to humans for another ninety million years, there might not have been a habitable planet for us to come to." He leaned forward, his expression cooling. "Your kind has turned out to be incredibly destructive, with your technology evolving much faster than your morals and common sense. When your Industrial Revolution began, we knew that we would have to intervene at some point because you were using up your planet's resources at an unprecedented pace. So we began preparations to come here because we saw the writing on the wall." He paused, taking a deep breath. "And we were right. Each generation has been more and more greedy, each successive advance in your technology doing more and more damage to your environment. As short-lived as you are, you think in decades—not even hundreds of years—

and that leads you not to care about the future. You're like a child who takes a toy apart for the fun and pleasure of it, not caring that tomorrow he won't have that toy to play with anymore."

Mia sat there, feeling like said child getting castigated by the teacher. The tips of her ears burned with anger and shame. Maybe what he was saying was the truth, but he had no right to sit in judgment of her entire species, particularly in light of what she knew about his kind. Humans may be primitive and short-sighted compared to the Krinar, but at least they had the wisdom—and morals—to stop enslaving intelligent beings.

"So you came to our planet to take it over for your own use?" she asked resentfully. "All under the guise of saving it from our environmentally unfriendly ways?"

"No, Mia," he said patiently, as though explaining the obvious to a small child. "We came to share your planet. If we had wanted to take it over, believe me, we would have. We've been more than generous with your species. Other than banning a few of your particularly stupid practices, we've generally left you alone, to live as you wish. That's far better than the way you have treated your own kind."

Seeing the stubborn look on her face, he added, "When the Europeans came to the Americas, did they let the natives live in peace? Did they respect their traditions and ways of life enough to let them continue, or did they try to impose their own religion, values, and mores on them? Did they treat them as fellow human beings or as savage animals?"

Mia shook her head in denial. "That was a long time ago. We've changed, and we've learned our lessons. We would never do something like that again."

"Maybe not," he conceded. "But you still have no

problem exterminating other species through negligence and willful ignorance. As recently as a few years ago, you treated the animals you raised for food as though they were not living creatures. And don't even get me started on the Holocaust and the other atrocities you've perpetuated against other humans during the last century. You're not as enlightened as you'd like to think you are."

He was right, and Mia hated him for it. As much as she would have liked to throw their own use of human slaves in his face, she was not supposed to know about that. So she asked instead, "If we're so awful, then why do you even want me? I certainly wouldn't want to be with someone of whom I had such a low opinion."

Korum sighed with exasperation. "Mia, I never said you're awful. Especially not you, specifically. Your species is still immature and in need of guidance, that's all."

"Plus, I'm just your fuck toy, right?" Mia said bitterly, not sure why she was even bothering to go there. "I guess it doesn't matter what you think of humans as a whole in that case."

He just stared at her impassively. "If that's how you want to think about it, fine. I certainly enjoy fucking you quite a bit." His eyes turned a deeper shade of gold, and he leaned toward her. "And you love getting fucked. So why don't you stop trying to slap labels on everything and just enjoy the way things are?"

Sitting back, he motioned to the waiter for the check. Mia's cheeks burned with embarrassment, even as her body involuntarily responded to his words with swift arousal.

He paid the bill, and they left, heading back to his penthouse.

As soon as they got into the limo, Korum pulled her onto his lap and thoroughly kissed her until all she could think about was getting to the bedroom. His hands found their way under the skirt of her dress, pressing rhythmically between her legs until she was moaning softly and squirming in his arms. Before she could reach her peak, they had arrived at their destination.

He carried her swiftly through the lobby of his building, and Mia hid her face against his chest, pretending not to see the shocked stares from the concierge and the few residents passing by. As soon as they were alone in the elevator, he kissed her again, his tongue leisurely exploring her mouth until she was nearly ready to come again. Without pausing to take off their clothes, he brought her inside the bedroom and threw her onto the bed.

At their entrance, the background music and soft lighting came on, creating a romantic ambiance. Mia hardly noticed, her arousal nearly at fever pitch. She watched hungrily as he stripped off his own clothes with inhuman speed, revealing the powerfully muscled body underneath. It was no wonder she was so addicted to him, she thought with some coolly rational part of her mind. He was probably the most gorgeous male she would ever be with in her life.

He came over her then and pulled off the dress, barely taking the time to unzip it. She was left lying there in her black pantyhose and high-heeled pumps, with her upper body completely exposed to his starving gaze. "You look so hot," he told her, his voice rough with lust. The thick, swollen cock pointing in her direction corroborated his words. Bending toward her breasts, he closed his mouth over her left nipple and sucked hard, making her arch off the bed with the intensity of the sensation. Doing the same thing to her other nipple, he simultaneously pressed at the throbbing place between her thighs, and Mia screamed as she came, her entire body shuddering from the force of her orgasm.

Before she could recover, he started kissing her again with an oddly intent look on his face. Starting at her lips, his warm mouth moved down her face and neck, lingering over the sensitive juncture of her neck and shoulder and making her shiver with pleasure.

Suddenly, there was a brief slicing pain, and Mia realized that he must have bitten her. She gasped in shock, but before she could feel anything more than a twinge of fear, hot ecstasy seemed to rush through her veins. Every muscle in her body simultaneously tightened and immediately turned to mush, and her skin felt like it had been set on fire from within. Her last rational thought was that it had to be the chemical in his saliva, and then she could no longer think at all, her entire being tuned only to the pull of his mouth at her neck and the feel of his body entering her own with one powerful thrust.

The rest of the night passed in a blur of sensations and images. She was vaguely aware that she climaxed repeatedly, her senses heightened to a nearly unbearable degree. All the colors seemed brighter, and she felt like she was floating in a warm sea, with the currents caressing her skin and lapping at her insides, making them clench and release in ecstasy. He was relentless in his passion, his cock driving into her in a savage, unending rhythm until she was nothing more than pure sensation, her essence reduced down to its very basics, her very personhood burned away in the all-consuming rapture.

Hours may have passed, or days. Mia didn't know and didn't care. At some point, her voice gave out from her constant screams, and she couldn't come anymore, her body wrung dry from the ceaseless orgasms. He came hard too, shuddering over her several times throughout the night, and then penetrating her again a few moments later. Finally exhausted, Mia literally passed out, falling into a deep and dreamless sleep that ended the most unbelievable sexual experience of her life.

CHAPTER NINE

Over the next couple of weeks, Mia settled into a routine—if sleeping with an extraterrestrial while trying to spy on him could be called anything that mundane.

He insisted on seeing her every evening, for dinner and beyond. She spent every night at his penthouse, no longer sleeping in her own apartment. During the day, he allowed her to attend class, go home to study, or spend time Skyping with her family. Her social life—never particularly active—now revolved around her relationship with him, and Jessie was horrified by that.

"I'm telling you, Mia," she earnestly tried to convince her, "I know you said it's only temporary, but I'm really worried about you. All you do is go to him—it's like you don't have a life anymore. It's not healthy, the way he just completely took over all your free time. I barely see you anymore—and we share an apartment. Can't you just spend one night away from him, just to hang out with the girls or go to a house party? You're in college, for Christ's sake!"

Mia shrugged, not wanting to get into an argument

with Jessie. Let her think that she was simply obsessed with her first lover. It was better than explaining the reality of her precarious situation.

John contacted her on Thursday, wondering if she had any useful information. Mia had nothing. Leeta and Rezav had come by Korum's place a few times, but they had gone into that room and Mia had been too scared to try spying on them again. Walking in Central Park, Korum and Mia had once been approached by a group of three Ks that she'd never seen before. Their attitude toward Korum had been somewhat deferential, giving Mia a glimpse of the power he supposedly wielded over the Krinar on this planet. However, they'd spoken in their own language, and Mia had no clue what they said. She was surprised to see them, however; she hadn't known that Manhattan was such a popular place for the Ks to hang out.

On Fridays and Saturdays, he took her out to see Broadway shows and new movie releases. Mia greatly enjoyed herself. For some reason, despite living in New York City, she rarely got a chance to go to the shows—and it was fun pretending to be a tourist for a night. He also took her out to expensive restaurants or made gourmet meals at home on the days that they stayed in. For an outsider looking in, her life was the stuff of every girl's fantasy—complete with a handsome, wealthy lover who drove her around in a limo and generally treated her like a princess.

Her wardrobe had undergone a complete change as well. The personal shoppers from Saks had gone all out, replacing every piece of Mia's clothing with something nicer, more flattering, and infinitely more expensive. Stylish new coats and fluffy parkas kept her warm and cozy in the unpredictable spring weather. All of her underwear was now mostly silk and lace, with a few cotton pieces mixed in for everyday comfort and exercise. Her bulky old sweaters and baggy sweatpants were exchanged for comfortable, but formfitting yoga pants and soft fleecy tops. Even her jeans were deemed to be too old and poorly fitting, and designer brands now proudly resided on her shelves. And, of course, the beautiful dresses that now hung in her closet were in a category of their own. Her shoes had not escaped either, with brand-new high-end boots, sneakers, flats, and heels taking place of her old Uggs and worn-out All Stars from high school.

Mia's strident objections at Korum's extravagant expenditures on her behalf were completely ignored.

"Are you under the impression that this is something more than pocket change for me?" he asked her arrogantly, arching one black eyebrow at her protests. "I like to see you dressed well, and I want you to wear these."

And that was the end of that topic.

The sex between them was explosive—literally and figuratively out-of-this-world. Korum was a very mercurial lover. One day, he could be playful and tender, spending hours massaging Mia with scented oils until she purred with pleasure; other times, he was merciless, driving into her with unrelenting force until she screamed in ecstasy. On days when he took her blood—not every day, because it could be addictive for them both, he'd explained—she thought she could easily lose her mind from the intensity of the experience. Although Mia had never tried the hard-core drugs herself, she knew about the effects of various substances on the brain through her Psychology of Addiction class, and she imagined that the sex-blood combo with Korum was probably like doing heroin at the same time as ecstasy.

She often felt bitter about that, knowing that she could never feel the same way with a regular human man. Even if she was able to return to her normal life some day, she knew that she would never be the same, that he was too deeply imprinted on her mind and body. With each day that passed, she grew to crave his touch more, every cell in her body aching for him when he was not around. All he had to do was smile or look at her with those amber eyes and she was ready, her body softening and melting in preparation for his.

The calm, rational Mia Stalis of the past twenty-plus years was replaced with an insecure, emotional wreck. When she was with Korum, feeling his touch and basking in his presence, Mia felt like she was floating on air. As soon as she stepped away, however, she was filled with self-loathing and gut-wrenching fear—fear of being caught spying, of being unable to carry out her mission before he tired of her, and, most of all, of losing him.

It was inevitable, she knew. Even if he hadn't been the enemy, even if his kind had not been enslaving her own, there was no future for them. They were different species, and, if that hadn't been enough of an obstacle, her life span was like that of a fruit fly compared to his. In another few years—a dozen years at most—she would begin the inevitable aging process, and his attraction to her would fade, assuming that it lasted that long in the first place.

In her darkest moments, a small insidious voice inside her head wondered if it would truly be that awful—being his charl in Costa Rica. Would he treat her any differently from the way he did today? If not, then what did it matter what label was placed on their relationship as long as she could continue to be with him? And then she would be disgusted with herself, sickened that she could even contemplate the idea.

Despite her best attempts to remain upbeat for them, her family had begun to notice that something was amiss. Her mom ascribed it to stress from the proximity of finals, but her dad was more observant. "Did you meet someone, honey?" he asked one day out of the blue, startling Mia. She had vehemently denied it, of course, but she could see that he still had some doubts. Out of her entire family, her father was the only one who could read the subtleties of Mia's moods, and she was sure that her artificially bright smile did little to conceal the turmoil within from his sharp gaze.

The only time she felt like her old self was when she would bury herself in the library, absorbed in her studies. The end of the semester was approaching quickly, and Mia's workload tripled, with papers and finals looming in the near future. Under normal circumstances, Mia would have been tense and snappy from the stress. These days, however, studying brought a welcome relief from the drama of the rest of her life, and she gladly pored over textbooks and practiced linear regression every chance she got.

The first days of May brought unseasonably warm weather to New York, and the entire city came alive, with residents quickly donning their new summer clothes and tourists arriving in droves.

As much as Mia would've liked to join the other students lounging on the lawn with their books, she needed four walls around her in order to concentrate. Korum was becoming increasingly reluctant to have her go to the library, given her tendency to forget about the time while there, so she tried to study more in his penthouse. He set up a desk and a comfortable lounge chair for her in a small sunny room next to his own office—the place where he had met with Leeta and Rezav—and she began spending hours there instead.

She was also starting to think about the summer. After finals, Mia was supposed to fly home to Florida to see her parents. She had been fortunate to get an internship at a camp for troubled kids in Orlando, where she would be one of the counselors. Since Orlando was only about ninety minutes away from Ormond Beach, she could easily visit her parents on the weekends or whenever she had days off. Although dealing with troubled children would not be the easiest gig, the experience was considered valuable for someone in her field and would greatly aid her on grad school applications.

She had no idea how Korum would react to her essentially leaving for the next couple of months. It was possible that in another couple of weeks he would be tired of her, and then the issue would never arise. Thus far, he had not prevented her from carrying on with her schoolwork, and she hoped they might be able to come up with a workable solution for the summer as well—if their relationship lasted that far. For now, she decided to keep quiet and not rock the boat.

Two days before her Statistics exam, with Mia beginning to think and dream in correlations, Korum got called away for some unknown emergency. Sitting in her study room, she heard raised voices speaking in Krinar across the wall. Minutes later, he came into her room and told her tersely that he would be away for the rest of the day.

"If you need to go home to study or you want to hang out with your roommate tonight, feel free," he added as an afterthought. "I may not be home tonight."

Surprised, Mia nodded in agreement and watched him depart swiftly, with only a quick peck on her cheek.

Her heart jumped into her throat as she realized that this may be the chance she had been waiting for.

She sat for a few minutes, making sure that he was truly gone. For good measure, she leisurely strolled to the bathroom and splashed cold water on her cheeks, trying to convince herself that there was nothing to worry about . . . that she was completely alone in the house. Her hands were shaking a bit, she noticed as she raised them to her face, and her eyes stood out against her unusually pale face. *You can do this, Mia. All you have to do is just take a look around.*

She casually walked toward his office, ready to run into her own study at the first sign of his return. The penthouse was eerily quiet, with only her footsteps breaking the uneasy silence. Her heartbeat thundering in her ears, Mia tiptoed toward the office door.

As before, the doors slid open automatically at her approach. Even though Mia had been expecting it, she still jumped at the quiet "whoosh." Stepping in, she quickly surveyed her surroundings.

The room was completely empty.

A large polished table stood in the center, dominating the space. There were a few chairs positioned around the table, with the whole setup reminiscent of a corporate conference room. Mia was not sure what she'd hoped to see—perhaps a few papers left lying around or a computer carelessly turned on. But there was nothing.

Of course, she realized, he would not be using anything as primitive as paper or a tablet computer. Whatever the K equivalent of a computer was, she likely wouldn't even recognize it as such given the state of their technology.

Not for the first time, Mia cursed her own technological ineptitude. Someone who had problems keeping up with all the latest human gadgets was particularly ill-equipped to spy on an alien from a much more advanced civilization.

Walking into the room, she carefully approached the table. It looked like a regular table surface, but Mia remembered the three-dimensional image she'd seen on it that one time. She tried to remember what it was that Korum did to make it disappear. Was it a wave of his hand?

Trying to imitate the gesture, she motioned with her right arm. Nothing. She waved her left arm. Still nothing. Frustrated, she stomped her foot. Unsurprisingly, that didn't do anything either.

Mia circled around the table, studying every nook and cranny. Getting down on her knees, she crawled underneath and tried to look at the underside in the crazy hope that there might be a recognizable button somewhere there. There wasn't one, of course. The surface above her was completely innocuous, made of nothing more mysterious than plain wood.

Trying to crawl out, Mia bumped against one of the chairs. Exactly like a corporate office chair, it had wheels and swiveled in the middle. A fleecy sweater Korum occasionally wore around the house was carelessly hanging on the back of it. She crawled around the chair, not wanting to disturb the arrangement in case Korum had a good memory for furniture placement.

Sitting on the cold floor next to the chair, Mia stared despondently around the room. It was hopeless . . . John had been crazy to think that Mia could help somehow. If they were truly relying on her, then they were doomed. She was, quite simply, the worst spy in the world.

Her butt was getting cold from sitting, and the whole thing was utterly pointless anyway.

Trying to get up, Mia inadvertently brushed against the chair and lost her balance for a second. Grabbing onto the chair for support, she accidentally pulled off Korum's sweater.

Great. She wasn't just a useless spy—she was also a clumsy one. Lifting the sweater, she brought it closer to her nose and inhaled the familiar scent. Clean and masculine, it made her warm deep inside. *You have it bad, Mia. Stop mooning over the enemy you're spying on.*

She tried to arrange the sweater back in its original position, and her fingers felt something unusual. A small protrusion on the edge of the sleeve that didn't seem to belong on a soft sweater like that.

Her pulse jumping in excitement, Mia lifted the sleeve to take a closer look.

On the bottom of the sleeve, a tiny chip was embedded in the fabric. It was the size of a small button, and it was sheer luck that Mia's fingers had landed on it—otherwise, she would not have noticed it in a million years.

A light went on in her head. Korum had been wearing this sweater when he waved his arm and made the image disappear, Mia remembered with chills going down her spine. He had literally had a trick up his sleeve!

Nearly jumping in excitement, Mia examined the little computer—or at least, that's what she presumed it was—with careful attention. The thing was tiny and had no obvious on or off button.

"On," Mia ordered, wondering if it would respond to voice commands.

Nothing.

Mia tried again. "Turn on!"

There was no response this time either.

This was frustrating. Either the chip did not respond to voice commands, or it did not understand English. Then again, it could be programmed to respond only to Korum's voice or his touch.

Maybe if she massaged it herself?

She tried it. Nothing.

Blowing in frustration at a curl that had fallen over her eye, Mia considered her options. If the thing responded to Korum's touch, then it probably knew his DNA signature or something like that. In which case, she had no chance of getting it to work.

Discouraged, Mia sat down on the floor again. It seemed to help the last time she was stumped. If only there was some way she could test her theory—like a chunk of his hair or something . . .

Suddenly hopeful, Mia jumped up and ran to the bedroom to see if she could find any stray hairs. To her huge disappointment, the room was utterly hair-free, except for a couple of long curly strands that could only be her own. Korum was either a clean freak, or he simply didn't shed his hair the way humans did.

Furiously thinking it through, Mia ran to the bathroom and grabbed his electric toothbrush. Maybe it had some traces of his saliva or gum tissue . . . She held up the toothbrush to the little device with bated breath.

The device blinked, powering up for a second, and then fizzled out again.

Mia nearly screamed in excitement.

She held the toothbrush even closer, nearly brushing the sweater with it, but the chip remained silent and dark.

Mia's teeth snapped together in frustration. She was on the right path, but she needed a bigger chunk of his DNA. His clothes might have some, his shoes, the sheets on the bed . . . But those would likely be trace amounts, like those on the toothbrush.

The sheets on the bed! A big grin slowly appeared on Mia's face. She knew exactly where to get that big chunk.

Going into the laundry room, she dug through the pile of towels and dirty linens that had piled up in the recent week. Korum tended to do his own laundry for some weird reason, and he usually did it on Mondays. Given that today was a Saturday, the room was chock-full of DNA tidbits, courtesy of their active sex life.

Mia pulled out a particularly stained pillowcase, blushing a little when she remembered how it got that way. Bringing it into the office, she held it up to the little device and waited, hardly daring to hope.

Without any sound, the chip blinked and turned on. A giant three-dimensional image appeared on the table surface. Her heart in her throat, Mia slowly hung the sweater back on the chair—which did not affect the image at all—and walked around the table, trying to make sense of what she was seeing.

CHAPTER TEN

Spread out before her was a giant three-dimensional map of Manhattan and the surrounding boroughs. It was like a much fancier, much more realistic version of Google Earth.

Slowly pacing around the table, Mia stared at the familiar landscape laid out in front of her. There was Central Park, right in the middle of the tall narrow island that was still the cultural and financial center of the United States of America. Much lower, all the way on the west side, Mia could see Korum's luxury high-rise, outlined in perfect detail.

Fascinated, she stretched her hand toward the small building image, wondering if it had any substance to it. Her fingers passed right through it, but she felt a small electric pulse run through her palm. All of a sudden, reality shifted and adjusted . . . and Mia cried out in panic as she found herself standing on the street and looking directly at the building itself—not its image, but the real thing.

Gasping, she stumbled backwards, falling and catching

herself with her hands.

There was no pain at the contact with rough surface of the sidewalk; in fact, the sidewalk felt like nothing at all. Everything seemed strangely muted and silent. There were no cars passing on the street and no pedestrians leisurely strolling by.

It had to be a dream, Mia realized with a shiver, or a really vivid hallucination. Maybe she was really dying from the contact with the alien technology, and this was her brain's last hurrah. It didn't feel like that, though—it just felt weird, like she had fallen into a reflective pool of something and the reflections turned out to be real.

Virtual reality.

Mia knew it with sudden certainty. Even today's human technology could give a weak imitation of it through all the three-dimensional movies and video games. The Ks could obviously do much better, making her feel like she was actually in the image herself. This had to be the K version of Google Maps, where, instead of placing the little orange figure on the digital map to look around via pictures, the map simply placed the viewer into the three-dimensional reality.

The question now was how to get out.

Maybe if she closed her eyes and reopened them, she would find herself back in the office. Squeezing her lids shut, Mia tried counting to five. Halfway through, she lost her patience and peeked. Nope, she was still definitely in front of the building.

Her next initiative was to pinch herself . . . hard.
Ouch.

She definitely felt that pain, but her view didn't budge. She stomped her foot. Her leg communicated that sensation to her brain as well, but Mia was still in that mysterious world.

Crap. She was starting to panic. What if she could never leave this place, or worse, what if she was still in it when Korum got home? He would know immediately that she had been snooping. There was no way to spin this in a positive light, or to pass it off as random curiosity. She had clearly gone to extraordinary lengths to access his files.

Think, Mia, think. If she had entered this world so easily, there had to be an equally easy way to get out. Something had to be real in this surreal place, even if everything seemed fake.

Raising her arms at her sides, Mia slowly turned in a circle. Initially, her outstretched hands encountered nothing but air. She took a step to the right and repeated the process. Then another step and another. On her fifth attempt, her fingers brushed against something soft and familiar. The sweater! She couldn't see it, but she could definitely feel it.

Grabbing it with a desperate grip, Mia attempted to locate the device. And there it was, a tiny nub near the edge of the sleeve. As soon as Mia touched it, the familiar electric pulse ran through her hand. For a second, she experienced that feeling of disorientation, and then she was standing on solid ground—on the floor of Korum's office inside the building she had just been looking at.

Nearly shaking in relief, she stared at the map still spread out before her. She'd done it! She—Mia Stalis, who had to be taught how to operate the latest iPads—had actually entered an alien virtual reality world and come out unscathed.

Of course, she still hadn't learned anything useful. As much as she wanted to stop and go back to memorizing the standard deviation formula, she had to explore this opportunity further.

This time around, Mia knew what she had to do to avoid getting lost in that strange world. She put on Korum's sweater herself. It was huge on her, nearly reaching down to her knees. His deliciously familiar scent surrounded her, almost as if she was standing in his arms. For some reason, she found it very comforting, even though she knew that he might kill her if he saw her in this moment.

Walking around the table, she examined the map in detail. The image seemed to pulse slightly, and there were areas that shimmered more than others. One particular building in Brooklyn almost had a glow around it.

A glow? Mia had to investigate it further.

Extending her hand toward the tiny image, she closed her eyes and braced for the reality shift. When she opened them, she was on the street, looking at a quiet tree-lined residential block populated by a row of red-brick townhouses.

To her surprise, the scene was far from empty. Stifling a startled gasp, she watched a man hurry into one of the houses. He walked right past Mia on the street, without even a cursory glance to acknowledge her presence. Of course, Mia realized, she wasn't really there from his perspective. She was either watching a live video feed—a very realistic one—or, more likely, a pre-recorded video.

A saying she'd once heard nibbled on the edge of her mind. Something about advanced technology being indistinguishable from magic. That's exactly what it was like with the Ks, thought Mia. She felt a little like Harry Potter in his invisibility cloak—though her adversary was admittedly much better-looking than Voldemort.

Gathering her courage, she followed the man up the steps and into the house. *This is not real, Mia. They can't see you. You can get out any time you like.* She opened the door—which was unlocked for some reason—and stepped inside.

There was no one in the hallway, but she could hear people in the living room. Her heart pounding in her throat, Mia slowly approached the gathering. The big sweater wrapped around her felt like a security blanket, giving her the nerve to continue.

Tiptoeing into the room, Mia hovered in the doorway, waiting for someone to yell out, "Intruder!" But the occupants of the room were unaware of her presence. Feeling much calmer, Mia began to observe the proceedings.

There were about fifteen people gathered there, of various ages and nationalities. Only three of them were women, including a middle-aged lady who looked like a professor. The other two women were young, probably around Mia's age, although the stressed look on their faces aged them somehow. A lean blond man was sitting with his back turned to Mia, but there was something about him that looked familiar.

"John," said the middle-aged woman, addressing the blond man, "we really need to work out these details. We can't just blindly trust them—"

He turned his head to respond, and Mia realized with a sinking feeling in her stomach that she knew this John—that she had spoken to him twice in the last few weeks. And that meant only one thing: what she was observing had to be a meeting of the Resistance— and if she was observing it through Korum's virtual reality video, then he was obviously onto them.

Oh dear God. They thought they were safe, that they weren't being tracked. Why else would they all be gathered here like this? John had said that Korum was specifically in New York to stamp out the Resistance movement . . . because they were getting close to some breakthrough. But clearly, Korum was even closer to his goal of hunting down the freedom fighters.

She had to warn them. They were sitting ducks in that Brooklyn house. Korum could ambush them at any moment.

Suddenly, Mia felt every hair on the back of her neck rising. The puzzle pieces snapped into place, and she gasped in horrified realization.

It may already be too late for John and his friends.

Why else would Korum leave so abruptly today? He knew exactly where they were. There was no reason for him to wait any longer. The ambush—if it hadn't occurred yet—was about to take place.

Without waiting a second longer, Mia touched the little device on her sleeve and was immediately transported back to Korum's office. Waving her hand as she had seen Korum do, she nearly collapsed with relief when the action actually worked and the map winked out of existence. Quickly taking off the sweater, she hung it on the back of the chair, making sure that no stray hairs from her head remained anywhere on the fleecy fabric. Then she positioned the chairs back to how she remembered them being and ran out of the room. Last minute, she remembered the pillowcase and grabbed that too, dropping it back in the laundry pile on her way out of the apartment. Two minutes later, she had her purse and shoes and was getting into the elevator.

She needed to contact John, right away.

Pulling out her old-fashioned pocket cell phone, Mia shot an email to Jessie, writing 'Hi' in the subject line. In the body of the text, she mentioned that she would be home tonight and asked if Jessie wanted to have a girls' night in. That should put John on alert, she thought, if he was indeed monitoring Jessie's account. Now all she could do was hope and pray that she was not too late.

Wanting to get home as quickly as possible, Mia hailed a cab. It was a wasteful extravagance, but if there was ever a good reason to hurry—this was it. Climbing in, she gave the driver her home address and leaned back against the seat, closing her eyes.

Thoughts and ideas zoomed around her brain, jumping from one topic to another. How did Korum know where they were meeting? He had to have bugged the fighters' house without their knowledge . . . But John had reassured her that he could tell if a room was bugged or not. Either John had lied to her or Korum was ten steps ahead of whatever knowledge John's crew thought they possessed. That last part made sense to her. Humans could never hope to win against the K technology. If Korum wanted to watch the Resistance, he could obviously do so without their knowledge.

The full danger of the game she was playing dawned on Mia. Depending on how long Korum had been spying on them, he could know all of their plans by now . . . and he could know about Mia's involvement, limited though it had been up until today. At that thought, Mia's stomach turned over and she felt a sickening cold spread down to her toes. She had never seen Korum truly angry, but she had no doubt it would not be a pleasant sight.

Arriving at her destination, Mia paid the driver with cold, clammy fingers and walked up the five flights of stairs to her apartment. Jessie wasn't home, and Mia enviously thought that she was probably out enjoying the beautiful day with her friends. Either that or studying for finals—and both options sounded amazing to Mia right about now.

She settled in to wait.

About a half hour had passed, and Mia had nearly worn a hole in the carpet pacing up and down the living room. Finally, just as she was about to go out of her mind with frustration, the doorbell rang.

John and one of the young women from the meeting were at her door. The girl's hair was a sandy shade of brown and cut short, almost like a man's. She also looked very athletic. If it hadn't been for her elfin features, she could have easily passed for a teenage boy.

"Mia, this is Leslie," said John. "Leslie—this is Mia, the girl I was telling you about."

Mia nodded in greeting and let them into the apartment.

"John," she said without a preamble, "I just learned that you're in danger."

"No shit," Leslie said sarcastically. "We had no idea."

Mia was taken aback. This girl had no reason to dislike her, yet her tone was almost contemptuous. She felt her own hackles rising. "That's right," she said coolly. "You obviously had no idea . . . else you wouldn't have had that meeting where Korum could get a nice video of you all—including you, Leslie."

John's eyes widened in shock. "What are you talking about? What video?"

"I'm not even sure if video is the right word for it. It's really more of a virtual reality show—"

She relayed to them exactly what she'd seen today. By the time she finished, John looked pale and Leslie's arrogant smirk had been wiped from her face.

"I don't understand," he said slowly. "How did he know where to find us? All of our regular meeting places get swept for bugs and tracking devices daily. We all get regular scans too—"

"It's obviously not enough," said Leslie. "Either that, or we were betrayed."

They looked at each other in dismay.

"How are you even doing this?" asked Mia. "How do you even know what to look for when you do your scans? They can hide their tracking devices in anything. You even told me I have them in me . . ."

"That's true," John nodded, "but we can still find them—"

"Usually," said Leslie.

"Right, usually, because we're not just relying on our own modern technology—"

"John," said Leslie warningly.

"Leslie, Mia should know. She clearly risked a lot finding this information for us tonight—"

"But how can you trust her? She sleeps with him every day!"

"She has no choice in the matter! And how else would she have come across this today? You should be kissing her feet that she risked her life like that—"

"Excuse me," interrupted Mia, flushed with anger and embarrassment, "what is it you think I should know?"

Leslie just stared angrily, looking like she wanted to hit John. He ignored her and said, "Look, Mia . . . I don't want you to think that we're just a bunch of idiots bumbling around, in over our heads. Maybe that's what the movement was in the early stages, when we had no clue what they were or what they were capable of. It's different now. We know our adversary well. And we have help—"

"Help from the Ks?" interrupted Mia, her heart beating faster at the thought.

"From the Ks," confirmed John. "As I told you before,

they're not all the same. Some of them believe it's wrong, the way the Ks have come to this planet to steal it from us . . . to enslave our population. They want to help us—to share their technology with us, to help us advance until we become their equals—"

"They're like the PETA version of the Ks," said Leslie, giving in to the inevitable, but with a frown still on her face. "We call them KETHs—Ks for the Ethical Treatment of Humans."

"KETHs, or Keiths, to make it easier to pronounce," clarified John.

Mia stared at them in amazement. He'd hinted at their powerful allies before, but this clearly went beyond just one or two rogue K individuals.

"What kind of pull do the Keiths have within their society?" she asked, trying to put it all into perspective.

"Not a ton," admitted John.

"They're kind of a fringe group, from what we understand," added Leslie. "But they do have access to K technology, and they supply us with what we need to stay ahead—the scanning tools we use, the shielding technology . . ."

"But to what end?" asked Mia, still not comprehending. "So you run around unseen—or not, as we learned today—but what can a fringe group do to really make a difference? You still can't fight them, even if you have a few bug scanning devices. Unless—"

She gasped in realization.

"Unless they were supplying us with more than a few scanning devices, that's right," John said helpfully.

"That's enough, John," Leslie said in a harsh tone. "Now she knows as much as most members of our group. If you tell her anything else and she gets caught—"

John sighed. "Leslie's right. Your lover already knows

everything we've told you so far. I can't tell you anything else without putting you in danger. In even greater danger, I mean . . ."

Mia nodded in understanding. There was no reason for her to know the particulars of the Resistance plans. The last thing she needed was to be tortured for information. Of course, she had no idea if she could withstand even the threat of torture. Just the thought of Korum being angry with her was frightening in and of itself.

"Okay, then," she said. "I have to ask you one thing . . . Since your security is not as good as you thought it was, is there a chance that Korum could know about me? Did you talk about me at any time in that place in Brooklyn? Because if you did—"

"No, Mia, you're safe." John understood immediately where she was leading. "There's always a chance that he could know . . . but I really doubt it. You're our secret weapon. I've never spoken about you with anyone. Except for Jason—and Leslie, who happened to be with me today when I saw your email—no one knows that you're working for us."

Seeing the surprised look on Mia's face, he explained, "I didn't want to put you in any unnecessary danger. If we were to get caught and interrogated, your name would not come up."

He paused, apparently thinking about his next words. "And, frankly, I wasn't sure you would be able to come across anything useful. What you just told us today is so far above my expectations . . . I can't even begin to tell you how grateful we are. You see, tonight we were supposed to have a final brainstorming session—more than thirty of our top fighters were scheduled to attend. Korum must know about this . . . We talked about it in the last meeting—the one that you partially saw. If he had ambushed us tonight, he could have dealt a serious blow to the movement. You probably saved many lives today, Mia."

Mia looked at him, her cheeks flaming with mixed emotions. She was glad she could help the Resistance and hugely relieved that her secret was safe for now. But she was also a little offended at his low opinion of her capabilities. Then again, it was sheer luck that she'd stumbled upon this information today. Prior to this, she really had been useless to the movement, so she could hardly blame him for thinking that.

"All right," she said. "I hope that you can reschedule whatever you've got planned for tonight. Korum said he may not be home at all this evening, so whatever he's doing is probably big."

CHAPTER ELEVEN

"Hey stranger, welcome back!"

Jessie had apparently gotten her email and came home, bubbling with enthusiasm.

Mia grinned back and gave her roommate a big hug, genuinely happy to see her cheerful face. Her meeting with the Resistance fighters had left her unsettled, and Jessie was exactly the distraction she needed.

"So tell me," Jessie joked, "how did the big bad K let you come out for a night? I was sure he was keeping you under lock and key there."

Mia flushed. It was a little too close to the truth for comfort. Shrugging, she said, "I think he has to work this evening or something. He wasn't sure if he'd be home at all, so he suggested we hang out."

"Wow, how nice of him," Jessie said, comically widening her eyes. "Do you know what this means?"

"No, what?" Mia said, laughing at the dramatic expression on Jessie's face.

"It means we're going out! It's a Saturday night, and we're going to party!"

Mia wrinkled her nose a little. "Really? Right before finals?"

"Damn right! Oh, don't give me that look. I know you've been cramming for weeks already. One evening out won't make or break your grade. But since your K overlord decided to let you out only for tonight, we're going to have ourselves a blast!"

Mia grinned. Jessie's enthusiasm was catching, and suddenly the idea of getting utterly wasted while dancing all night sounded just about perfect.

Two hours later, the girls began preparations for the night out. Showering and shaving every inch of her body, Mia washed her hair and thoroughly conditioned it. The regular use of Korum's shampoo had turned it soft and silky, infinitely more manageable, and blowdrying resulted in a soft mass of well-defined dark curls cascading halfway down her back.

Makeup was next, and Mia went for the dramatic smoky-eye look, keeping the rest of her face neutral. Her wardrobe, however, presented a dilemma, for which she needed expert advice. "Jessie!" she yelled for the expert.

Her roommate came in, dressed to the nines herself. In her short red dress and sky-high heels, she looked like a million bucks. "Let me guess. You still don't know what to wear?" she asked with a big grin.

"I need your help." Mia gave her a helpless look, motioning toward the closet.

"Okay, let's see, what have we got here... Prada, Gucci, Badgley Mischka—oh poor you, you really have nothing to wear!" Jessie shook her head in mock reproach. "This is unbelievable, Mia—he totally spoils you. No wonder you never come home anymore."

Digging through Mia's closet, Jessie pulled out a risqué Dolce & Gabbana dress and thrust it at Mia. "Here, try this one on."

Mia eyed it doubtfully. "Won't I be cold?" There wasn't much to the dress. It looked like two scraps of purple fabric held together by a few hooks and zippers.

"Dancing in a hot, crowded club? Oh please." Jessie snorted dismissively. "And if you wear this, I can guarantee you we won't have to stand in line outside."

Mia decided to listen to the expert. Shimmying into the dress, she walked out of the room to show it to Jessie.

"Wow." Jessie was almost speechless. "I don't know what he's been feeding you, but you look amazing. I mean, you always looked cute—but this is a whole other level."

Mia blushed a little. The dress was definitely sexy, showing off her legs and exposing her back and shoulders. It was a bit too provocative for Mia's taste, with the flimsy ties around her neck being the only things holding the top in place. She couldn't wear a bra with it, given the low cut in the back, and she felt like her nipples were visible under the clingy fabric. To complete the look, she slipped on a sexy pair of heels and grabbed a tiny sparkly purse.

She was ready to party.

* * *

For the club, they chose the trendiest place in the Meatpacking District. It was a popular destination for celebrities, models, model wannabes, and any other beautiful people who liked to party. Pre-Korum Mia would have never gone to such place, sure that she wouldn't make it through the door without waiting for two hours in the cold. However, her newly confident well-dressed self had no such qualms.

Strolling right up to the bouncer, Mia and Jessie gave him big sexy smiles. He eyed them with a purely masculine appreciation and lifted the rope, letting them through without a word.

"Nicely done," Jessie whispered as they walked down the steps toward the deafening music.

Even at 11 p.m. the club was packed and happening. The music was excellent, a mix of old hip-hop favorites and some of the latest dance-hop. The dance floor was not particularly large, and every inch of it was filled with gorgeous girls grinding against each other and the few lucky guys who'd managed to get past the bouncer thus far. Sometimes it was really nice to be a girl, Mia thought. The only way most men could get into a place like this was by spending a ridiculous amount of money, whereas the girls were let in for free—as bait, of course.

Going up to the bar, the two girls quickly found a pair of stools and ordered four vodka shots. A couple of guys immediately offered to buy them drinks, and Jessie declined with a giggle. "Too early for that," she told Mia. "We want to dance, not hang out with these bozos all night."

Mia laughingly agreed, and they did their first shot, biting into a lemon afterward.

The evening got even brighter, taking on that special sparkle that only the first glass of alcohol and anticipation of a fun night could bring. Mia felt young and pretty—and, for the moment, utterly carefree. Tomorrow she could worry again, but tonight—tonight she was going to party.

"Cheers!"

The second shot went down even smoother, and things acquired a pleasant fuzzy glow in Mia's mind. The dance floor beckoned, the pulsating rhythm of the music reverberating in her bones. Grabbing Jessie's hand, she pulled her toward the gyrating crowd.

For the next hour, they danced nonstop. One good song after another came on, driving the dance floor into a frenzy. Mia danced with Jessie, with two other girls who had danced up to them, with a group of Wall Street types who kept trying to touch her naked back, and with Jessie again. She danced until she was hot and sweaty and breathless, her leg muscles quivering from all the squatting motions that a proper grinding dance entailed. She danced until she could no longer remember why she'd felt so crappy earlier today and what tomorrow could bring.

"Need water!" Jessie yelled out, trying to be heard above the music. Laughing, Mia accompanied her back to the bar. They each got a glass of tap water and another round of vodka. This time, Jessie was too buzzed to refuse when a handsome guy who looked vaguely familiar—a reality TV star, perhaps—offered to pay for their shots.

Edgar—who turned out to be an actor in a recently canceled drama—hit it off with Jessie right away. Her roommate, flattered by attention from a celebrity, flirted and giggled for all she was worth. Feeling slightly left out, Mia went to the bathroom by herself.

When she came back, a couple of Edgar's friends had joined them at the bar. They were both cute in that slightly boyish way that was popular now, and looked to be in great shape. They introduced themselves, and Mia learned that they were from the show as well. Peter was a stunt double, while Sean was a member of the supporting cast. "What is this, *Entourage*?" Mia joked, and they laughed, agreeing that their lives had much in common with the old show.

Apparently realizing they were horning in on a girls' night out, the guys ordered another round of drinks for everyone. It was tequila this time, and Mia nearly gagged at the strong taste that remained in her mouth even after biting into her lime. Her alcohol-barometer nose was long past its itching point, and she knew she would probably regret this tomorrow. But at this particular moment, with vodka and tequila surging through her system, she couldn't bring herself to care.

Mia wasn't planning on chatting up any guys, but Peter turned out to be a surprisingly good conversationalist. His voice was deep enough that it carried above the loud music, and she learned that they had Polish ancestry in common. His parents had actually come to this country fairly recently, even though he was an American citizen and had no accent. He had recently graduated from NYU himself—the Tisch School of the Arts—and wanted to be a film producer longer term. Since he had always been athletic, stunt-doubling was the best way for him to break into the field and start getting to know people, and he had been lucky enough to land a spot on the recently cancelled show.

He also seemed genuinely interested in Mia, his blue eyes sparkling whenever he looked at her. With his wavy blond hair, he looked like a mischievous angel, and Mia couldn't help laughing at some of the over-the-top compliments he directed her way. Under normal circumstances, a fun, outgoing guy like that would never have been interested in someone as shy and studious as Mia—and she couldn't help but be flattered by his attention. So when Peter asked for her number, she gave it to him without thinking, the alcohol in her veins slowing her thinking just enough to remove all caution.

They went on the dance floor again—Edgar and Peter

joining her and Jessie. Sean, probably feeling like a fifth wheel, left to join another group of girls. They danced as a group at first, and then Peter starting dancing closer to Mia, his movements graceful and athletic. She smiled, closing her eyes and swaying to the pulsing rhythm, and it didn't occur to her to move away when he put his hands on her waist.

It felt good to just dance with a regular guy she liked, whose intentions she had no need to second-guess. Nothing could come of this, of course, but some silly drunk part of her hoped that maybe—if she survived all this and was still in New York when Korum inevitably tired of her—she could look up Peter on Facebook one day. Out of all the guys she'd met in recent years, she liked him the most, and she could easily envision herself becoming friends with him . . . and maybe something more.

A new song came on, with even more explicit lyrics. The crowd let out a whoop, and the movement on the dance floor picked up. Peter stepped closer to her, his hips rubbing suggestively against her own. He was of average height, and Mia's high heels put the top of her head nearly at his temple. He smiled at her, eyes twinkling, and Mia smiled back, experiencing a pleasantly mild attraction—nothing like the maddening, all-consuming heat Korum made her feel. And even though her stupid body was wishing that it was Korum who was holding her like this, she still enjoyed the sexy dance with a cute guy . . . who, under different circumstances, could have been her date.

"You're really pretty," said Peter, practically yelling it over the music.

Mia grinned, moving to the rhythm. It was always nice to get compliments. "Thanks," she yelled back, "so are you!"

Her head was spinning from the drinks, and the whole night started to seem a little surreal—right down to the angelically handsome guy dancing with her. Still dancing, she closed her eyes for a second while holding on to Peter's waist to combat a slight dizziness. Mistaking her actions, he leaned toward her, and his mouth brushed against her lips for a brief second.

Startled, Mia pushed Peter away, taking a step back. Embarrassed, she looked to the side and suddenly froze, paralyzed with dread.

Looking directly at her from the edge of the dance floor was a familiar pair of amber-colored eyes. And the icy rage reflected in them was the most terrifying thing she had ever seen in her life.

CHAPTER TWELVE

He knew.

In the suffocating panic engulfing her, Mia had only one clear thought: Korum knew. Somehow, he had found out about today—about what she'd done for the Resistance fighters—and he had come here to find her.

Her survival instinct kicked in, and a surge of adrenaline cleared the alcohol-induced fog from her mind. She fought a desperate urge to run, knowing that he would hunt her down in a matter of seconds. Instead, she just stood there, watching as he stalked toward her through the dance floor crowd, his eyes nearly yellow with fury.

Through the pulsing music and the terrified pounding of her own heart, she heard her name.

"Mia! Mia!" It was Peter, and he was talking to her. "Hey Mia, listen, I didn't mean to be so pushy—"

He broke off in the middle of his apology and followed her gaze. "What the hell . . . is that your boyfriend or something?"

"Or something," Mia said dully, staring at Korum easily pushing his way through the normally impassable mob. Her stomach churned with nausea and fear. Would he kill her on the spot or bring her elsewhere to interrogate first?

And then he was there, standing right in front of her.

"Hey man, listen, I think there's been a misunderstanding—" Peter bravely stepped up, not realizing in the darkness what he was dealing with. In a blink of an eye, Korum's hand was wrapped around Peter's throat.

"No!" screamed Mia as Peter was lifted off the floor, feet kicking in the air and hands clawing helplessly at the iron grip around his throat. "No, please, let him go—"

"You want me to let him go?" Korum asked calmly, as though he was not killing a grown man with one hand in a crowded club.

"Please! He had nothing to do with it," begged Mia, horrified tears running down her face.

"Oh really?" said Korum, his voice dripping with sarcasm. "So my eyes deceived me then. He wasn't the one just pawing you . . . It was someone else?"

Pawing her? Korum was upset that she had danced with Peter? Her brain could barely process the implications.

"Korum, please," she tried again, "you're mad at *me*. He didn't do anything—"

"He touched what's mine." The words sounded like a verdict.

"Korum, please, he didn't know! It was all me—"

The dancers around them realized that something unusual was going on, and a ring of spectators was starting to form around them.

"Please, don't kill him!" she begged, grabbing at Korum's arm in desperation. "Please, I will do anything—"

"Oh, you will," he said softly, "you will do anything I want regardless."

Peter's face was turning purple, and the frantic clawing of his fingers was slowing. There were panicked cries from the crowd, but no one dared to intervene.

"PLEASE!" screamed Mia hysterically, tugging uselessly at his arm. He didn't even look at her.

And then he suddenly released Peter, letting his body drop to the floor with a thump.

The crowd gasped as Peter drew in air for the first time, choking and gagging.

Sobbing, Mia nearly collapsed in relief. Her hands were still holding Korum's forearm, and she let go, taking a step back.

He didn't allow her to get far. His hand shot out, steely fingers wrapping around her upper arm.

"Let's go," he said quietly, his tone leaving no room for arguments.

And Mia went with him, ignoring shocked stares from the people around her.

She was certain now that she would not survive this night.

There was no limo waiting for them. Instead, he hailed a cab and tersely gave the address of his building to the driver.

The ride was mercifully short. He didn't speak to her at all, the silence in the cab interrupted only by the sound of her quiet weeping.

She'd always known that Ks had great capacity for violence, but she had never witnessed it in person. Korum had always been so careful, so gentle with her . . . It had been difficult for Mia to imagine him tearing apart a human being—like those Ks had done with the Saudis. But now she knew that he was no different, that he could snuff out a human life as casually as swatting a fly.

She didn't want to die. She felt like she had barely started living. Thoughts tumbled around in her mind, frantically searching for a way out and finding none. Would he interrogate her first? She didn't know anything of significance, but he might not believe her. She shuddered at the thought of torture. She'd never experienced real pain, and she didn't know if she could withstand it. The last thing she wanted was to die like this, sniveling and begging for her life. If only she were braver—

They arrived at the building, and he dragged her out of the cab, still holding her arm. Her legs were weak with fear, and she stumbled on the stairs. He caught her and lifted her in his arms, carrying her through the lobby and into the penthouse elevator. The warmth of his body felt wonderful against her frozen skin, reminding her of the other night he'd carried her like this—under vastly different circumstances.

Once inside the apartment, he set her down on the couch and went to the closet to hang up his jacket. Of course, Mia thought resentfully, he wanted to be as comfortable as possible for the upcoming torture and mutilation.

To her utter mortification, she felt a strong urge to pee, her bladder nearly bursting from all the earlier drinks. She desperately wanted to hold on to her last shreds of dignity—dying while peeing her pants seemed like the ultimate humiliation.

"Please," she whispered, her voice trembling, "can I go to the bathroom?"

He nodded, a small mocking smile appearing on his lips.

Mia went as quickly as her shaking legs could carry her. Once inside, she quickly relieved herself and washed her hands. Her fingernails had a faint bluish tinge, she noticed, and the warm water felt almost scalding on her icy hands.

Finishing, she stared at the closed door and the flimsy lock on it. It was useless, she knew. But she didn't want to go out there. For some strange reason, the thought of her blood spilling all over the cream-colored furniture was too disturbing. She would wait here, she decided. He would undoubtedly come get her in another few minutes. But when these might be the last moments of her life, every second counted.

She sat down on the edge of the jacuzzi and waited. It felt like an eternity had passed. Her reflection in the mirrored wall looked nothing like her normal self, from the provocative purple dress to the raccoon-like circles around her eyes from the smeared mascara. It was oddly fitting that she would die looking like this—not at all like the Mia Stalis from Florida that her family knew and loved. At the thought of their grief, a sharp pain sliced through her chest, and Mia nearly doubled over from the force of it. She couldn't think about this now. If she did, she would break down and plead for her life, and it was strangely important to retain at least a semblance of pride—

There was a knock on the door.

Mia stifled a hysterical giggle. He was being polite before he killed her.

"Mia? What are you doing? Open the door and come out." He sounded annoyed.

Mia didn't respond, her eyes trained on the entrance.

"Mia. Open the fucking door."

She waited.

"Mia, if you make me open this door myself, you will regret it."

She believed him, but she refused to go meekly, like a lamb to the slaughter. At the very least, she wanted him to have to deal with some house repairs afterwards.

The door flew off the hinges, crashing onto the floor. Even though she expected it, Mia still jumped from the suddenness of the violent action.

Korum stood in the doorway, looking magnificent and angry. His high cheekbones were flushed with color, and his eyes were almost pure gold.

"Are you seriously hiding from me in my own bathroom?" he asked, his tone dangerously quiet.

Mia nodded, afraid that her voice would tremble if she spoke. Despite her best intentions, fat tears kept sliding down her cheeks.

He came toward her then, and Mia shut her eyes, hoping that it will be over quickly. Instead, she felt his hands on her naked shoulders, lightly stroking her skin.

Her eyes flew open, and she stared up at him.

"Get in the shower," he said. "You have his stink all over your body."

In the shower? He wanted her clean. Mia's stomach churned with nausea at the realization that he intended to have sex with her—maybe for the last time—before he killed her.

She shook her head in refusal.

His expression darkened. Before Mia could further contemplate the wisdom of her actions, the little dress lay in shreds on the floor and he was carrying her—naked and squirming—to the shower stall. A surge of adrenaline kicked in, and she arched in mindless panic, furiously kicking and scratching anything she could reach. Suddenly, she was standing on her feet inside the stall, and he was looming over her with an incredulous look on his face.

"Are you insane?" he asked her softly. "Did all that alcohol fuck with your brain?"

Panting from exertion and fear, she stared up at him defiantly through the tears blurring her vision. "If you're going to kill me, just get it over with! I don't want to be fucked first!"

His eyebrows rose, and he looked genuinely taken aback. "You think I'm going to kill you?" he asked slowly, as though not believing his ears.

"You're not?" It was Mia's turn to be surprised. Her heart pounded as if she'd run a marathon, and she could barely think.

He took a step back. He was still wearing his clothes, she noticed now. The expression on his face was strange. If she hadn't known better, she would have thought she'd wounded him somehow.

"Mia," he said wearily, "just because I'm angry with you doesn't mean that I'm going to hurt you in any way, much less kill you."

"You're not?"

She had difficulty processing this. Ever since she'd laid eyes on him at the club, she'd been so certain that she would not survive the discovery.

"Of course not," he said, still looking at her with that strange expression. "You betrayed my trust tonight, but you were drunk and stupid—"

Mia blinked. Something didn't add up.

"—and I should have known better than to let you out like that on a Saturday night."

She stared at him in confusion, hardly daring to hope. "You're upset that I went out clubbing?"

"Upset is a very mild term for what I feel right now," he said quietly. "You let that pretty worm put his hands all over you, and you kissed him right in front of my eyes. No, Mia, upset doesn't even begin to approximate it."

He didn't know.

Her knees almost buckled in relief, and she grabbed the shower wall for support. As unbelievable as it seemed, his anger tonight was due to misplaced jealousy and had nothing to do with the Resistance movement.

It was a mind-boggling realization, and Mia desperately wished that she could think past the fog that seemed to permeate her every thought. She shook her head in an attempt to clear it. "I'm sorry," she said cautiously. "I didn't think you'd care if I went out tonight. I just wanted to have fun with Jessie and . . . I didn't think you'd care either way. I wasn't going to do anything but dance, I swear . . ."

He just continued looking at her, as though trying to decipher her thoughts.

"All right, Mia," he said slowly, "just take that shower now, okay? We'll talk when you're done."

And then he left, walking around the broken door lying on the floor.

CHAPTER THIRTEEN

She was going to live. He said he wasn't going to hurt her, despite his anger.

Korum didn't know about her real betrayal. She had gotten incredibly lucky.

Her head spun, and every muscle in her body trembled in the adrenaline rush aftermath. As she stood there, she felt her stomach twist with sudden nausea. Scrambling for the toilet, Mia barely made it before the contents of her stomach came up, the toxic brew of alcohol and residual terror proving too much for her system to handle.

Mortified, she kneeled naked in front of the toilet, shaking uncontrollably. Flushing the disgusting mess, she used her remaining strength to crawl back into the shower stall and turn on the water, shuddering in relief as the warm stream poured over her frozen body.

The hot shower worked miracles. After a few minutes, Mia felt well enough to get up off the floor. She washed and shampooed every inch of her body, rinsing away all traces of the horrible night. When done, she toweled herself off, put on a big fluffy robe, and brushed her teeth twice to remove the unpleasant taste in her mouth. She was now ready to face Korum again, even though all she wanted to do was pass out and sleep for the next ten hours.

He was waiting in the living room, again looking at something on his palm. At her tentative entrance, he looked up and motioned to have her come closer. Mia cautiously approached, still feeling wary.

"Here, drink this."

He had picked up a glass filled with a pinkish liquid from the table next to him and was holding it out to her.

"What is it?" asked Mia with visible nervousness.

"Not poison, so you can relax." At her continued reluctance, he added, "Just something to reduce the strain on your liver from all the crap you drank tonight."

Mia flushed with embarrassment. He had clearly heard her vomiting earlier. Without further arguments, she took the glass and tried the liquid. It tasted like slightly sweet water and was wonderfully refreshing. She gulped down the rest of the glass.

"Good," said Korum. "Now sit down and let's talk about expectations in our relationship . . . specifically, my expectations for your behavior."

Mia swallowed nervously and sat down next to him. The liquid was already working its way through her system, and she felt the cobwebs clearing from her mind.

He turned toward her and took one of her hands in his, lightly stroking her palm. His eyes were nearly back to their normal shade of amber, with only a few traces of the dangerous yellow flecks.

"You're mine, Mia," he told her, his thumb caressing the inside of her wrist. "You've been mine from the moment I saw you in the park that day. I don't share what's mine. Ever. If you so much as look at another male—human or Krinar—you will regret it. And whoever lays a hand on you will be signing his own death warrant. Do I make myself clear?"

Mia nodded, unable to speak past the volatile mixture of emotions brewing in her chest.

"Good. The pretty boy you were dancing with tonight is very lucky he walked away. If there's ever a next time, I won't be so merciful."

Her free hand curled into a fist on the couch.

"You acted foolishly tonight. Two pretty girls going out dressed like that—any number of bad things could have happened to you. And drinking until you throw up—you might as well schedule a liver transplant for yourself in the near future. Your human body is already fragile, and I won't allow you to abuse it like this."

Mia's nails dug into her palm in frustrated anger. To be lectured like this, as though she was a stupid teenager, was beyond humiliating.

"If you want to go out dancing, I will take you. And no more nights out with your roommate—the two of you clearly cannot be trusted."

Mia just stared at him with a mutinous look on her face.

"And now," he said softly, "we should discuss your little misconception earlier . . . the fact that you actually believed that I would kill you for kissing a boy in a club."

"You nearly killed Peter," said Mia, frantically searching for an explanation for her earlier panic. "Why are you so surprised that I was scared?"

"*Peter* deserved exactly what he got for touching what's mine." He leaned toward her. "*You*, on the other hand, have nothing to fear from me. When have I ever hurt you—aside from the loss of your virginity?"

It was true. He had never caused her physical pain—at least not of the unpleasant kind. He was always very careful not to hurt her with his much greater strength. Of course, he didn't know she was helping the Resistance.

"Mia, I know we literally come from different worlds, but some things are universal across both species. I sleep with you every night, I kiss and caress your body, I take great pleasure in having sex with you—and you think that I could just snuff out your life like that, with no regrets?"

He still might, if he discovered her true betrayal.

Taking her silence for the affirmative, he shook his head in disappointment. "Mia, I'm really not the monster you've made me out to be in your mind. I would not hurt you—ever, under any circumstances. Do you understand me?"

"Yes," she whispered, suppressing a slight yawn. She felt completely drained, exhaustion creeping up on her during their conversation. Even after the restorative potion he'd fed her, she was more than ready to go to sleep. Tomorrow she would gladly analyze all the ins and outs of his words, but for tonight—she was completely done.

"All right," he said, "I can see that you're tired. Let's go to bed. You'll feel much better after some rest."

Mia nodded gratefully, and he picked her up, carrying her to the bedroom.

Entering the room, he placed her gently on the bed.

Too tired to move, Mia just lay there, watching as he stripped off his clothes. His body was truly beautiful—all muscle, covered with that smooth golden skin. All of his movements were inhumanly graceful and carefully controlled. For the first time, Mia realized that he probably exerted a lot of effort to reign in the enormous strength she'd witnessed today.

He came toward her, his cock already stiff, and opened her robe. "You're so lovely," he murmured, studying her body with obvious appreciation. Despite her exhaustion, she felt her inner muscles clenching in anticipation.

Climbing over her, he bent down and kissed the sensitive part of her neck. Mia held her breath, waiting for the familiar rush of bite-induced ecstasy, but he just continued nibbling his way down the rest of her body, with only his lips and tongue touching her. She moaned softly, wanting more, but he was ruthlessly slow, branding every inch of her skin with his mouth.

He reached her feet, and Mia giggled, feeling his lips closing over one of her toes. And then his warm hands touched her foot, massaging with a light yet firm pressure, and Mia arched in unexpected pleasure as his thumb found a spot that sent sensations directly to her nether regions. All of a sudden, she didn't feel like giggling anymore as tension started building in her sex. He gave her other foot the same treatment, and she cried out, feeling as if he was touching her clit instead.

He flipped her over then and removed the robe completely. Grabbing a pillow, he placed it under her hips, elevating her butt. For some reason, Mia felt very vulnerable, lying there face down, with her back exposed to the predator she was sleeping with.

Leaning over her, Korum lifted the dark mass of curly hair off her shoulders, revealing the tender spot of her nape. Bending down, he kissed it lightly, his mouth feeling hot on her sensitive skin. She shivered from the sensation, and he moved lower, kissing his way down each vertebra of her spine until he reached her tailbone. His hands touched her butt, lightly squeezing the pale globes, and she felt his mouth leisurely making its way down to the opening of her sex, teasing the crevice between her cheeks on the way with his tongue. She jumped, startled by the unfamiliar sensation, and he laughed softly at her reaction. "Don't worry," he whispered, "we'll leave that for another time."

And then playtime was over.

He settled over her, his legs pushing between her own, opening her wider. Mia gasped as she felt the heavy force of his cock pushing into her. Despite her wetness, he felt impossibly big in this position, and she whimpered slightly, her muscles quivering, trying to adjust to the intrusion. Sensing her difficulty, he paused for a second and reached under her hips, applying steady pressure to her clitoris even as he moved his pelvis in a series of small, shallow thrusts, working himself deeper into her. With his much larger body over her like that, she felt completely dominated, unable to move an inch, and she groaned in frustration, hovering on the verge of relief yet not climaxing. He moved deeper still, touching her cervix, and she froze as every nerve ending stood on edge, waiting for something—pleasure, pain, she didn't care which as long as she could reach the elusive peak.

He withdrew halfway then and slowly worked himself back in. The tension was becoming unbearable, and Mia resorted to begging, pleading him to do something, to make her come. "Not yet," he told her, moving in that maddeningly slow rhythm that kept her at an agonizing intensity level. Whenever he sensed her orgasm approaching, he would slow down further, and then thrust faster when the sensation receded a bit. It was literally torture, and Mia realized that this was to be her punishment for tonight.

"Korum, please," she begged, but he was intractable. The slow drag and thrust of his cock was driving her insane. In any other position, she would have been able to do something, to move her hips in a way that speeded up the climax. But lying there like that, with his heavy body pressing her down, she could only scream in frustration.

"You're mine, do you understand it now?" he said hoarsely, still keeping up that mercilessly slow pace. "Only I can give you this—what your body craves. No one else . . . Do you understand that?"

"YES! Please, just let me—"

"Let you what?" he panted, the torture exerting a toll on him as well.

"Just let me come! Please!"

And he did. His thrusts gradually picked up speed, winding her up even tighter, and her screams got even louder . . . and then she went over the cliff, her entire body pulsing and spasming in a release so powerful that every muscle in her body trembled in its aftermath. Her orgasm sent him over the edge as well, and he came deep inside her with a hoarse groan, his seed spurting in warm bursts inside her belly.

Mia lay there afterwards, feeling his weight pressing her down. She couldn't breathe easily, but she didn't care. She felt utterly boneless, unable to move in any case. And then Korum rolled away, freeing her. She shivered slightly at the feel of cool air on her naked sweaty back. He picked her up and took her into the shower again, for a quick rinse this time. And then they finally slept, with him cradling her possessively even in his sleep.

CHAPTER FOURTEEN

Mia woke up the next morning feeling surprisingly well. Dry mouth, a pounding headache, and the generally shitty overall state that came with the morning after clubbing—none of these were present today, likely due to Korum's magic potion.

As usual, she was alone in the bedroom. She had learned that Ks needed significantly less sleep than humans—some as little as a couple of hours a night—so Korum was a very early riser. It was just as well. She wasn't sure she was eager to face him this morning.

For some reason, she had never expected him to be jealous. With his looks and skills in bed, she couldn't imagine that any female would prefer another man over him. Her light flirtation with Peter last night had been just that—harmless fun that would've never led anywhere.

Most of the time, she had trouble deciphering his emotions. He usually seemed so calm and controlled, with that slightly mocking expression on his beautiful face. She knew she frequently amused him, and he often liked to tease her just to see her temper flare up. She imagined she was something like a kitten to him, a little creature that he liked to pet and play with on occasion. His reaction last night did not jive with that casual attitude, however. The extreme possessiveness he'd displayed didn't make sense in light of what their relationship really was. He definitely liked having sex with her, but she could not imagine that she meant anything more to him than that.

Then again—although she might have misinterpreted his expression last night—it seemed like he'd been genuinely hurt that she'd thought him capable of killing her. Could it be? Did he actually care for her as a person—as something more than his human toy? At this thought, an odd ache started in her chest. It couldn't be, of course, but if he really did care for her . . .

And then she remembered a little tidbit about life on Krina. They were territorial, he'd said, and didn't like to live right on top of each other.

And she wanted to cry.

It was all clear now. Of course he had been mad at Peter last night: the poor guy had inadvertently infringed on Korum's territory. As far as Korum was concerned, she belonged to him now, for as long as he wanted to keep her.

She was another one of his possessions. And he didn't like to share.

As much as she wanted to laze in bed all day, there were things to be done. Her Stat final was tomorrow, and she still didn't feel fully ready. The last thing she needed was the distraction of her screwed-up love life.

Getting up, Mia brushed her teeth and got breakfast. Korum wasn't home at all, and she wondered where he went.

Before she settled down to study, she decided to check her phone to make sure that Jessie got home safely last night. Sure enough, there were about a dozen missed calls from her roommate and an equal number of texts and emails—each getting progressively more worried. Mia groaned. She should've texted Jessie last night before falling asleep, but it had been the last thing on her mind at the time.

There was no help for it. Studying would have to wait. She called Jessie instead.

Her roommate picked up at the first ring. "Oh my God, Mia, are you all right?!? What the fuck happened last night? If that alien bastard hurt you in any way—"

"No, Jessie, he didn't! Look, I'm totally fine—"

"Totally fine? Everybody was talking about it last night—how he dragged you off after nearly killing Peter! I came back from the bathroom, and you were gone, and the poor guy was still choking on the floor—"

"Is he all right now?" interrupted Mia, suddenly overcome by guilt.

"He was taken to the hospital, but it was mostly swelling and bruises, they said. He's probably going to have difficulty speaking for a few days, and I'm sure he was scared out of his mind . . ."

"Oh my God, I am so sorry about that," Mia groaned. "I should have never put him in danger like that—"

"Him? What about yourself? Mia, this K of yours is insane! He was about to kill a person for dancing with you—"

"Kissing me actually . . ."

"Whatever! It's not like you slept with the poor guy, but even if you had . . . that's just crazy!"

Mia sighed. "I know. I learned too late that they're apparently very territorial and possessive. If I'd known before, I obviously would've never gone to the club in the first place—"

"Territorial and possessive? More like homicidal! Mia . . . you really need to leave him. I'm scared for you . . ."

"Jessie," said Mia softly, wondering how to best phrase it, "I'm not sure that I can leave him yet."

"What do you mean? Like he would force you to stay somehow?"

"I don't really know, but I don't think it's the best idea to break up right now—"

"Oh my God, I knew it! You *are* afraid of him! Did he threaten you in any way?"

"No, Jessie, it's not like that . . . He said he would never hurt me. I just think it's best to let the relationship play out naturally. I'm sure he'll get bored soon and move on—"

"And you're okay with that? Just waiting around until he tires of you? Wait, what about the summer, when you go home to Florida?"

"Um, I'm not really sure how that's going to play out yet . . . I haven't really talked to him about that—"

"Well, you better, because it's coming up! Finals are next week, and then you're gone. What is he going to do then? Not let you go home?"

Jessie had a valid point. Mia had no idea what would happen at the end of next week. For some reason, she had thought that Korum might get bored of her before Florida became an issue. His actions last night, however, were not those of someone who was getting bored with his new toy; in fact, he seemed very determined to hold on to said toy. Mia was starting to worry, but Jessie didn't need to know that.

"No, I'm sure we'll figure something out. Look, Jessie,

I know it sounds bad, but he's really not mistreating me or anything. If I just act more considerately, everything will be totally fine. He'll go back to his K Center soon, and I will have lots of interesting stories to tell my grandchildren . . ."

"I don't know, Mia. This is starting to sound like he's almost holding you captive—"

"Don't be silly! Of course he's not!"

"Uh-huh," said Jessie skeptically, "sure he's not. You can just go anywhere you want, do anything you want—"

"Well, no," admitted Mia, "not exactly—"

"Not at all! He's keeping you prisoner there—"

"No, he's not," protested Mia. Taking a deep breath, she added, "But even if he was, there's nothing anyone can do about it. You saw it last night—they can nearly kill someone in public and nobody will say boo. Whether we like it or not, they are not subject to our laws. Jessie— please, just let it go . . . I know how to handle my relationship with him. Obviously, it's not like dating another NYU student, but it's not all bad—"

"Not all bad? You mean the sex is good?"

Mia blushed, glad that Jessie couldn't see her. "Well, definitely that—it's actually pretty amazing . . . but also just spending time with him. He can be really fun . . . and romantic, and he's a great cook—"

"Oh, don't tell me . . . are you falling in love with him?"

"No! Of course not!" Mia sincerely hoped she wasn't lying. "He's not even human—"

"That's right! He's not human! Mia, he's dangerous. Please be careful, okay? If you feel like you can't break up with him yet, then don't . . . but just don't fall for him, okay? I don't want to see you get hurt . . ."

"Of course, Jessie. Please don't worry so much—I'm

totally fine. But enough about me," Mia said with false brightness. "What's the deal with that hot actor you were flirting with all night?"

"Oh, he was a total sweetheart. I gave him my number, and he said he will call today—"

And Jessie told her all about the cute guy and how he was in town for at least a few more months, and how they both enjoyed Chinese food and had the same taste for nineties music . . . It was all so uncomplicated, and Mia envied her roommate for being able to fret over something as ordinary as whether Edgar would call today as promised.

They wrapped up the conversation, and Mia promised to see Jessie the next morning after the Stat exam. And then she settled in to study for the rest of the day.

CHAPTER FIFTEEN

On Monday morning, Mia walked out of her Stat exam feeling like she had conquered the world. She'd known the answer to every question and finished the test in half the time. Now she only had to turn in three papers, and the school year would be officially over.

Elated, she texted Jesse to let her know that she was done. Her roommate was probably still taking her BioChem final, so Mia decided to chill in the park for a bit and wait for Jessie to finish up.

Parking herself on a bench, she pulled out her phone to call her parents and let them know that the test had gone well. But before she could even press a button, a man sat down right next to her, and Mia found herself looking into a familiar pair of blue eyes.

"John! What are you doing here?" Mia asked in surprise. She had always seen him inside her apartment, and it was a bit of a shock to see him out in the open like this.

"I wanted to talk to you about something important,

and I wasn't sure when you would be home next," he said. "But first, let me ask you . . . are you all right?"

"Uh, yeah." Mia flushed a little. "Why, did Jessie talk to Jason again?"

"No, but we heard about what happened. Your Saturday night adventure made the local papers."

Mia shuddered. That was embarrassing. A scary thought occurred to her. "Was my name in the paper? If my parents find out—"

"No, there was only a description. I doubt your family will make the connection."

Mia exhaled in relief. "Yeah, well, as you can see—I'm totally fine."

"Why did he attack that guy like that?"

Mia shrugged. "He's just possessive, I guess. I was really scared, actually, because I thought he'd found out I was helping you. Turns out I was wrong, but there was a very unpleasant hour when I was certain he would kill me."

John regarded her with a calm, level gaze. "It's a risk that we all run, unfortunately," he said.

Mia shivered slightly. She didn't want to think about the nearly paralyzing terror that had gripped her that night. Instead, she asked him brightly, "So how did things work out for you guys this weekend? You moved your meeting, right?"

"We did. That's why I'm here to talk to you today. There's been a change of plans."

"What kind of change? But, wait, first—did you figure out how he was videotaping you?"

"Do you remember the Keiths that we mentioned the last time?

Mia nodded.

"They were able to find the devices. They were

embedded in the curtains and the couch fabric—even the tree branches outside. It was a new and different technology—something that they must've developed recently. We are lucky that one of the Keiths has a design background and was able to figure out what the things were based on their new nano-signature."

Mia listened in fascination. "So what now?"

"We got very lucky that you came across that information. The Keiths thought so too—"

"They know about me now?" Mia wasn't sure if she should worry about that.

"Yes. We had to explain how we learned about being recorded in the first place."

The expression on her face must've seemed concerned because he added, "Look, I promise you they're not all the same. The Keiths really believe in our cause—they won't do anything to put you in danger."

"I don't understand something," said Mia. "Are these Keiths openly walking around their communities talking about their views and the fact that they're helping you guys?"

"No, of course not! If Korum knew who they were, he would quickly neutralize them. They have a lot to lose if their identities are discovered before we put our plan into action."

"Okay," said Mia, "so what's the plan? And should I really know about it, given my proximity to you-know-who?"

"Unfortunately, you do have to know... because you're a big part of this plan now."

Mia felt her heart skip a beat. "Okay," she said slowly, "I'm all ears."

"Do you remember when I told you that Korum is one of the key reasons they came here? That his company essentially runs the K Centers?"

Mia nodded.

"Well, the reason why he has all this power is because his company developed a lot of proprietary, classified technology that's not available to the general Krinar population. We don't know much about their science, but we think they probably have mature nanotechnology—"

"What does that mean, mature nanotechnology?" asked Mia.

"Basically, we believe they can manipulate matter on an atomic level. As the Keiths have explained to us, they can create almost anything using technology that's right in their homes—as long as they have simple input materials and the design for it. Their designers—which are a bit like our software engineers—create the nano blueprints for all the things they use in daily life, as well as for their weapons, ships, houses, et cetera . . . Do you understand what I'm saying?"

Mia didn't fully understand, but she nodded anyway.

"Korum is one of their most brilliant designers. A lot of the blueprints that he and his company have created are not available to the general public. That includes the design of their ships—that's highly classified information—and many of their security details, including shields and weapons for the K Centers. If you're a regular run-of-the-mill K, you can easily go on the Krinar version of the Internet and get yourself a design for their standard weapons and technologies. That's how the Keiths have been helping us until now— by providing us with the basic tools we need to evade capture and some simple weapons. Ultimately, the goal was to use their own weapons to attack their Centers and kick them off our planet.

"But, like I said, the K Centers are protected by

technology that only Korum and his trusted lieutenants have access to. One of the Keiths has spent months trying to hack into their files . . . but with no success. We thought we were close to being able to penetrate their defenses, but we learned this weekend that we're as far away as we've ever been. Korum continues to develop newer and more complicated designs—the devices he used to spy on us are particularly ingenious—"

"Can't the Keiths reverse-engineer these designs?" interrupted Mia. Not that she knew anything about technology, but that seemed logical.

"Most of Korum's designs contain a self-destruct feature that gets triggered when you try to take apart the device on the molecular level—which is what you'd have to do to figure out the structure of it. That's how he has a monopoly on this stuff—the patent or copyright protection is built into the design itself."

"Okay, so let me see if I understand this . . . The Keiths are willing to help you attack their own Centers, but they can't break the code on the technology that protects the settlements? Am I getting that right?"

"Exactly. There are fifty thousand Ks and billions of us. They may be stronger and faster, but we could easily overtake them if they didn't have their technology. If we could somehow disable their shields and get our hands on some of their weapons, we could take our planet back."

Mia rubbed her temples. "But why would the Keiths help you so much against their own kind? I mean, I understand that they think it's wrong the way humans have been treated . . . But to endanger the lives of fifty thousand other Ks for the sake of helping us? That doesn't fully make sense to me—"

"We promised to minimize the Krinar casualties as much as possible and to grant them safe passage back to

Krina. We also promised that the Keiths—and whoever else they think can be trusted—can stay here on Earth and live among humans, as long as they obey our laws.

"You see, Mia, they would be our teachers, our guides . . . bringing us into the new technological era and greatly accelerating our natural progress. They would be heroes to all of humankind, their names revered for ages. They would help us cure cancer and other diseases, and give us ways of extending our lifespan." His face was glowing with fervor. "Mia . . . they would be like gods here on Earth, after all the other Ks leave. Why wouldn't they want that instead of leading the regular lives they've already led for thousands of years?"

Mia was reaching her own conclusion. "So they're bored and looking to do something epic?"

"If you want to think about it that way. I believe they're genuine in their desire to help our species evolve to a higher level."

"Okay, so let's go back for a second. If they can't hack into the files, then what are you going to do? Sounds to me like Korum is winning the war before you even got a chance at a single battle."

"Not quite," said John, his eyes burning with excitement. "We can't hack into the files—but we can steal the information anyway."

Mia didn't like where this was going. "Steal it how?" she asked slowly.

"Well, the rumor is that Korum keeps many of his particularly sensitive designs on him at all times. For instance, have you ever seen him doing anything like looking into his palm or at his forearm?"

"I've seen him looking into his palm," said Mia reluctantly, starting to get a really bad feeling about this.

"Then that's where he has one of their computers

embedded. I use the term computer loosely, of course. It has as little in common with human computers as our computers do with the original abacus. Still, he has information stored there—literally in the palm of his hand. We could never hope to get to it because even if we captured and immobilized him—which is a nearly impossible task—he would probably be able to wipe the data in a matter of seconds."

"So what can you do then?" asked Mia in confusion.

"*We* can't do anything . . . but *you* can. You're the only one who gets close enough to him to be able to gain access to that information—"

"What? Are you insane? It's in his palm—how would I get to it? It's not like he's just going to hand it over!"

"No, of course not," sighed John. "But we do have this . . ."

He was holding a small silver ring.

"What is it?" asked Mia warily.

"It's a device that scans data. The Keiths deliberately made it look like jewelry, so you could wear it without raising suspicions. If you could somehow hold it to Korum's palm for about a minute, it should be able to access his files and get us the blueprints."

"Hold it for a full minute against his palm? What, like he wouldn't find it suspicious?"

"Not if he was otherwise distracted . . ." His voice trailed off suggestively.

"Oh my God, are you serious? You want me to steal data from him during sex?" Mia's stomach turned over at that thought.

"Look, the when is up to you. He could be sleeping—"

"He only sleeps for a few hours, and I'm usually passed out during that time."

"Okay, then, do you ever go anywhere with him when"

he just holds your hand?"

Mia thought about it. When they walked somewhere together, she would usually put her arm through the crook of his elbow. Or sometimes he would put his hand on the small of her back. If he ever held her hand, it was usually for a brief period of time only. "Not really."

"Well then, it has to be when it wouldn't be strange for you to be touching him . . ."

"So you do mean during sex?"

"If that's the only time, then yes."

Mia stared at John in shock, unable to believe he was asking her to do this. "John," she said slowly, "I'm not some femme fatale who can just do stuff like this. The last time, when I thought that Korum had caught me, I was completely freaking out. I'm not cut out to be a spy, not even close. And Korum knows me by now—if I suddenly start acting weirdly, he'll catch on right away—"

"Look, I understand that it's not going to be easy. You're right—you're not a seasoned agent. But you're literally our last hope. The Keiths believe that Korum is getting closer to figuring out who they are. He knows that we're getting help from the inside, and the Keiths think that their ruling council will not look kindly on those who pose a threat to the Centers here. At best, they're looking at forced deportation to Krina and some serious punishment there. At worst, well . . ."

"John," said Mia wearily, feeling the beginnings of a headache, "I just can't—"

"Mia, please, just wear the ring. That's all I will ask you to do. If you get an opportunity, great. If not, well, at least we will have tried."

"And if I get caught wearing this device? If Korum is as brilliant as you say, won't he recognize their technology from a mile away?"

"He has no reason to suspect you. You're just his charl. He won't be expecting a threat from you. And here, see, the ring is truly nice-looking. You could claim that it's a gift from your sister if he asks."

Mia stared at the device. The little silver circle was thin and stylish, and it probably wouldn't look out of place on her finger. To confirm that theory, she extended her hand. "All right, let me try it on—see if it's even my size."

John gave her the ring with a relieved smile. Mia slid it on the middle finger of her right hand. It fit perfectly. If she hadn't known its purpose, she would have never thought it was anything other than a simple piece of jewelry. She hoped that Korum would be fooled as easily.

With his mission accomplished, John rose to his feet. "Mia," he said, "I hope you realize that if this works, if you succeed, then our species will enter into an entirely new era. We will have our planet back, and our freedom. And we will have a lot more knowledge—science and technology that we wouldn't have had for hundreds or maybe thousands more years. You will be a hero, your name written in the history books for generations to come—"

Mia felt chills going down her spine.

"—and you will have nothing to fear from him again, ever. And girls like my sister will finally be reunited with their families, and they would be able to lead normal lives again—as will you."

He painted a compelling picture, but Mia couldn't imagine how she could possibly bring something like this pass. "John," she said, "I'll try. That's all I can promise you."

"That's all I want." He put his hand on her shoulder and gave it a reassuring squeeze. "Good luck."

And then he walked away, leaving Mia with the alien

device that was supposed to determine the future of humankind sitting innocuously on her finger.

CHAPTER SIXTEEN

Jessie joined Mia in the park a few minutes later. "Ugh," she said, "I hate BioChem. So glad that torture is over."

Mia smiled at her. "No one said it's easy being a pre-med."

"Yes, well, not all of us chose the easy route with a psych major—"

"Easy, please! I have to write three papers by Thursday, and I'm only done with one so far!"

"My heart bleeds for you . . . it really does—"

"Oh shut up," said Mia, and they both grinned at each other.

"So what are you doing now? Going to the library?" asked Jessie, wrinkling her nose.

"Nah, I think I'll head back to Korum's place. All my books and stuff are there now—"

Jessie's expression immediately darkened. "Of course. I should've known."

"Jessie," said Mia tiredly, "please don't give me a hard time over this. One way or another, I'm sure this relationship will be over soon—"

"Mia, is there something you're not telling me?" Jessie was looking at her suspiciously.

"No! I just meant that I will be going home to Florida—and he may not want to continue seeing me when I return, that's all."

"You've talked to him about this already?"

Mia shook her head. "I'll do it tonight."

"Okay, good luck with that. Let me know how that goes." She paused and then added, "Oh, and by the way, Edgar said that Peter's been asking about you."

"What? Why?"

Jessie shrugged. "I guess he's suicidal. That, or he really likes you. It's hard to tell, you know?"

"Is he feeling better now?"

Jessie nodded. "He seems to be fine, just some residual bruising."

"Well, I'm glad. Listen, tell Edgar that Peter should just forget about my existence. If it's ever safe, when this thing with Korum is over, I'll contact him myself."

Jessie promised to do so, and they chatted some more about Edgar. Jessie was supposed to see him tonight, and Mia again envied the ease and simplicity of her roommate's life.

Mia was now literally wearing the fate of her species on her finger, and the burden felt far heavier than the light silver circle could ever be on its own.

* * *

That night, Korum made dinner for them again. After agonizing over the best way to approach summer plans, Mia decided to just tell him straight out. First, though, she wanted to make sure that he would be in a good mood and receptive to the idea.

The dinner was delicious, as usual. Mia gladly consumed another creatively made salad—she had definitely developed a taste for them—and a bean crepe wrapped in seaweed with a spicy mushroom sauce.

If she succeeded in her mission, there would be no more dinners like this. Korum would be forced to go back to Krina—if he even survived the attack on their settlements.

At that thought, Mia felt a strange squeezing sensation in her chest. She didn't want him killed. He might be the enemy, but she didn't want to see him get hurt in any way.

Furiously thinking about this, she resolved to ask John to grant Korum safe passage—if she did get her hands on the data. Of course, even the thought of him simply leaving the planet was oddly agonizing. *You silly twit, he did manage to get under your skin.*

"A penny for your thoughts," teased Korum, apparently noticing the introspective look on Mia's face.

"Um, I'm just thinking about all the stuff I still have to do before the end of the week—turn in all those papers and then start packing..." Mia let her voice trail off. It seemed like a good segue into what she wanted to discuss today.

"Packing?" A slight frown appeared on his smooth forehead.

"Yes, well, you know the semester will be over soon," Mia said cautiously, her heart rate beginning to increase. "After finals, I have to go home, to Florida, to see my parents, and then I have an internship in Orlando—"

His expression visibly darkened. "And when were you going to tell me about this?" His voice was deceptively calm.

Mia slowly chewed the last bite of her food and

swallowed it. "I thought you knew everything about me already, including my summer plans." The evenness of her tone matched his, despite the pounding of her heart.

"The background check I did on you a month ago was not sufficiently comprehensive, I guess," he said, still dangerously calm.

Mia shrugged. "I guess not." She was proud of how bravely she was handling this discussion. Maybe she would make a decent spy yet.

"I don't want you to go," he said quietly. His eyes were taking on that golden tint that she now associated with all kinds of strong emotions.

"Korum, I have to." Mia tried to think of ways to convince him. "I have to see my parents and sister—she's pregnant, actually—and then I have a really good internship lined up at a local camp, where I would be a counselor for children who are going through a difficult time . . ."

He just looked at her, his lack of expression scaring her more than any outward anger.

"All right," he said. "I will take you to see your family this summer . . . just not next week. I can't leave New York quite yet. And if you want, I will find you an internship here as well, something within your field that you would enjoy."

Mia felt a cold sensation radiating from her core all the way down to her toes. Up until now, even though she knew he regarded her as his pleasure toy, their relationship had a semblance of normality. He might have considered her his human pet, but she could still pretend he was her boyfriend—an arrogant and domineering one, for sure . . . but still just a boyfriend. Now that illusion was broken. If he really did go so far as to disregard her summer plans made months in advance, then he had absolutely no respect for her rights as a person—and probably no qualms about keeping her as his charl indefinitely, until he got bored with her.

Her fists were tightly clenched on the table, she noticed, and she forced herself to relax her fingers before proceeding. "And when you're done with your business in New York," she asked quietly, "what happens then?"

He regarded her with a level gaze. "Why don't we cross that bridge when we come to it?" he suggested gently. "That might not be for a while."

"No," said Mia, past the point of caring. "I want to cross that bridge now. If your business gets done next week, what would happen then?"

He didn't answer.

Mia could feel herself getting even colder inside. Slowly getting up from the table, she searched for something to say. There was really nothing. She wanted to yell and scream and throw something at him, but that would not accomplish anything. The clueless Mia that she was supposed to be would not read anything particularly sinister into his silence. It was only Mia the spy who knew what could happen to a girl that a K regarded as his charl.

So she acted the way he would expect any normal girl to act when her boyfriend was being unreasonable. "Korum," she told him with a stubborn expression on her face, "I'm going to Florida this summer—and that's that. I have a life that doesn't just revolve around you. I made these plans months before I knew you, and I can't change things around just because you want me to—"

"Mia," he said softly, "you *can* change things around and you will. If you try to leave at the end of the week, I will stop you. Do you understand me?"

She did. She understood him perfectly. But the Mia she was pretending to be wouldn't.

"What, you're going to prevent me from getting on the airplane? That's ridiculous," she said, even as her stomach twisted with fear.

"Of course," he said. "All I have to do is make one phone call, and your name will be on a no-fly list at all your human airports."

She stared at him in shock. Somehow, she hadn't expected him to go to such lengths to detain her. She figured he might lock her in the apartment or something. But it made perfect sense ... Why do something as crude as physically restraining her when he could simply exercise his power with the U.S. government?

She felt tears welling up in her eyes, and she held them back with great effort. "I hate you," she told him, barely able to speak past the constriction in her chest. And she really did in that moment. If she'd had any doubts about helping the Resistance, they dissolved as she stared at his uncompromising expression. He had no right to do this to her, to take over her life like that—and his kind deserved exactly what they got. If Mia could really make a difference in the fight against the Ks, then she had an obligation to do so—even if it meant losing her life in the process.

He got up then and came toward her. "You don't hate me," he said in a silky tone. "You may wish you did, but you don't ..." He grasped her chin, forcing her to meet his gaze. His eyes were nearly yellow at this point. "You're mine," he said quietly, "and you're not going anywhere without me. The sooner you come to terms with it, my darling, the easier it will be for you."

And so the gloves had come off then. He was not going to hide his true colors any longer.

Mia's fists clenched with impotent rage.

"I'm not coming to terms with anything," she hissed

at him. "I'm a human being. I have rights. You can't order me around like this—"

"That's right, Mia," he said in that same dangerously smooth tone. "You're a human being—the creation of my kind. We made you. If it weren't for the Krinar, your species would not exist at all. Your people came up with all kinds of imaginary deities to worship, to explain how you came to be on this Earth. The things you have done in the name of your so-called gods are simply preposterous. But *we* are your true creators—*we* made you in our image. The only reason you have the rights you think you have is because we choose to let you have them. And we've been extremely lenient with your species, interfering as little as possible since we came to your planet." He leaned closer to her. "So if I want to keep one little human girl with me, and I have to order her around because she's too inexperienced to realize that what we have is very special—well, then, that's the way it's going to be."

Mia could barely think past the fury clouding her brain. Staring up at his beautiful face, she felt a surge of hatred so strong that she would have gladly stabbed him in that moment if she'd had a knife nearby. "Screw you," she told him bitterly, taking a step back to avoid his touch. "You and your kind should just go back to whatever hell you came from and leave us the fuck alone."

He smiled sardonically in response, letting her go for the moment. "That's not going to happen, Mia. We're here and we're staying—you might as well get used to it."

No, they weren't. Mia would make sure of that.

But he couldn't know that yet, so she said nothing, just looking up at him in defiance.

"And Mia," he added gently, "I can be very nice . . . or not—it's really up to you."

"Fuck you," she told him furiously, and watched his eyes flare even brighter.

"Oh, you will—and gladly." He smiled in anticipation.

Mia wanted to hit him. If he thought she would melt into a puddle at his touch, he had another thing coming. Unless . . .

"Fine," she said slowly, "but I call the shots tonight." And she smiled back at him, ignoring the rapid beating of her heart.

His eyes glittered with sudden interest. "Oh really? And why is that?"

"Because that's the only way I'm having sex with you tonight . . . willingly, I mean." Her smile took on a taunting edge. "You can always force me, of course— maybe even make me enjoy it. But I will always hate you for it . . . and you will ultimately regret it."

"Okay," he said softly, the bulge in his pants growing before her eyes, "let's pretend you're calling the shots . . . What would you like to do?"

Mia moistened her suddenly dry lips with the tip of her tongue and watched his eyes follow the motion with a hungry look. "Let's go into the bedroom," she said huskily, and walked past him, making the safe assumption that he would follow her there.

CHAPTER SEVENTEEN

They entered the room.

Mia walked over to the bed and sat down on it, fully dressed. He was about to do the same, but she stopped him with a shake of her head. "Not yet," she murmured, and watched him pause in response.

"I want you to take off your clothes," she said quietly, and waited to see what would happen.

To her surprise and growing excitement, he did as she asked, removing his T-shirt with one smoothly controlled motion. She inhaled sharply, the sight of his muscular half-naked body making her inner muscles clench with desire. Watching her with an amused half-smile, he unzipped his jeans and lowered them to the floor, stepping out of them gracefully. His erection was now covered only by a pair of briefs, and Mia could feel herself getting even wetter inside.

"Okay," he said softly, "now what?"

Mia's heart was galloping in her chest. "Lie down on the bed," she said, hoping she didn't sound as nervous as she felt.

He smiled and obeyed, sprawling out on his back, his

hands behind his head.

Mia got up and started taking off her own clothes, watching the bulge in his briefs growing even larger as she shimmied out of her jeans and unbuttoned her shirt. Still wearing her bra and underwear, she climbed on top of him, straddling his hips. All of a sudden, he no longer looked amused, his entire body tensing up as her sex pressed against his erection, with only the two layers of underwear standing in the way of his cock.

Mia smiled triumphantly and put her hands on his chest, feeling the powerful muscles bunching under her fingers. The game she was playing was incredibly dangerous, yet she couldn't help but be aroused by the control she was exerting over her normally dominant lover. Running her hands over his chest, she leaned forward and touched the flat masculine nipple with her tongue, loving the way his cock jumped beneath her at the simple action.

"Give me your hands," she whispered, her hair brushing against his naked chest. He reached for her, but she intercepted him, grabbing his wrists. His eyebrows rose in surprise, but he let her stop him, observing her actions with a heavy-lidded amber gaze.

She twined her fingers with his and pressed his hands into the pillow above his head, as though her small human hands could contain his Krinar strength for even a second. His eyes burned brighter with lust, but he did not resist, letting her hold him captive for now. She leaned closer to him and kissed his neck, and he arched beneath her with a sharp hiss. Reveling in his response, she lightly scraped the area with her teeth and was rewarded with a low growl. Rising up a bit, she repeated the action on the other side of his neck. By now, his body was nearly vibrating with tension, and she wondered hazily how much longer he would allow her to tease him like that. Still holding his hands, she kissed him on the lips, her tongue tentatively entering his mouth. He kissed her back with barely controlled aggression, and she sucked lightly on his tongue, causing him to buck underneath her. Leaving his mouth, she nibbled his neck again, focusing on the tightly corded muscle connecting it to his shoulder, and he groaned as though in pain.

Loving her newfound power, Mia licked the side of his neck and tongued his ear, softly biting the earlobe. His hips thrust at her in response, but the underwear was in the way of his penetration. She moaned, her panties getting soaked with her juices as his erection rubbed against her clit.

"Keep your arms raised," she whispered, finally letting go of his palms.

He did, and Mia could see the effort it took him not to touch her in the sweat beading up on his forehead. She moved down his body then, licking and kissing every inch of skin along the way until her mouth reached his flat stomach. His abdominal muscles quivered in anticipation, and she smiled with excitement, gently squeezing his balls through the briefs as her lips followed the dark trail of hair down from his navel to where it disappeared into his underwear. He groaned her name, and she hooked her fingers into his briefs, slowly pulling them down. As he lifted his hips to help her, his cock sprang up at her, the bulbous shaft stiff and the tip glistening with pre-ejaculate.

Mia swallowed with nervousness and excitement, wondering what would happen if he lost control—if she drove him as crazy as he could make her.

Grasping his shaft with one hand, she lowered her head and slowly licked the underside of his balls, which were tightly drawn against his body with extreme arousal. He hissed at her action, torso arching and cock jumping in her hand, and Mia let go of it, using her hands to cup his balls instead. Simultaneously, she closed her lips around the tip of his cock and moved to take him further into her mouth, stopping only when he reached the back of her throat. She could taste the saltiness of his pre-cum, and her sex contracted in excitement. His body vibrating from the tension, he growled low in his throat, hips thrusting at her in a wordless demand to take him deeper, but Mia resisted, moving her lips up and down his shaft in a torturously slow and shallow rhythm.

And then he snapped.

Before she even realized what happened, he had her on her back, her panties ripped to shreds and his cock pushing into her in one heavy stroke. She cried out in shock, her nails digging into his upper arms as he penetrated her all the way without giving her any time to adjust to his fullness. She was dripping wet, but it didn't matter, and her inner muscles trembled in the desperate attempt to accommodate the invasion. There was pain, but there was pleasure too, as his hips hammered at her in a merciless, driving rhythm. She screamed—in agony, in ecstasy, she didn't know which—and felt him swell even more, becoming impossibly harder and thicker, and then he was coming, his head thrown back with a roar and his pelvis grinding into her sex. Mia cried out in frustration, her own release only a few elusive seconds away, and then his teeth sank into her shoulder, and her entire world exploded from the sudden rush of heated ecstasy through her veins.

It was not enough for him, of course, with the taste of her blood driving him into a frenzy, and his cock stiffened again inside her before her pulsations even ended. And

Mia could no longer think at all, the drug-like high from his saliva turning her body into a pure instrument of pleasure, her skin unbearably sensitized to his touch and her insides burning with liquid desire. He drove into her relentlessly, and she screamed from the excruciating tension until she climaxed, over and over, in a never-ending cascade of orgasmic peaks and valleys, the night turning into a nonstop marathon of sex and blood.

Finally passing out toward the morning, Mia slept, her body still joined with his and her mind void of any thoughts.

* * *

Mia woke up the next day to the feel of someone's hand gently playing with her hair.

Surprised, she opened her eyes just a bit and saw Korum sitting by the edge of the bed, looking oddly concerned.

"Wh-what are you doing here?" she muttered sleepily, blinking in an attempt to focus.

"How are you feeling?" he asked quietly, brushing back a stray curl that fell over her eye.

"Um . . ." Mia tried to think. Moving a little, she became aware of various aches and pains, as well as an extreme soreness between her thighs.

Obviously not satisfied with her response, Korum pulled off the blanket, uncovering her naked body to his eyes. Her mind still feeling fuzzy, Mia followed his gaze as it lingered on the faint bruises covering her breasts and torso, many in the shape of finger marks.

His face darkened with guilt, and he groaned. "Mia, I'm so sorry about this . . . I should've never let you play that game with me last night. I can usually control myself with you because I know how small and fragile you are, but I completely lost it last night . . . I never meant to hurt you like this—please believe me . . ."

Mia nodded, still trying to understand what happened. All she could recall was the mind-blowing sex, mixed with the ecstatic rush from his bite.

He gently stroked her shoulder, caressing the soft skin. "I am really sorry about this," he murmured. "You're so delicate . . . I should've never lost control like that. I'll make you feel better, I promise—"

The events of last night were slowly coming back to Mia. Her hand clenched into a fist as she remembered what had led her to tease him like that, and the feel of the ring on her finger was utterly reassuring.

She might be sore this morning, but she was also hopeful that the little device had worked as promised. There was no guarantee, of course, but her finger's proximity to Korum's palm last night should've been sufficient to get access to the necessary blueprints. Now she just had to get the ring over to John and, for that, she needed Korum to leave her alone.

"It's all right," she mumbled, trying to think of something appropriate to say. He was obviously feeling guilty about leaving a few bruises on her body. It struck her as hypocritical, this extreme concern for her physical well-being, since he obviously had no problem causing her emotional pain by upending her entire life. Then again, her being sore could interfere with their sex life, and he probably didn't want that.

"I'll bring something, okay?" he said, and disappeared from the room with inhuman speed.

Mia buried her head in the pillow while waiting for his return, desperately thinking of ways to get the information over to John quickly. She still needed to write her papers, so maybe she could tell Korum she had to get some books from the library.

He was back a minute later, carrying the familiar device that had "shined" her and something else that she'd never seen before. The second object looked most like a lipstick tube, but was made of some strange material.

"Um, I'm all right—really, there's no need for this," said Mia quickly, not wanting him to plant any additional tracking devices on her. For all she knew, the next batch of nanotechnology in her body might broadcast her every thought to him, and that was the last thing she wanted.

"There's every need," he said, obviously surprised at her reluctance. "You're hurt, and I can fix it. Why not?"

Why not indeed. She didn't have a good answer for that, and protesting further would make him suspicious. Getting caught so close to the end of her mission would be stupid, and it's not like she didn't already have the tracking devices embedded in her palms. What's a few more?

So she just shrugged her shoulders in response, letting him do as he wanted.

He activated the "shining" device and ran the warm red light over her bruises. Seeing it work the second time was still incredible, with the marks on her skin disappearing as though they were never there. He was very thorough, inspecting every inch of her skin, and Mia blushed slightly at having so much attention paid to her naked body in broad daylight. Once he was done, he took the tube-like device in his hand and brought it toward her thighs.

"What are you going to do with that?" she asked suspiciously, eyeing it with distrust. There was only one place remaining on her body that still hadn't been healed, and the red light from the device could not reach there. She hoped the little tube wasn't really going where it looked like it could go.

Korum sighed and said, "It's something we use for deep internal damage, when you have to heal various organs before you can mend the outer layer of the skin. I know it's overkill for what you've got, but it's the only thing I have in this apartment that can reach inside you to help you with the soreness."

So it was going there. Mia's blush got worse. The thing was about the size of a tampon, and the thought of having something medical like that inserted in broad daylight was embarrassing.

"Seriously?" he asked with incredulity. "After last night, you're going to blush at this?"

Mia refused to look at him. "Just do it already," she mumbled, plopping down and hiding her face in the pillow.

He laughed softly and did as she requested, sliding the little device inside her sore and swollen opening. It went in easily, and Mia didn't feel anything for a few seconds until the tingling began.

"It feels funny," she complained, still shielded by the pillow.

"It's supposed to—that means it's working."

The tingling went on for a couple of minutes and then it stopped. She didn't feel sore anymore, which was nice, although the feel of the foreign object inside her was disconcerting.

"It should be done by now," said Korum, reaching inside her with his long fingers and pulling out the tube. "That's it—all finished. You can stop hiding now"

"Okay, thanks," muttered Mia, still refusing to meet his eyes. "I think I'm going to shower now."

He laughed and kissed her exposed shoulder. "Go for it. I have some things to take care of, so I'll be out the rest of the day. The dinner will probably be a late one, so be sure to grab a good lunch."

And then he walked out of the room, finally leaving Mia alone to carry out the rest of the plan.

CHAPTER EIGHTEEN

As soon as Korum left, Mia sprang into action, her heart pounding at the magnitude of what she was about to do.

Before hopping into the shower, she sent a quick 'Hi' email to Jessie, letting her know that she would be stopping by the apartment today and asking how Jessie's Anatomy final had gone. Hopefully, John would see the email and contact Mia quickly. It was already early afternoon; due to her complete exhaustion, Mia had slept far later than planned, and there was a lot to get done before this evening.

Korum had thoughtfully left her a sandwich for lunch, and Mia gratefully gobbled it down before heading out the door. When he did things like that—considerate little gestures—she could almost believe that he genuinely cared about her, and she would feel an unwelcome pang of guilt at betraying his trust. Even today, after everything that happened last evening, the thought of him coming to any harm made her feel sick. It was ridiculous, of course; he would most likely be fine—and even if he wasn't, it was his own fault for invading Earth and trying to enslave her species. Still, she would much rather see him safely deported back to Krina, so she could resume her normal life knowing that he was thousands of light years away and would never bother her again.

Or so she told herself.

Deep inside, some silly romantic part of her wanted to cry at the thought of never seeing Korum again—never feeling his touch or hearing his laughter, never glimpsing the dimple that so incongruously graced his left cheek. He was her enemy, but he was also her lover, and she had gotten attached to him despite everything. The pleasure that he gave her went beyond the sexual; just being with him made her feel excited and alive, and—if she ever let herself forget the exact nature of their relationship— oddly happy.

She could not imagine having sex with someone else after experiencing Korum's lovemaking. It would be like eating sawdust for the rest of her life after first tasting ambrosia. It made perfect sense that he would be a good lover, of course; aside from whatever special chemistry he said they had together, Korum was also thousands of years old—and had had plenty of time to learn exactly how to please a woman. How could a human man compare to that? And she didn't even want to think about how he made her feel when he took her blood. She wasn't sure that it was healthy, to feel a pleasure so intense, but the thought of never experiencing it again was nearly more than she could bear.

For the first time, she wondered about the xenos she'd heard about before. The motives of these people—who supposedly advertised online with the goal of entering into sexual relations with the Krinar—had always been a mystery to her. But she wondered now if they were perhaps truly addicted . . . if they'd had a taste of paradise and knew that everything else would pale in comparison.

Korum had warned that addiction was a possibility for both of them if he took her blood too frequently. Mia shuddered at the thought. That was the last thing she needed—to actually develop a physical need for him. It was enough that she would probably miss him with every fiber of her being when he was finally gone from her life; the last thing she needed was to crave some elusive high that she could only achieve with him.

There was no other alternative for her; she had to complete the mission. Their relationship was bound to end—it was just a matter of time. Even if she were willing to put up with his autocratic nature—or if she even went so far as to accept being his charl—he would tire of her in a few short years and then she would be alone anyway, completely heartbroken and devastated at his desertion.

No, she had to do this. There was no other way. She couldn't have lived with herself knowing that she'd had a chance to make a real difference in the course of human history and failed to do so because of her weakness for one particular K—for someone who regarded her as nothing more than his plaything.

Arriving at her apartment, Mia was surprised to see that John was already there. So were Jessie and Edgar, the actor her roommate had apparently started seeing.

As soon as she walked through the door, John asked if they could speak in private. Mia nodded and led him into her room, closing the door behind her. Before the door was fully shut, Mia heard Edgar ask Jessie if her roommate was seeing John as well, but Jessie's reply was already inaudible.

"I think I have it," said Mia without any preamble.

John's entire face lit up. "You do? That's great! How

did you manage it so quickly?" Seeing the color flooding her face, he added hastily, "Never mind, that's not important."

Mia shrugged and pulled the ring off her finger. There was a little indentation left behind on her skin. She sincerely hoped that Korum was not particularly observant when it came to women's jewelry; otherwise, he might wonder why she'd worn that ring once and never again.

"I need you to promise me something," Mia said slowly, still holding on to the ring.

"What?"

"Promise me that Korum will not be harmed in whatever you're planning to do."

John hesitated, and Mia's eyes narrowed. "Promise me, John. You owe me that much."

"Why? He doesn't deserve it—"

"It doesn't matter what he does or does not deserve. This is my condition for helping you. Korum gets safe passage home."

John looked at her and then sighed heavily. "All right, Mia, if that's what you truly want. We'll make sure that he gets safely deported."

Mia nodded and handed him the ring. "So what now?" she asked. "How long do you think it will take your Keiths to do something with this information?"

He grinned at her, looking like a kid at Christmas. "They'll have to look at it and make sure that it's not more complicated than they think, but if they're right . . . we could be looking at a potential attack within days."

Days? That was much faster than Mia had ever thought possible.

"Won't it take them time to make . . . well, whatever it is that those blueprints are for?" she asked hesitantly.

He shook his head. "No, not that much time at all. Remember what I told you about how they manufacture everything using nanotechnology—and can make things almost instantly if they have the design for it?"

Mia vaguely recalled something like that, so she nodded.

"Well, they will now have the blueprints, and they already have the technology to create those designs. They just need to get that technology to a safe location outside of their settlements, and then they can manufacture the necessary weapons to penetrate the K Center shields. Once the shields are gone, the human forces will be ready."

Forces?

"Is the government in on this?" asked Mia with surprise.

John hesitated. "Not exactly. But there are those within the government who believe that it was wrong to sign the Coexistence Treaty, to allow them to build the settlements. These individuals are sympathetic to our cause and they have the ability to bring us reinforcements. Some of these are highly placed people in the Army and the Navy, as well as within the CIA and other equivalent agencies worldwide."

Mia looked at him in shock. She hadn't realized the full scope of the anti-K movement. For some reason, she'd envisioned it as being a few hundred suicidal individuals within the Resistance—or those like John, who had a personal vendetta against the Ks—helped by a few human-sympathizing aliens. But it made sense, of course, that the freedom fighters couldn't have come as far as they did—and gained the assistance of the Keiths—if they hadn't had at least a decent chance of success.

"Wow," she said softly, "so it's really happening then?

We're kicking them off our planet?"

John nodded with barely contained glee. "It's happening, Mia. If the information on this ring is as good as we hope it is, we're looking at Earth's liberation within a week—a couple of weeks at the most."

That was crazy. Mia tried to imagine what would happen when the Ks learned that they were being attacked. She remembered the days of the Great Panic and shuddered.

"John," she said slowly, "would they really go without a big fight? You know what happened before . . . how much damage they could do even with bare hands—"

"That's true," agreed John, "they could definitely fight back—and it could get very bloody for both sides. That's why the information you got for us is so crucial. You see, if the Keiths are right, these blueprints also contain the design for one of their most advanced weapons. Once the shields are down and we let the Ks know that we have this weapon, they would be suicidal to do anything but surrender. Because if they fight, we *will* use it—and every K in their colonies would be turned to dust."

"Turned to dust? What kind of weapon can do that?" asked Mia in horrified shock.

"It's weaponized nanotechnology on a massive scale. It can be programmed with very specific constraints, so we could set it to only destroy Ks within a certain radius and to spare whatever humans may be in the area at the time."

Mia's eyes widened, and John continued, "Of course, we still expect some Ks to try to escape from the colonies when they learn of the attack, so we'll have our fighters stationed all around to capture and contain those—and that could get bloody. We might still end up suffering heavy casualties, but we stand a very real chance of winning here."

Mia swallowed, feeling nauseous at the thought of any bloodshed. Knowing that something she did led to "heavy casualties" or extermination of thousands of intelligent beings—she didn't know how she would handle that kind of responsibility.

But there was no choice now, not that there had ever been any for her. Ever since she'd laid eyes on Korum at the park, her fate had been decided. Her only choice had been to meekly accept being his charl or to fight back—and she had chosen to fight. And now that decision might result in the loss of many lives, both human and Krinar.

Mia bitterly wished she'd never gone to the park that day, had never learned about what goes on in the K Centers. If she could somehow turn back the clock and go back to her regular life, knowing next to nothing about the Ks, she would gladly do so—and leave the liberation of Earth to someone better equipped to deal with it. But she knew, and that burden felt unbearably heavy right now as she looked into John's glowing face and imagined the upcoming bloody battle.

"Mia," said John, apparently sensing her distress, "please don't forget: *they* came to our planet, *they* imposed their rules on us—and killed thousands of people in the process, until we had no choice but to give in. Do you remember how it was during the Great Panic?"

Mia nodded, thinking of the terrifying chaos and bloody street fights of those dark months.

Satisfied, John continued, "I know that your only exposure to them has been through Korum, and he has probably treated you nicely so far . . . because he thinks of you as his current favorite pet. But they're not nice at all. They're predators by nature. They evolved as parasites, as vampires, sustaining themselves by consuming the blood of other species. In fact, they developed humans for that purpose—to satisfy their own perverse urges with us—"

That wasn't exactly what Korum had told her, but she didn't feel like arguing that point right now.

"—and they have no regard for our rights. Most of them view us as inferior, and they would not hesitate to enslave us completely if it suited their purposes."

"I know," said Mia, rubbing her temples to get rid of the tension. "I know all of that—that's why I'm helping you, John. I just really wish there was another way . . . some way we could just make them go away without spilling any blood."

"I wish there was too," said John, sighing heavily. "But there isn't. They invaded our planet with force—and now we take it back from them in the same way. And if some lives have to be lost in the process—well, we just have to hope that not too many of them are on our side. It's war, Mia—the real *War of the Worlds.*"

John left, and Mia sat down on her bed to digest everything.

How had she—a regular college student—managed to get involved in a war? Spying was something she'd always associated with glamorous secret agents, men and women who've had extensive training in everything from martial arts to defusing a bomb. A psychology major from NYU just didn't fit the bill. Yet here she was, supposedly aiding the Resistance in their most important fight against the Ks.

A terrifying thought occurred to her. Once Korum knew what was happening—that their settlements were being attacked—would he realize that she was the one responsible? Would he make the connection between his carefully guarded blueprints being stolen and the human girl he slept with every night? Because if he did—and he was still in New York at the time—then her days were likely numbered as well.

A tentative knock on her door interrupted her dark musings.

"Yes, come in!" she called out, relieved to have a distraction from that line of thinking.

To her surprise and dismay, it was not Jessie. Instead, Peter stood in her bedroom doorway, his wavy blond hair and blue eyes looking even more angelic in the bright light of the day. There were still black and blue marks on his throat.

"Peter!" she exclaimed. "What are you doing here?"

"I came to see you," he said. "Your roommate told Edgar that you would be home today, and I just wanted to make sure you were all right after what happened that night—"

"Oh gosh, Peter, that's really nice of you," said Mia, desperately trying to think of the quickest way to get rid of him. She couldn't imagine that Korum would be pleased to know that Peter was anywhere near her right now, much less in her bedroom. He probably wouldn't find out, but she didn't want to chance it. It was enough that she had almost gotten him killed in that club.

Peter was looking at her with a concerned expression. "What happened that night, Mia? Did that monster hurt you in any way?"

"No, of course not," she tried to reassure him. "He just got jealous—I never expected him to react like that, believe me. I'm really sorry about everything that happened. I should've never danced with you that night. You got hurt because of me—"

He waved his hand dismissively. "It's not a big deal. I was once beaten up in high school because the head quarterback thought I was flirting with his girlfriend. Believe me, this was nothing in comparison." And he grinned at her, his smile utterly infectious.

Mia smiled back a little. It was good to hear that he didn't hold a grudge against her. But he still needed to go away for his own safety.

"Listen, Peter, thanks for checking up on me," she said. "That was really sweet of you. But we now know that my boyfriend is not too keen on our friendship—and it's really for the best if he doesn't find out you were here—"

"Mia," said Peter seriously, his smile completely gone, "are you really dating that creature? I just never pictured you as a xeno—"

"I'm not!"

"You're not a Krinarian, are you?"

"Of course not! I'm not religious at all!"

"Then why are you seeing him?"

Mia sighed. "Look, Peter, that's not really any of your business. He's my boyfriend—that's all you need to know. I'm sorry I didn't tell you that when we first met. I was just having a fun time at a girls' night out. I really didn't mean to mislead you in any way—"

"That's bullshit," said Peter vehemently. "A boyfriend—that's a human guy, not some vicious alien who drags you out of the club like that." He paused for a second and asked quietly, "Mia, is he forcing you to be with him?"

"What? Why would you think that?" Mia stared at him, wondering what would make him ask something like that.

He looked back at her, his brows furrowed in a frown. "You just don't seem like the type to seek out one of these monsters."

"What type is that?" wondered Mia, genuinely curious to hear the answer.

He tugged at his ear in frustration. "Well, a lot of people in the entertainment industry actually . . . models, actresses, singers—they get bored and look for something to spice up their lives . . . They're shallow, and many of them are stupid—all they see are the pretty faces and not the evil underneath—"

"Evil underneath?" asked Mia, surprised that he felt so strongly about the Krinar. Prior to her own close encounters with Korum, she'd had zero exposure to the invaders and no real opinion about them. Maybe Peter was religious himself and believed the claim that the Ks were demons?

He grimaced. "I've seen people disappear, Mia, when they get involved with these creatures. That, or end up really messed up at the end. It's not natural for us—to be with their kind. It never ends well . . ."

Mia took a deep breath and said firmly, "Peter, look, I appreciate the concern, but there's really no need in this case. I know what I'm doing. I'm neither shallow nor stupid—"

"I never said you were," protested Peter.

"—and I don't really appreciate you implying anything about my relationship. I'm with Korum because I want to be, and that's all there's to it."

She sincerely hoped that was enough to get Peter to go away. The last thing she needed was a bumbling white knight trying to save her from the evil monster—a white knight who would definitely end up getting slain in the process. Maybe later, if she survived the next couple of weeks, she would apologize to Peter for being so harsh. She liked him, and it would be nice to become friends with him, particularly if her life ever got back to normal.

He looked slightly hurt. "Of course, I'm sorry, I didn't mean to imply anything. Obviously, you can be with whomever you choose. I just wanted to make sure you were all right, that's all."

Mia nodded and gave him a faint smile. "I understand. Thanks again for stopping by." Reaching into her bag, she pulled out the laptop and a couple of books.

Peter immediately got the hint. "Sure. I'll see you around, okay?" he said, and walked out of the room. Mia heard him talking to Jessie and Edgar for a minute, and then he was gone, the front door closing decisively behind him.

Mia plopped down on her bed with relief. How had it happened that a cute guy—with whom she actually had a decent connection—had come along at such a wrong time in her life? Had she met him two months ago, she had no doubt that she would have been ecstatic to have him pay attention to her like that—but it was too late now.

Like those people he knew, she would likely end up messed up in the end—either that or dead at the hands of her alien lover.

CHAPTER NINETEEN

Shortly after Peter left, Edgar departed as well. Mia heard them kissing and giggling by the door, and then there was silence. Almost immediately afterwards, Jessie came into her room.

"So," said Mia, smiling at her roommate, "I take it things are going well with Edgar?"

Jessie gave her a huge grin. "They are going *very* well. He's just so nice, and so fun, and so cute . . ."

Mia laughed and said, "I'm glad for you. You deserve a good guy like that."

"That I do," said Jessie without any false modesty, still grinning. And then her expression abruptly became serious. "And so do you, Mia—"

Uh-oh, thought Mia. Here comes the lecture.

"—and you're clearly not getting it."

"Jessie, please, let's not beat a dead horse—"

"A dead horse? I'd like to beat up a certain K!" Jessie took a deep breath, clearly riled on Mia's behalf. "Peter is such a nice guy, and he seems to really like you—to come all the way here like this after everything that happened . . . and you're stuck with that monster!"

Mia rubbed the back of her neck to get rid of some tension there. "Jessie, please stop worrying about my relationship . . . everything will get resolved in its own time

"Speaking of getting things resolved, did you talk to him about the summer?"

Mia bit her lip. She hated lying to Jessie, and she so badly wanted to talk to someone about the whole maddening mess. If John was right about the Keiths' timing, her trip to Florida would be merely delayed—and not even by all that much. Of course, that assumed she would still be alive at the time. Mia decided on a slightly edited version of the truth.

"I have," she said slowly.

"And?"

"And we agreed that I'll go later in the summer, and do an internship here in New York instead."

Jessie stared at her in shock. "What internship?"

"I'm not sure yet. Korum promised to find me something in my field."

"Oh my God, he's not letting you go, is he?" Jessie looked completely horrified.

"Not exactly," admitted Mia. "He did say, though, that we'll go to Florida together once his business in New York is done."

"Together? What, he's going to meet your family?" The expression on Jessie's face was utterly incredulous.

"I have no idea," said Mia, and she really didn't. She hadn't had a chance to think about it, with everything that had gone on—but she couldn't imagine her normal down-to-earth family interacting calmly with her alien lover. "We didn't get as far as discussing the particulars—"

"That bastard! I can't believe he's doing it to you! No wonder you're helping the Resistance—you probably hate his guts."

Mia couldn't believe her ears. "What? What did you just say?"

"Oh come on, Mia," said Jessie calmly. "I'm not an idiot. I can put two and two together. John was waiting for you here in the apartment even before you showed up. Clearly, he knew you were coming. You're communicating with them, aren't you?"

Damn it. Sometimes Mia forgot just how astute her pretty, bubbly roommate could be. Denying it any longer would be pointless, but Jessie could not know the extent of Mia's involvement—it would be much too dangerous for both of them.

Mia gave her a piercing look. "Jessie, listen to me, don't ever say something like that—and don't ever talk about it with anyone, not even Edgar. Do you promise me?"

Jessie nodded, her eyes narrowed. "I would never say anything. When Edgar asked me if you and John were dating, I just said that he was an old friend of your family's."

"That's good," said Mia with relief. Then she added, "Look, I am not doing anything too crazy, I promise. John just asked me to keep an eye on Korum's activities and report to him occasionally. That's all I was doing today. Korum met a couple of other Ks recently, and I just wanted to tell John about it. Turns out he already knew, so it really wasn't a big deal." Mia had no idea where she had learned to lie so smoothly.

"Not a big deal? Mia . . . you're dealing with an extraterrestrial who has no regard for human life. You saw what he did to Peter—and that was just for dancing with you! If he catches you spying, he would kill you for sure! Of course, it's a big deal!" Jessie blew out a frustrated breath.

There was nothing Mia could really say to that, so she just shrugged.

"And it's all my fault for blabbing about you to Jason! I can't believe those bastards decided to use you like that."

Mia rubbed her neck again. "They just saw an opportunity and decided to use it. It doesn't really change my situation. I'm still with Korum, whether or not I'm spying on him. So I might as well try to help out, you know?"

Jessie gave her a frustrated look. "I can't believe all this shit is happening to you. You're the most by-the-book person I know . . . and you end up sleeping with a K and spying on him."

Mia sighed heavily. "I know. I'm so screwed, Jessie— and not just in a good way."

A small smile broke out on Jessie's face, and she shook her head in reproach. "Mia . . ."

Mia grinned at her. "I know, I know, that was pretty bad."

"Not James Bond caliber, that's for sure." And Jessie grinned back.

* * *

That evening, Korum got home around eight o'clock. Mia was already back at his place and frantically working on her paper.

He entered her study room and came up to kiss her. "Hey there, looks like somebody is hard at work," he teased, brushing his lips briefly against her cheek.

Mia gave him a little frown. "Yeah, I have to finish this paper tonight. I have this and my Child Psychology paper due Thursday, and I'm not done with even one of them."

"Sounds terrible," Korum said, the slight curve of his lips giving away his amusement.

"It is!" said Mia, her frown getting worse. Couldn't he see she was stressed? He didn't have to laugh at her just because her worries seemed minor to him.

"Do you want some help with it?" he asked, causing Mia to give him an incredulous look.

"Help with my papers?" Was he serious?

"Isn't that what you're stressing about?" He didn't look like he was joking.

"Uh . . ." Mia was speechless. Finally finding her tongue, she mumbled, "That's okay, thanks . . . I should be able to handle it."

Stifling a grin, she imagined turning in a paper on the effects of environmental factors in early childhood development—written from the perspective of a two-thousand-year-old extraterrestrial. The look on Professor Dunkin's face would be priceless.

"I can write in English, you know," said Korum, apparently offended by her reluctance.

Mia smiled with some condescension. "Of course you can." This was the strangest conversation ever. "But there's more to writing an academic paper than just knowing the language. You have to have read all these books and attended the lectures . . ." She gestured toward the big pile of paper books sitting at the corner of her desk.

"So," said Korum, shrugging nonchalantly, "I can read the books right now."

Mia gave him a dumbfounded look. "There's about ten of them . . ." She swallowed to get rid of the sudden dryness in her throat. "H-How fast do you read?"

"Pretty fast," he said. "I also have what you would call a photographic memory, so I don't need to read the material more than once."

Mia stared at him in shock. "So you can read all these books in a matter of hours?"

He nodded. "I would probably need about two hours to finish them all."

That was incredible. "Is that normal for your kind?" Mia asked, still digesting that shocking tidbit.

"Some of us have that ability naturally, while others choose to enhance it with technology to keep up. I was born this way."

Mia could feel her heart rate picking up. She'd known that he was very smart, of course, and John had told her that Korum was one of the best designers among the K. She just hadn't expected him to have what amounted to superhuman intelligence.

"I probably seem really stupid to you then," Mia said quietly, "given how long it takes me to do all this—"

He sighed. "No, Mia, of course not. Just because you're lacking certain abilities doesn't mean you're not smart."

Yeah, right. "What else can you do?" asked Mia, realizing how little she still knew about her alien lover.

He shrugged. "I can probably do some math in my head that you would need a calculator for."

This was fascinating and scary at the same time. "What's 10,456 times 6,345?" she asked, simultaneously reaching for her phone to check the answer.

"66,343,320."

That was exactly right. And he'd given her the answer before she even had time to input the numbers into the calculator on her phone. Mia swallowed again.

"So do you want my help with the paper or not?" Korum was beginning to look impatient.

Mia shook her head. "Uh, no—that's all right, thanks. I'm sure you could write a great paper—probably better than me—but I still have to do this myself."

"Okay, sure, whatever you want," he said, shaking his head at her stubbornness. "Are you hungry? Do you want me to make something?"

Mia had snacked throughout the day, so she wasn't starving. "I don't know," she said tentatively. "I don't think I have time for a sit-down meal today." She looked up at him, hoping that he would understand.

"Of course," he said, "I'll bring you something to eat here." Giving her a quick smile, he left the room.

Mia stared at the door in frustration. Why did he have to be so nice to her today? It would be so much easier if he treated her with cruelty or indifference. The guilt burning her up inside made no sense; she knew she was doing the right thing by helping the Resistance. The Ks had invaded their planet, not the other way around; liberating her species should not make her feel like this— like she was betraying someone she cared about.

Taking a deep breath, she tried to focus back on the paper. It was an impossible task. Her thoughts kept wandering, jumping from one unpleasant topic to another. Had she set in motion something that would result in the loss of thousands of lives? And would Korum be one of the casualties? It still didn't seem entirely real to her, the potential impact of her actions.

Korum came back a few minutes later. He had made some kind of sushi-like rolls with crunchy lettuce and peppers and an apple-walnut dish for dessert.

Mia thanked him and gladly dug in, finding that she was quite hungry after all.

He smiled at her and bent down to kiss her forehead. "Enjoy. I'll be next door if you need me."

And then he left, letting her work on her papers—and battle her own dark thoughts.

CHAPTER TWENTY

That night, he was incredibly tender with her.

His fingers unerringly finding every knot and tense muscle, he massaged every inch of her body until she lay there in a boneless puddle of contentment. Once he was satisfied that she was fully relaxed, he flipped her over onto her back and began kissing her, starting with the tips of her fingers. His lips were soft and felt warm on the skin of her hand, and when he sucked her index finger into his mouth and swirled his tongue around it, Mia moaned from the unexpectedly erotic sensation.

Leaving her fingers alone, his mouth traveled up her palm, licking the sensitive spot on the inside of her wrist, and then further, up her arm, until he reached the arched column of her throat. Mia held her breath, waiting for the familiar biting pain, but he merely placed a series of light kisses there, sending goosebumps down her leg and arm, and nibbled softly on her earlobe. Mia moaned again, overcome by the pleasure of his touch, and buried her fingers in his hair, pulling his face down for a deep French kiss.

He kissed her back, passionately and intensely, and

Mia felt the strength of his desire in the rigid erection brushing against her thigh. His hand found her breasts, gently squeezing and massaging the small globes, and his thumb flicked across her left nipple, causing it to stiffen further.

Lifting himself up on his elbows, he looked down at her with a warm golden gaze. "You're so beautiful," he murmured, staring into her eyes, and the tender expression on his face made her want to cry. Why was he doing this to her today of all days? This might be one of the last few times she was having sex with him, and she didn't want to remember it like this—like the lovemaking that it could never be.

He kissed her again, and she sucked on his tongue, hoping to make him lose control, so she could forget everything in the mind-bending ecstasy and finally turn off her brain. He groaned in response, and she felt his cock jump against her leg, but his touch on her body remained exceedingly gentle, with none of the raw lust from last night.

Frustrated, Mia pushed at his shoulders. "I want to get on top," she told him huskily. He was clearly doing penance for his roughness yesterday, but that wasn't what Mia wanted tonight.

His eyes widened a little in surprise, but he rolled off her onto his back. Mia climbed over him and grabbed his head with both hands, bringing his face to hers for a deep tongue-filled kiss while simultaneously rubbing her sex on his without allowing actual penetration. He wrapped his arms around her in response, so tightly that she could barely breathe, and kissed her back with the intensity she was seeking. She could see a fine layer of sweat on his forehead as his body strained with the effort of holding himself back. Mia moved her hips suggestively then, grinding against his cock, and his hips lifted off the bed, trying to get more. His embrace loosened slightly, and Mia worked her right hand in between their bodies and wrapped her fingers around his shaft. He hissed, his body tensing up, and she carefully guided his cock to her opening, starting to lower herself onto him in a maddeningly slow motion.

He growled low in his throat and his hips thrust up, penetrating her in one powerful stroke. Mia cried out, feeling her muscles quivering, adjusting to the extreme fullness. He grasped her hips, his thumb finding her clit through the closed folds and pressing on it, his touch torturously light, bringing her closer to the desired peak without sending her over. Mia moaned, her sex clenching around his cock. She wanted more—more of the madness, of the mindless bliss that only he could make her feel. "Bite me," she told him, and watched his eyes turn even more yellow even as he shook his head in denial. "You don't know what you're asking," he muttered roughly, and rolled over so that he was over her again, their bodies still joined.

Before she could say anything else, he twisted his hips slightly, and the head of his cock nudged the sensitive spot deep inside. Mia moaned, arching toward him, and he repeated the action, again and again, until the monstrous tension coiling inside her became unbearable, and she screamed, raking her nails down his back as the long-awaited climax finally rushed through her, obliterating all rational thought in its wake.

But he wasn't done with her yet. He still hadn't come, despite the rhythmic squeezing of her inner muscles, and his shaft was lodged inside her, as hard and thick as ever. Burying his hand in her hair, he kissed her deeply and began thrusting, alternating a shallow stroke with a deeper one, until the tension started building again and every cell in her body was crying out for the release. She tried to move her hips, to force him into that constant pace she needed to reach her climax, but he wouldn't let her, his large, powerful body holding her down. His kiss was relentless, his tongue ravishing her mouth, and Mia felt like she would explode from the intensity of the sensations. And then suddenly she was there, her entire body convulsing in his arms, and he was coming as well, his pelvis grinding into her own as his cock pulsed inside her, releasing his semen in short, warm bursts.

Afterwards, he rolled off her and gathered her to him, leaving her lying partially on top, her head on his chest and her left leg draped over his hips. They were both slick with sweat, and Mia could hear the rapid beating of his heart gradually beginning to slow as his breathing returned to its normal pace.

She didn't really know what to say, so she didn't say anything. The sex had been incredible, and she hated the fact that he could make her feel like this—even without any chemical enhancers.

Why did it have to be him, she thought bitterly, looking at his flat bronzed stomach moving up and down with every breath. Why couldn't she have fallen for a normal human guy instead of an alien genius whose kind was taking over her planet?

She felt the hot prickling of tears behind her eyelids and squeezed them tightly, not letting the moisture escape. Her body felt languid and tired in the aftermath of the sex session, but her mind kept buzzing, working overtime, looking for a solution where none could be found. Even if he cared for her in his own way, those feelings would turn to hatred once he learned the depths of her betrayal—and the hands that held her so gently now would likely end up wrapped around her throat.

She must have tensed at the thought because he pulled away to look at her face and asked curiously, "What's the matter?"

When she hesitated, a worried frown appeared on his face. "Mia? What's the matter? I didn't hurt you, did I?"

Mia shook her head, trying not to look him directly in the eyes. "No, of course not," she said huskily, "it was wonderful . . . you know that—"

"Then what?" he prodded, reaching out to grasp her chin and force her to meet his gaze.

Mia tried to control herself, but the stupid tears wouldn't leave her alone, welling up in her eyes.

"It's nothing," Mia lied, silently cursing the fact that her voice was shaking, "I just . . . g-get this way when I'm stressed—"

His frown got deeper. "Why are you so stressed? Is it your papers?" he asked, studying her with a perplexed look in his eyes.

Mia nodded slightly, squeezing her eyes shut and trying to calm herself. He might become suspicious if her tears didn't have a good explanation. Unless . . .

Opening her eyes, she looked at him, no longer caring if he saw the glimmer there. "I really miss my family," she confessed, and it was the truth. In this moment, she desperately wanted to be a child again, safe and sound in her parents' house, with her mom making chicken soup with matzah balls and her dad reading a newspaper on the couch. She wanted to turn back the clock and go back to the last decade, to a time before people knew that there was life on other planets—and that their own planet would not belong to them much longer. To a time before she met the alien who was staring at her now with his beautiful amber eyes—the lover whom she had no choice but to betray.

Korum seemed to accept her explanation. "Mia," he said quietly, letting go of her chin, "you'll see them soon, I promise. I'm getting closer to completing my business here, and then I will take you there—"

"I haven't even told them yet that I'm not coming," said Mia, her voice thick with tears. "They're expecting me this Saturday, and my plane ticket is nonrefundable—"

He looked exasperated. "Are you worrying about money now? I will refund you the cost of the ticket—"

"My parents are the ones who bought it."

"Okay, then I will refund the cost to your parents." Taking a deep breath, he added, "Mia, you don't ever have to worry about these logistics when you're with me. I'll always take care of you and your family—you don't need to stress about money ever again. I know your parents' finances are tight, and I would be more than happy to assist them financially—or in whichever way they need."

Mia swallowed a sob, feeling like an iron fist was squeezing her heart. As arrogant and high-handed as that statement was, she had no doubt that he was genuine in his offer. "Th-thank you," she whispered, her voice breaking, "that's very . . . generous of you—"

"Mia," he said softly, "I care about you, okay? I want you to be happy with me, and I will do whatever I can to make that happen."

His every word felt like he was cutting her with a knife, and she could no longer hold back. Burying her face in the pillow, she turned away from him and broke down crying, her entire body shaking from the force of her sobs.

"Mia?" His voice sounded uncertain for the first time since she'd met him. "What . . . Why are you crying?"

She cried even harder. She couldn't tell him the truth, and the guilt was like acid in her chest, eating her up inside.

Tentatively touching her back, he stroked it in a soothing manner, murmuring little endearments. When that didn't seem to help, he pulled her into his arms, letting her bury her face in the crook of his neck and cry while he stroked her hair.

So Mia cried. She cried for herself, and for him, and for the relationship that could never be . . . not even if he weren't the enemy that she'd been spying on.

After a few minutes, when her sobs began to quiet down, he reached somewhere and handed her a tissue, letting her wipe her face and blow her nose before asking softly again, "Why?"

Mia looked at him, her vision still blurry with tears. The full truth was out of the question, of course, but she could tell him something that had been tormenting her for a while. "This is not right," she whispered, her voice rough with residual tears. "You, me—it's not right, it's not natural . . . And it can never last—"

"Why not?" he said softly. "It can last for as long as we want it to last."

"You're not human," she said, looking at him in disbelief. "How could it ever work for us?"

He hesitated for a second and then said, gently brushing her hair off her face, "It can—just trust me on that, darling. I can't really say more right now, but we will talk about it later . . . when the time comes."

Mia blinked in surprise, staring at him. This was something she hadn't expected. Did he mean that there was some way for them to be together . . . as an actual couple? The implications of that were too big to contemplate right now, with her head pounding and her mind barely functioning in the aftermath of her emotional storm.

He pulled away then and got off the bed. "I'll bring you something to make you feel better," he said, and left the room.

Mia looked at the door, stifling a hysterical giggle at the thought that this was becoming a nightly occurrence. She just hoped he didn't bring back the little tube.

He brought back a glass filled with some kind of milky liquid and handed it to her.

"What is it?" she asked, sniffing it with suspicion. It didn't smell like anything.

He grinned at her, showing the dimple. "Not poison, I promise. It's just a little something to help you sleep better and take away your headache."

How did he know that her head was hurting? Mia blinked at him again.

As though reading her mind, he said, "I know how humans feel after crying. This drink is meant more for helping with a cold or a flu, but it doesn't have any harmful side effects, so you might as well drink it now and feel better."

Mia nodded in agreement and tasted the liquid. It didn't have any flavor either; if not for the color, she would have thought she was drinking water. She felt dehydrated, so she gladly drank the entire glass. Almost immediately, the painful pressure around her temples eased, and the congested feeling in her nose disappeared. Another K wonder drug, apparently.

"Why do you have all these medicines for humans?" she asked, the thought only now occurring to her. "Do you also use these for yourself?"

He shook his head, smiling. "No, they're human-specific. We have other ways to heal ourselves."

"So why have it then?" Mia persisted.

He shrugged. "I knew that I would be living among humans and interacting with them. It only made sense to have a few basics handy in case of various emergencies."

Interacting with humans at his apartment? Mia suddenly felt an unwelcome pang of jealousy at the thought of other women being here, in this very bed. It wasn't surprising, of course; he was a healthy, attractive male with a strong sex drive—it was perfectly normal for him to have had other sex partners before her, both human and K.

Or so she told herself. The green-eyed monster inside refused to listen to reason.

Something of her thoughts must have shown on her face because he said softly, "And no, none of those interactions have been human women in recent months—definitely none since I met you."

"What about K women?" she blurted out, and then mentally kicked herself. She had no right to be jealous after what she'd done. He was her enemy, and she had treated him as such. It was absurd to feel so relieved that she was the only woman in his life right now. Their days together were numbered, and it shouldn't matter whether Korum had been faithful to her or if he had fucked a hundred women in the past month. Yet somehow it mattered to her—and it mattered a lot.

"None since we've met," he said, smiling. He seemed pleased by her jealousy, and Mia nearly broke down crying again. Taking a deep breath, she controlled herself with great effort. A second crying fit would be even more difficult to explain.

"Let's go to sleep, shall we?" he suggested softly. "You still seem stressed, and you'll probably feel better in the morning."

Mia nodded in agreement and lay down, covering herself with the blanket. Korum followed her example, pulling her toward him until they lay in his favorite spooning position.

Against all odds, Mia drifted off to sleep as soon as she closed her eyes, feeling comforted by the heat of his body wrapped around her own.

CHAPTER TWENTY-ONE

Mia woke up on Wednesday morning with a sense of dread in her stomach.

Today she had to tell her parents that she wasn't coming to see them on Saturday. She still hadn't come up with a good reason to explain the delay, especially since she was supposed to start her internship at the camp on Monday.

And if Korum discovered her involvement in what was about to befall the K colonies, then it might be the last time she was speaking to her family in general. That made it even more imperative that she present an upbeat and positive image today, so as not to make her parents worry prematurely. It would be better if she left only good memories behind when she disappeared from their lives.

At that thought, stupid tears threatened again, and Mia took a deep breath to control herself. She didn't have time for this right now; she still had to write the last paper. Although it made no sense to care about something so trivial in her precarious situation, not writing the paper would be like giving up—and some small part of Mia was still hopeful that there might be light at the end of this tunnel, that some semblance of a normal life was still possible if she made it through the next couple of weeks unscathed.

Clinging to that thought, Mia dragged herself out of bed and into the shower. Korum was nowhere to be found in the apartment, and she guessed he was off doing whatever he normally did during the day. It probably had something to do with tracking the Resistance fighters, but she had no way of knowing that for sure. Grabbing a quick breakfast, she headed to the library in the hopes that she might be better able to concentrate there.

The day was beautiful and sunny—a perfect foil for her gloomy mood. Under normal circumstances, Mia would have taken a nice lengthy walk to the library, but time was of essence and she took a cab instead. Staying at Korum's place and eating nearly all her meals with him, Mia was flush with cash for the first time in her college career. The student grants that helped pay for tuition and books also provided a minimal allowance for food and other living expenses, but it was usually just enough for her to survive on. Eating out in restaurants or taking cabs were indulgences that Mia could not normally afford, and it was nice to be able to splurge now that she didn't worry so much about the cost of food.

The library was a zoo. Just about every NYU student was there, frantically cramming for exams and writing papers. Of course, Mia realized, it was finals week. She should've just stayed in the comfortable study room Korum had set up for her, but she'd wanted to be some place where nothing reminded her of the mess that her life had become.

After wandering around for a good fifteen minutes, she finally located a soft chair that had just been vacated by a pimply red-headed boy who looked like he was all of twelve years old. Quickly occupying it before anyone else saw her prize, Mia smiled to herself. Not that she was all that old, but some of the freshmen looked ridiculously young to her these days.

Five hours later, Mia triumphantly finished the last sentence and saved her work. She still had to proofread the damn thing, but the bulk of the job was done. Gathering her things, she left the library and went to her own apartment, hoping to see Jessie and have a chance to talk to her parents.

Jessie wasn't home when she got there, so that left only the parents. Taking a deep breath, Mia turned on her computer and prepared to be as bright and bubbly as any college student who was almost done with finals week.

"Mia! Sweetheart, how are you?" Her mom was in fine form today, her blue eyes sparkling with excitement and a huge smile on her face.

Mia grinned back at her. "I'm almost done! Just have to proofread the last paper, and then the school year is officially over for me," said Mia, keeping her voice purposefully upbeat.

"Oh, that's great!" her mom exclaimed. "We can't wait to see you this weekend! Marisa and Connor are coming over on Sunday, and we'll have a big dinner. I'll make all your favorites. I already bought some eggs and even a bit of goat cheese—"

"Mom," interrupted Mia, feeling like she was dying a little inside, "there's something I need to tell you . . ."

Her mom paused for a second, looking puzzled. "What is it, honey?"

Mia took a deep breath. This was not going to be easy. "One of my professors asked me for a big favor this week," she said slowly, having come up with a semi-plausible story in the last few minutes. "There's a program here at NYU where psychology students go and spend some time with disadvantaged high school kids from some of the worst neighborhoods . . ."

"Uh-huh," said her mom, a small frown appearing on her face.

"It's a great program," lied Mia. "These kids don't really have anyone to help them figure out the next steps, whether they should go to college or not, how they should apply if they decide to go . . . And you know, that's exactly what I want to do—provide that type of counseling . . ."

Her mom's frown got a little deeper.

Mia hurried with her explanation. "Well, I didn't know about this program before, but I was chatting with my professor this week and mentioned my interest in counseling to him. And that's when he told me about this program, and that he was actually desperately looking for a volunteer to help out for a week or two this summer—"

"But you're flying home on Saturday," her mom said, looking increasingly unhappy. "When would you be able to do this?"

"Well, that's the thing," said Mia, hating herself for lying like this, "I don't think I can come home this weekend, not if I do this program—"

"What! What do you mean, you can't come home this weekend?" Her mom appeared livid now. "You already have a ticket and everything! And what about your camp internship? Aren't you supposed to start that on Monday?"

"I already spoke with the camp director," lied Mia again. "He's fine with pushing back my start date by two weeks. I explained the whole situation, and he was very understanding. And my professor said he'll reimburse me for the cost of the ticket and even buy me another one to make up for this—"

"Well, that's the least he could do! What about the money you were going to earn during those two weeks of your internship?" her mom said angrily. "And what about the fact that we haven't seen you since March? How could he ask you to do something like that, so last-minute?"

"Mom," said Mia in a pleading tone, "it's a great opportunity for me. This is exactly what I want to do career-wise, and it'll really boost my chances of getting into a good grad school. Plus, the professor said he'll write me a glowing recommendation if I do this—and you know how important those are for grad school applications . . ."

Her mom was blinking rapidly, and there was a suspicious glimmer in her eyes. "Of course," she said, a wealth of disappointment in her voice, "I know that stuff is important . . . We were just so looking forward to seeing you this Saturday, and now this—"

Every word her mom said was like a knife scraping at Mia's insides. "I know, mom, I'm really sorry about this," she said, blinking to hold back her own tears. "I'll see you in a couple of weeks, okay? It won't be so bad, you'll see . . ."

Her mom sniffed a little. "So no family dinner this Sunday, I guess."

Mia shook her head with regret. "No . . . but we'll have one in two weeks, okay? I'll cook and everything—"

"Oh, please, Mia, you couldn't cook to save your life!" her mom said irately, but a tiny smile appeared on her face. "I've never met anyone who couldn't manage to boil water— "

"I can boil water now," said Mia defensively. "I've

been living on my own for the last three years, you know, and I can even make rice—"

The tiny smile became a full-blown grin. "Wow, rice? That *is* progress," her mom said with barely contained laughter. "I honestly don't know what you're going to do when you meet someone . . ."

"Oh, mom, not this again," groaned Mia.

"It's true, you know. Men still like it when a woman can make a good meal, and keep the house—"

"And do laundry, and be a general domestic slave, and yadda yadda yadda," finished Mia, rolling her eyes. Her mom could be amazingly old-fashioned sometimes.

"Exactly. Mark my words, unless you find some guy who likes to cook, you'll be stuck eating takeout for the rest of your life," her mom said ominously.

Mia shrugged, biting the inside of her cheek to avoid bursting into semi-hysterical laughter. The irony of it was that she had actually found such a guy—except he wasn't human. She wondered what her mom would say if she told her about Korum. *He's great: he loves to cook and even does laundry for us both. Just one tiny issue—he's a blood-drinking alien.* No, that probably wouldn't go over well at all.

"Mom, don't worry about me, okay? Everything will be fine." At least Mia sincerely hoped that was the case. "We'll see each other soon, and maybe I'll really try to learn how to cook this summer. How about that?" Mia gave her mom a big smile, trying to prevent any more lectures.

Her mom shook her head in reproach and sighed. "Sure. I'll tell your dad what happened. He'll be so disappointed . . ."

Mia felt terrible again. "Where is he?" she asked, wanting to speak to her father as well.

"He's out getting the car fixed. The damn thing broke again. We should really get a new one . . . but maybe next year."

Mia nodded sympathetically. She knew her parents' financial situation was not the best these days. Her mom was currently between jobs. As an elementary school teacher, she was usually in demand. However, the private school where she had taught for the past eight years had closed recently, resulting in a number of teachers losing their positions and all applying for the same few openings in the local public schools. Her dad—a political science professor at the local community college—was now supporting the family on his one salary, and they had to be careful with bigger expenses, such as a new car. In general, her family, like many other middle-class Americans with 401(k) retirement plans, had suffered in the K Crash—the huge stock market crash that took place when the Krinar had arrived. At one point, the Dow had lost almost ninety percent of its value, and it was only about a year ago that the markets had recovered fully.

"All right," said Mia, "I'll try to log back in later, see if I can reach dad."

"Call Marisa too," her mom said. "I know she was really looking forward to seeing you on Sunday."

Mia nodded. "I will, definitely."

Her mom sighed again. "Well, I guess we'll talk to you soon then."

"I love you, mom," said Mia, feeling like her chest was getting squeezed in a vise. "I hope you know that. You and dad are the best parents ever."

"Of course," her mom said, looking a bit puzzled. "We love you too. Come home soon, okay?"

"I will," said Mia, blowing an air kiss toward the computer screen, and ended the conversation.

Her sister was next. For once, she was actually reachable on Skype.

"Hey there, baby sis! What's this text I just got from mom about you not coming home?"

Mia hadn't seen her sister since she got pregnant, and she was surprised to see Marisa looking pale and thin, instead of having that pregnancy glow she'd always heard about.

"Marisa!" she exclaimed. "What's going on with you? You don't look well. Are you sick?"

Her sister made a face. "If you can call having a baby sickness, then yes. I'm throwing up constantly," she complained. "I just can't keep anything down. I've actually lost five pounds since I got pregnant—"

Mia gasped in shock. Five pounds was a lot for someone her sister's size. While a little taller and curvier than Mia, Marisa was also small-boned, with her normal weight hovering somewhere around 110-115 pounds. Now she looked too thin, her cheekbones overly prominent in her usually pretty face.

"—and my doctor is not happy about that."

"Of course, he's not happy! Did he say what you should do?"

Marisa sighed. "He said to get more rest and try not to stress. So I am working from home today, preparing my lessons for next week, and they got someone to substitute for me for a few days."

"Oh my God, you poor thing," said Mia sympathetically. "That sucks. Can you eat anything, like maybe crackers or some broth?"

"That's what I'm subsisting on these days. Well, that and pickles." Marisa gave her a wan smile. "For some reason, I can't stop eating those Israeli pickles—you know, the little crunchy ones?"

Mia nodded, stifling a grin. Her sister had always been a pickles fan, so it really wasn't surprising she was going pickle-crazy during her pregnancy.

"So anyway, enough about my stomach issues . . . What's going on with you? Why aren't you coming this Saturday? We were all ready and excited to come over, see you and the parents—"

Mia took a deep breath and repeated the whole story to Marisa. She was getting so good at lying that she could almost believe herself. Maybe she should think about starting such a program at NYU next year—if she was still alive and attending school at that time, of course.

Her sister listened to everything with a vaguely disbelieving expression. And then, being Marisa, she asked, "Is the professor cute?"

To her horror, Mia felt her cheeks turning pink. "What? No! He's old and has kids and stuff!"

"Uh-huh," said Marisa. "So I'm supposed to believe you would be willing to do something like this at the request of an ugly professor? Just to pad your resume a little?" She shook her head slightly. "Nope, I just don't see it." A sly smile appearing on her face, she asked, "Just how old is old?"

Mia cursed her poor acting skills. Now Marisa would probably go blabbing to their parents that Mia had a crush on her professor. She tried to imagine liking Professor Dunkin that way and shuddered. Between his receding hairline and the yellowish spittle that frequently appeared in the corners of his mouth when he spoke, he was probably one of the least attractive individuals she'd ever met.

"Old," Mia said firmly. "And unattractive."

Marisa grinned, undeterred. "Okay, then, who is he?" she persisted. "I know you, baby sis . . . and you're hiding something. If it's not the old and unattractive professor you're staying in New York for, then who is it?"

"No one," said Mia. "There's no man in my life . . . you know that." And she wasn't lying. There wasn't a human man—just an extraterrestrial of the male variety. Who was also old—a lot older than her sister could imagine.

"Oh, please, then why are you acting so weird? You've been kinda strange for the past month, in fact," said Marisa, looking at her intently. "Mia . . . is something wrong?"

Mia shook her head in denial and silently cursed Marisa's sisterly intuition. It had been so much easier to fool her mom. "No, everything's fine. It's just been stressful, you know, with finals and all . . ."

"Uh-huh," said Marisa, "you've had finals for the past three years, and it's never been like this. I can see you're not yourself, Mia. Now fess up . . . what's happening?"

Mia shook her head again, and tried putting on a bright smile. "Nothing! I don't know what you're talking about—there's absolutely nothing wrong. I just got a great opportunity to get some valuable work experience, and I am taking advantage of it. I'll see you soon, just in a couple of weeks. There's nothing to worry about—"

"Have you already bought tickets?" interrupted Marisa. "Do you have a set date when you're flying in?"

"Not yet," Mia admitted. "I'll do that soon. The professor said he'll buy me a new plane ticket, so there's nothing to worry about about—"

"Nothing to worry about? Mia, I know when you're lying," said Marisa, giving her a strict look. "You're terrible at it. You've been such a good girl your whole life, you've had absolutely no practice deceiving your parents—or me. You've never even snuck out to a party in high school . . ."

Mia bit her lip. How did Marisa get to be so observant? This was a big problem. Maybe if she told her a partial truth . . .

"Okay," said Mia, choosing her words carefully. "Let's say that there's something to what you're saying . . . If I tell you, do you promise not to tell the parents? They'll worry, and it's really not necessary—"

Marisa looked at her, her blue eyes narrowed in consideration. "Okay," she said slowly, "you can always talk to me, baby sis, you know that. I'll keep your secret . . . but only if it's nothing life-threatening that parents must know about."

It actually *was* something life-threatening, but parents definitely didn't need to know about that. Mia sighed. Since she started going down this path, she might as well tell her sister something, or else her entire family will be calling in panic within a half-hour.

Taking a deep breath, Mia said, "You're right. I did meet someone—"

"I knew it!" yelled Marisa triumphantly.

"—and he's not exactly someone you'd be happy to see me with."

Marisa stared at her in surprise. "Why? Who is he? Another student?"

Mia shook her head. "No, that's the problem. He's older, and he's not exactly first-boyfriend material."

"Are we talking about the professor now?" asked Marisa in confusion.

"No, the professor is just the professor. It's someone else. He's actually a senior executive in a tech company," fibbed Mia, trying to stick as close as possible to the truth.

"I met him in the park one day, and we've been sleeping together—"

"What?" Her sister was gaping at her in disbelief. "Is he married? Does he have any children?"

"No, and no. But I know it's just a temporary fling for him, so I really didn't want to go into any details with you and the parents . . ."

As Mia was speaking, a big smile slowly appeared on Marisa's face. "A fling? Wow. When my baby sis decides to finally lose her virginity, she does it with style! A senior executive no less . . ."

Mia shrugged, trying to be nonchalant about the whole thing.

"What's his name?"

"Uh, I'd rather not say," mumbled Mia. "He'll be leaving in a couple of weeks, and there's no point in discussing the whole thing—"

"Leaving to go where?"

"Um . . . Dubai." Mia had no idea why she'd chosen that particular location, but it seemed to fit the story.

"Dubai? Is he from there originally?" Her sister's curiosity knew no bounds.

Mia sighed. "Marisa, listen, there's really no point in discussing it. He'll leave, and that's that."

Her sister cocked her head to the side, studying Mia's face. "And you're okay with that, baby sis?" she asked quietly. "Your first lover leaving just like that?"

Mia looked away, trying to hide the moisture in her eyes. "He has to leave, Marisa. There's no choice. It doesn't matter if I'm okay with it or not."

"Of course, it matters," said Marisa. "Do you think he cares for you at all? Or are you just a pretty college girl he's sleeping with while in New York?"

Mia shrugged. "I don't know. I think he might care

about me a little."

"But not enough to stay?"

"No, he can't stay," said Mia. "And it doesn't matter. We're not right for each other, anyway. The relationship was doomed from the start."

"Why did you start it then?" asked Marisa, eyeing her with bewilderment. "Is he really good-looking? Did he sweep you off your feet or something?"

Mia nodded. "He's gorgeous, and he's smart, and he knows a lot about everything..." Those were all true statements. "And he took me out to all kinds of fancy restaurants and Broadway shows—"

"Wow, Mia," said Marisa, looking envious for the first time in Mia's memory, "that sounds like a dream guy."

Mia smiled. "And he's also a great cook, and does laundry—"

"Oh my God, where did you find this paragon?"

"I know, right? Mom would have a cow if she heard about this."

And the sisters grinned at each other in perfect understanding.

Then Marisa got serious again. "So why can't it work out for the two of you? He sounds perfect. Does he have some major character flaw that you can't stand?"

"Well, he's very bossy and autocratic," admitted Mia, "so I definitely have a problem with that. And where he comes from, they don't necessarily view, um, women... as equals, if you know what I mean?" That was as close to the truth as she could get.

Marisa's eyes widened in understanding. "Ohhh, is he one of those Middle Eastern types? With a harem and all... who require their women to be veiled from head to toe?"

Mia shrugged. "Something like that. So it could never

really go anywhere. We come from very different worlds."
Mia meant that in the literal sense, but Marisa didn't need
to know that.

"Wow, baby sis." Marisa was looking at her with
newfound respect. "I have to say, you've surprised me.
No boring college boys for you . . . oh, no—you've gone
straight for the big leagues. A sheikh from Dubai, huh?"

Mia flushed. "He's not a sheikh, just an executive."

"Wow." Her sister was still looking impressed. "So did
he give you any fancy gifts or jewelry?"

Mia smiled. Her sister was so predictable sometimes.
Even though she lived a simple life for the most part,
Marisa definitely appreciated the finer things in life—nice
hotels, designer clothes, beautiful accessories.

"He bought me a whole new wardrobe from Saks Fifth
Avenue," admitted Mia. "He really didn't like my old
clothes—"

"OH MY GOD, FROM SAKS?" Marisa's shriek was
ear-piercing. "Are you serious? You've gotta let me
borrow something when you come!"

Mia laughed. "Of course! Whatever you want, it's
yours."

"Oh crap, never mind," said Marisa, "I just realized
that soon I won't be able to borrow anything from
anyone—especially from my tiny baby sister. In a couple
of months, I'll be a total cow."

"Oh please," said Mia, laughing at the image of her
svelte sister looking even remotely cow-like, "you'll look
like one of those actresses in Hollywood—all normal, just
with a cute little baby bump."

Marisa shuddered. "I certainly hope so. But I have to
say, so far, pregnancy is nothing like what I'd imagined."

Mia looked at her sympathetically. "That sucks. Hang
in there, okay? It's just a few more months, and then

you'll have a beautiful child . . ."

Marisa beamed at her. "That's true. And you too, baby sis, hang in there, okay? Call me if you ever want to talk about Mr. Gorgeous again. And I promise I won't say anything to the parents. You're right—they would worry unnecessarily. This type of stuff is best left for talks with your sister."

Mia smiled and said, "That's what I thought. I love you. Say hello to Connor for me, okay?"

"Will do," said Marisa, and disconnected with one final wave.

Relieved, Mia stared at the blank computer screen. She had lied to her family, but at least she'd managed to prevent them from freaking out completely. In a way, the conversation with Marisa had been therapeutic. Although she couldn't tell her sister the whole truth, she'd been able to share enough details to make herself feel much better about the situation. Marisa's nonjudgmental, sympathetic ear had been exactly what she'd needed at this point.

Now she had to finish editing the paper—and then she will have completed everything she'd set out to do for the day.

CHAPTER TWENTY-TWO

Now that she was done with studying, Mia had no idea what to do with herself. Waking up on Thursday morning, she submitted her papers online and decided to go for a walk in Central Park. Korum again left early in the morning, before she had woken up, so she was on her own for the day. She texted Jessie, but her roommate had her Calculus exam in the afternoon and was frantically cramming. Mia wished there was someone else she could hang out with, just to avoid being alone with her thoughts, but most other students were too busy packing for the summer or still in the middle of finals.

The middle of May was usually a 'hit-or-miss' weather in New York. This year, it seemed like summer had started early, and the temperature that day was a balmy seventy-five degrees. Mia gladly put on one of her new spring dresses, a simple blue cotton sheath, and a pair of cream-colored sandals that managed to be both comfortable and stylish. And then she headed out to join the hordes of New Yorkers and tourists that came out to enjoy Central Park.

It was hard to believe that only a month ago Mia had

been walking here by herself, with no real knowledge of the Ks, thinking about nothing more than her Sociology paper. She hadn't met Korum yet, and had no idea what a drastic turn her life would take in the next few minutes. What would have happened if she hadn't sat down on that bench that day? Would she even now be packing to go home on Saturday?

As though her feet had a mind of their own, Mia found herself heading toward Bow Bridge, the place of her first close encounter. Unlike the last time, the little bridge was teeming with people today, all seeking to take photos of the picturesque view. Mia found herself a spot on a bench next to a young couple and settled in to read the latest bestselling thriller—something she only had time to do when school wasn't in session.

After a half hour, the couple left, and Mia got the entire bench to herself. Before she could enjoy it for long, however, she heard her name being called. Startled, she looked up and saw a young woman, dressed in a pair of ripped jeans and a white sleeveless shirt, approaching the bench. Her short sandy hair was tousled, like a boy's, and her arms were sleekly muscled. It was Leslie, the girl she'd met that one time with John—one of the Resistance fighters.

"Hey Mia," she said, "do you mind if I join you for a minute?" Without waiting for a response, she sat down on Mia's bench.

"Sure, be my guest," said Mia, somewhat rudely. Leslie was not her favorite person, and she really didn't feel like being tasked with something else right now. As far as Mia was concerned, she had carried out her mission, and all she wanted was to be left alone.

"Look," said Leslie, her tone far friendlier than before, "I know we got off on the wrong foot. I just wanted to say thanks for what you did, and to give you something from John." She held out a small oval object that looked vaguely like a garage opener or an automatic car key.

"What is it?" asked Mia warily, not taking it from her.

"It's a weapon," said Leslie, "a weapon that you can use to protect yourself in case Korum figures out what happened before we have a chance to neutralize him."

"Neutralize him?"

Leslie sighed. "As per your request, we'll try to capture him alive, so he can be deported back to Krina. It's not going to be easy, but we'll do our best."

Mia swallowed. "What . . . um, when are you going to do it?"

"We can't do it before the shields are down, and the attack on the K Centers is underway. He might be able to warn them, or get reinforcements, if we try to take him now, so we can't risk it. It'll have to be almost simultaneous. He's not the only one. There are other Ks who are outside their Centers right now. As soon as they learn of the attack on their colonies—and they'll learn it almost immediately—they will join in the fight. But they're not in some remote areas—they are in our cities, near our government centers. If they realize that we've broken the treaty, they will attack us—and many civilian lives will be lost before we would be able to stop them. So we need to plan everything very carefully, or else it's going to turn into a bloodbath."

This was bad, thought Mia. Really bad. She hadn't thought of that aspect—other Ks who, like Korum, were living among humans for whatever reason. Strong, fast, and armed with K technology, even one individual could inflict a tremendous amount of damage on the human population. She tried to imagine Korum fighting to protect his kind, and shuddered at the thought. Just that one brief glimpse of his rage in the club had been frightening. She had no doubt that he could be truly brutal if the occasion called for it.

Turning her attention back to the little object, Mia asked, "So what is this weapon supposed to do?"

"It dissolves molecular bonds, breaking down everything in its path," said Leslie. "Essentially, it'll turn whatever you want into dust. It's a simple miniature version of the big weapon we intend to use to make the Ks surrender."

Aghast, Mia stared at the small, harmless-looking device in Leslie's palm. "So it could turn a person to dust?"

Leslie nodded. "It'll work on whatever is in its path. The nanomachines it releases work for a period of only about thirty seconds before they become inactive, but that time is usually enough to completely dissolve a person. You don't even need to worry about shooting him in the chest or whatever—if the nanos get on any part of his body, he's toast."

Mia nearly gagged at the thought. "What? No! I could never do something like this!" she exclaimed in horror. "I can't use it on him—"

"You can, and you will," said Leslie, "if your life is at stake. I have no idea if he'll make the connection between what's happening in the K Centers and you—but he's supposed to be some kind of a genius, so I wouldn't be surprised if he did." Running her hand through her short hair in a frustrated motion, Leslie added, "And it's best if you do it quickly, before he has a chance to react. Just point and shoot, no thinking . . . do you understand me? They're fast, Mia, really fast."

Mia shook her head. "I won't do it. I can't—"

Leslie shrugged. "That's your call. If you'd rather die,

then so be it—it's none of my business. John asked me to give it to you, and here it is. You can take it and not use it, if that's what you want. But at least you won't be completely helpless when all this shit goes down." She put the device on Mia's lap. "If you want to use it, just feel for the little indentation on the side—if you press firmly there, it's going to go off. Just be sure to point the rounded end toward him—"

Mia shook her head again. "I won't use it," she said with firm conviction.

Leslie looked at her with something resembling pity. "You idiot," she said softly, "you've fallen for the monster, haven't you?"

Mia looked away. "That's none of your business," she said quietly, examining her fingernails. "I did what needed to be done. He'll leave, and that's all there is to it."

"You stupid girl," said Leslie in a contemptuous tone, "you're nothing to him—less than nothing. He'll crush you like a bug if you're anywhere in the vicinity when we attack. Just because he likes to fuck you doesn't mean he'll have mercy on you if he learns what you've done. He's slept with hundreds of women just like you— thousands, probably—and you're nothing special—"

"You don't know anything!" interrupted Mia, feeling each word like a stab in the heart. "You've never even met him—"

Leslie's eyes narrowed. "I don't need to meet him to know exactly what he's like—what all of them are like, Mia. They have no regard for us, for human life. We're just an experiment to them, something they've created. As far as they're concerned, we're their creatures—theirs to do with as they please. And if it pleases them, they will get rid of us and take over our planet for their own use.

And you're a fool if you think he's somehow different. He's as bad as they come—he's the one who led them here..."

Leslie was right. Mia knew all of that with the rational part of her mind, but her stupid heart refused to get with the program. The knowledge that he would be gone from her life in a few short days was strangely painful, and the thought that he might be harmed in the process made her stomach twist with fear. And yet Leslie was right—he probably would not hesitate to kill her if she learned that her actions had threatened the Ks' agenda here on Earth.

She didn't want to die, but she didn't think she could kill him, not even in self-defense.

Taking a deep breath, Mia asked, "When is it happening? How long until the attack takes place?"

Leslie hesitated, apparently wondering if Mia was still trustworthy.

"Leslie," Mia said wearily, "I know what would happen if he found out I was helping you. I won't warn him. I can't, not without losing my life in the process. I have no regrets about what I've done. Just because I can't kill someone I've been intimate with for the past month doesn't mean I would betray our cause. I just want to know how much longer I have—"

"Until tomorrow," said Leslie. "You have until tomorrow. My advice is to disappear in the morning—get away as far as you can. Don't pack, don't do anything to raise his suspicions. Just leave. One way or another, everything will be over by this weekend."

* * *

That evening, Korum came home late, closer to nine o'clock.

Mia found herself pacing back and forth in the living room starting at five o'clock, unable to sit still or relax in anticipation of what was to come. If Leslie had told her the truth, this would be her last night together with Korum . . . and maybe the last night she was alive. To maximize her chances of survival, she decided to follow Leslie's advice about leaving first thing in the morning. Korum would likely be gone from the apartment by then, and she would have a chance to escape—maybe taking the subway to one of the boroughs. The dissolver, as she'd decided to call it, was sitting in her purse, safe and sound. She had no intention of using it on Korum, but it was still good to know that she had something she could defend herself with, in case all hell did break loose on Friday.

Just to keep herself busy, she went through her closet and tried on a few of her new dresses. Her wardrobe was so large now that many of her clothes still had tags on them, and she had no idea what she owned. Everything fit her perfectly, of course; the shoppers from Saks had done their job. After an hour of trying on one outfit after another, Mia settled on a simple grey sleeveless dress, made of some cotton-silk blend, that hugged her upper body and flared gently from the waist down to her knees. Despite the conservative color and cut, it looked stylish and sexy—as did most of what Mia wore now. To go with the dress, Mia decided to apply some makeup, putting on one coat of mascara and a light dusting of powder. She had no idea why it was suddenly so important to look good tonight, since she didn't normally obsess over such things, but she wanted to appear particularly attractive to Korum this evening. Finishing the outfit with a pair of strappy black heels, Mia resumed her impatient pacing.

He had given her a phone number where he could be reached in case she needed him, but Mia had never used it before. As eight o'clock rolled by, however, she seriously contemplated calling him to find out his whereabouts. But that would be so far out of character for her that he might wonder—and she didn't want to chance his getting suspicious.

Finally, the door opened at a quarter to nine. He came in, dressed in a simple pair of blue jeans and a black T-shirt. It didn't matter what he wore, of course; he would have looked stunning in rags. At the sight of her standing there, a wide dimpled smile appeared on his beautiful face, lighting his features and making those amber eyes crinkle at the corners. And then a familiar golden glow lit his gaze.

Before she had a chance to say anything, he was next to her, lifting her up effortlessly for a deep, thorough kiss. His tongue stabbed into her mouth, and Mia wound her arms around him and kissed him back, passionately and a little desperately. Her legs found their way around his hips, and they stayed like that, locked in each others' arms, until Mia was gasping for breath and writhing against him, her breasts rubbing against his chest and her sex grinding on his pelvis. He groaned low in his throat, and she could feel his erection grow even bigger, pressing into her nether regions through the material that separated them. Holding her up with one arm, he found the lacy scrap of material that covered her pussy and tore it off, his fingers petting and exploring her moist folds. Mia moaned, driven nearly mindless with desire, and heard the sound of a zipper sliding down. And then he was inside her, his cock thrusting up into her even as he still held her like that, lifted up against him while he was standing in the middle of the living room.

Shocked at the suddenness of his penetration, Mia cried out, her inner tissues struggling to accommodate the intrusion, and he paused for a second, letting her get used to the feel of him in the unfamiliar position. And then he started moving, raising her up and down with one hand while his other hand buried itself in her hair, bringing her mouth back toward him. There was no slow and gentle build-up this time, as everything inside Mia tensed simultaneously, and then she was hurling into the climax, her muscles clamping down on his shaft, and he was coming too, so deeply inside her that she felt his contractions in her belly.

Panting, Mia collapsed against him, unable to believe that this happened just now, in the span of all of two minutes. His breathing was heavy as well, and she could feel his powerful chest moving up and down as she hung in his grasp, his cock still inside her. Once the pulsations of his orgasm ended, he lifted her up and placed her carefully on the ground, his hands still wrapped around her waist. Mia's legs were shaking, and she clung to him, grateful for the support.

Staring up at him, Mia noticed that his eyes were returning back to their regular amber color. His lips curling into a small, wry smile, he said huskily, "I guess I have to apologize again—clearly I don't have any control where you're concerned. I really didn't mean to jump you like that first thing. You're probably hungry too . . ."

Mia actually was, but it didn't matter. Blushing a little at the feel of his semen sliding down her leg, she mumbled quietly, "No, no need for apologies . . . you know that I really enjoyed it too . . ."

His smile now held purely masculine satisfaction. "I'm glad," he murmured. "Now how about some dinner?"

Mia nodded in agreement, and blushed even more when he disappeared for a second and came back with a paper towel that he handed to her. Embarrassed, Mia looked away as she cleaned off the remnants of their passion.

He laughed softly. "You're still such a prude," he teased gently. "We'll have to cure you of that at some point. It's all natural, you know."

Mia shrugged, purposefully not meeting his eyes. For some reason, she still had these occasional bouts of shyness around him, despite all the hot and raunchy sex they've had in the past month.

Korum laughed some more, and then asked, "Since you're dressed so nicely, how do you feel about going out for some French cuisine?"

Mia felt great about that, and she told him so.

"Okay, then, let me take a quick rinse and change, and we'll go," he said, stripping off the T-shirt on the way to the bathroom. The sight of his lean, muscled back made her insides clench with desire again. Why him, she wondered again in desperation, why did he have to be the one to make her feel this way? And how would she be able to bear it when he was gone for good?

The dinner was at a little French place Mia had never heard of. Nonetheless, the meal was outstanding, from the ratatouille Mia had gotten for her main course to the super-light pastry they ended up sharing for dessert.

"So are you now officially done with school for this year?" Korum asked, taking a sip of his red wine. He seemed to like wine and champagne, Mia had noticed, although she had never seen it have any effect on him. Then again, she'd never seen him have more than a couple of glasses.

"That's it," she replied, spearing a piece of zucchini with her fork. "The school year is officially over for me. I turned in all the papers today, and now I can be a total bum."

He grinned. "Somehow I can't quite envision you bumming around all day. Ever since I've known you, you've been busy studying or doing something for school." Reaching for her, he lightly stroked her cheek, his expression becoming more serious. "It'll be nice to have you relax a little. You've been working way too hard in these past couple of weeks. I don't think all that stress is good for your health."

Mia gave him a surprised look. "I'm fine," she protested. "I feel great—it's really not a problem at all."

Korum regarded her intently, a concerned expression on his face. "I don't know," he said, shaking his head. "Your immune system is so delicate, so fragile—it's really not good for you to overload yourself like that."

Mia shrugged, wondering what got him started on that topic. "My immune system is fine," she said. "It's as strong as that of any other human. You really don't need to worry about me—I don't get sick often or anything like that."

"As strong as any human is not all that strong," he said, a slight furrow between his dark brows. He looked at her speculatively, and Mia had no idea what he was thinking. Whatever it was, he apparently came to some conclusion, because his forehead smoothed out. Changing the topic, he asked about her day, and the conversation again flowed casually and easily.

As the dinner went on, Mia couldn't help but stare at him, drinking in the sight of his face, the animated gestures he used when he spoke about something he found exciting, the way his tall, muscular body moved in his chair—even the smallest of motions endowed with that athletic, inhuman grace. Her flesh craved him sexually, but it now went beyond that. Every cell in her body yearned to be with him, and the thought of tomorrow filled her with a cold, sick horror. She couldn't tell him, couldn't warn him of what was to come, but she could try to remember every moment of this evening, to commit to her memory the curve of his mouth, the bold slashes of his eyebrows, the way his laugh sounded when she said something amusing.

An agonizing realization tore through her then: she loved him. Despite everything she knew about him, despite everything he'd done to her, despite the fact that he was her enemy and she'd betrayed him—despite all that, she loved him with every fiber of her being.

And tomorrow, she would lose him forever.

CHAPTER TWENTY-THREE

A faint but steady sound of rain woke up Mia the next morning. Still half-asleep, she stretched, reluctant to face the day for some reason—and then her brain connected the dots and she sat up, gasping at the realization of what was to take place this morning.

Jumping out of bed, she forced herself to walk to the restroom and brush her teeth, following her usual morning routine in case Korum was still in the house. Once done, she pulled on a pair of jeans and a comfy long-sleeved shirt and carefully ventured out into the living room to check on the situation.

The living room and the kitchen areas were empty, and Mia almost shuddered with relief. Korum must have followed his usual routine, leaving for the day to do whatever it was that he did. And after the wave of relief came disappointment. Rationally, she knew that she should be glad she would have a chance to get away, that fate was being kind by enabling her to avoid one last— potentially deadly—encounter with her alien lover, but that didn't help the gaping wound in her heart that had opened at the recognition that she would never see him again.

Last night had been incredible, the sex between them as close to lovemaking as Mia had ever experienced. He had treated her like a princess, worshipping her with his body, and Mia had cried again in the aftermath, unable to stem the flood at the knowledge of what tomorrow would bring. He had tried to soothe her, to find out what was causing her distress this time, but Mia had been incoherent. And finally, he had simply taken her again, his body driving into hers in a savage, relentless rhythm until she could not think about anything at all, her worries burning up in the heat of passion—until she screamed in ecstasy as he brought her to peak, over and over again. And then she had simply passed out, too exhausted to remember why she had been crying in the first place.

But she couldn't think about that now. Not if she wanted to get out alive.

Grabbing her purse, Mia laced up her sneakers and prepared to leave Korum's apartment. With one last look at the cream-colored furniture and leafy plants, she walked toward the door, each step feeling heavier than the rest.

She wasn't sure what made her turn back, to go toward his office, leaving her purse sitting on the couch in the living room. Was her subconscious still clinging to the hope that he was here? That she might be able to see him one final time? She didn't think so, but her feet appeared to have a mind of her own, bringing her toward the sliding doors that parted at her approach.

There was no one in the room, but a giant three-dimensional map shimmered before her, looking like nothing she had ever seen before.

Her heart hammering in her chest, Mia stepped into the room, as though drawn in by an invisible string.

This was not New York spread out before her; she would have recognized that at a glance. In fact, it was not like a city at all. Vegetation was everywhere. Lush green plants seemed to dominate the landscape, ranging from the familiar to the exotic. Pale-colored oblong structures could be seen peeking through the trees, looking a bit like strange mushroom caps. If it hadn't been for the structures, Mia would've thought she was looking at a park or a forest in some tropical country. The place was beautiful . . . and alien. Every little hair on her nape stood up as Mia realized exactly what she was looking at.

It had to be a K Center . . . perhaps even their main one in Costa Rica. Lenkarda, Korum had called it once.

Her heart racing, Mia assessed the situation. She needed to leave, and she needed to do so now. Why would Korum be looking at a map of one of the K Centers? Was he suspecting something? And why would he be so careless as to leave it visible like that? Did he suspect her after all? Was this a trap?

At the last thought, Mia felt a cold wave of terror rushing through her veins. She had to leave right now.

Yet she couldn't tear her eyes away from the incredible picture in front of her. How many humans had seen such an amazing sight? The K Centers were closely guarded, with a no-fly zone established over them. Even human satellites could not view them; the Krinar shields had rendered the settlements all but invisible to human electronics. And here was a chance for her to look at an alien colony, to see where Korum had lived.

A terrible curiosity drove Mia now. Ignoring all reason and common sense, she stepped further into the room, slowly circling around the table and studying the tableau laid out in front of her.

The buildings—if that's what they were—were spaced widely apart and blended harmoniously into their surroundings. There were no paved roads or sidewalks as far as Mia could see; instead, each structure stood alone, right in the middle of all the greenery. And there were no windows or doors, Mia realized—at least none visible to her eyes. Each building was light in color; ivory, cream, and soft beige were the most prevalent, although light grey and pale peach shades could also be seen.

Toward the center of the map, there were several larger structures, including one big circular dome. They were purely white in color. Mia surmised that those were probably common gathering areas. There were no sidewalks or roads leading to them either, and no visible entrances or exits.

On the outer edges of the settlement, some smaller circular buildings were spaced evenly apart, surrounding the entire perimeter. They were green and brown and blended into the scenery so well that Mia had to look carefully to discern their presence. It was like camouflage, she realized. If it hadn't been for a slight shimmer that the buildings seemed to emit, she wouldn't have known they were there. Mia wondered if these were some kind of guard posts. The Ks were in hostile territory after all, far outnumbered by the natives; it only made sense that the security in their colonies would be strong.

Beyond the green-brown buildings lay more greenery, the plant life dominating everything in sight. And to the west, Mia saw a large body of water—perhaps an ocean of some kind. If this was Costa Rica, then it was likely the Pacific; although the country had two coasts, the Guanacaste region that Korum had mentioned was located on the Pacific side.

As Mia stared in wonder at the three-dimensional images, she noticed a familiar glow surrounding one of the areas near the ocean. Peering closer at it, she saw a small wooden structure that looked human in origin— like a hut of sorts. Hardly daring to breathe, Mia extended her hand toward it, and then jerked back, remembering what had happened the last time she entered this virtual reality world without a way to get back. Casting a desperate glance around the room, she saw Korum's sweater hanging on the back of one of the chairs. Ah-hah!

Quickly putting on the sweater, Mia touched the glowing image with her hand, bracing for the reality shift she'd experienced before.

And then she was there, standing on the beach, breathing in the salt-scented breeze, feeling the warm sun on her face, and hearing the roar of the ocean. A dragonfly whizzed by, followed by a bee. She could see a little crab-like creature scuttling across the sand a few feet away from her. It all seemed so real, yet she knew she was probably in a recording of some kind.

Squinting against the brightness, Mia stared at her surroundings. There was a little path leading from the beach toward the hut-like building she saw nestled among the trees. Feeling a bit like Alice in Wonderland, she headed toward it, unbearably curious to see what was inside.

The hut looked old and decrepit, even more so on closer inspection. It had to be human-made; judging by the condition of the wood, it definitely predated the Ks' arrival. It also had a door, which meant that Mia could go inside and explore. Holding her breath in anticipation, she pushed open the door, wincing at the squeaky sound of the rusted hinges.

The interior of the hut was immaculately clean, free of cobwebs and other unpleasant things one might expect to find in an abandoned building. The furniture was old and plain, but still serviceable, with a small table and a few chairs arranged around it. There was also a pallet on the floor, apparently for sleeping. And the place was completely empty. Disappointed, Mia looked around. Why did Korum have this recording? Clearly, nothing was happening.

And then the door opened, and a male K came in. He looked very typical of their kind, tall and good-looking, with black hair and darkly bronzed skin. He wore a pair of grey shorts made of some unusual material, a loosely fitting sleeveless top, and some type of thin sandals on his feet. Hardly daring to breathe, Mia stared at him, but he was obviously unaware of her presence. He did seem nervous, however. Casting a brief, furtive look around, he walked toward the table. Just in case, Mia scooted out of his way, climbing onto the pallet, uncertain what would happen if she physically touched someone in this strange virtual world.

The K moved the table to the side and squatted, looking at something on the floor. Then he pressed on one of the floorboards, and it seemed to give under his fingers. Loosening it further, he pulled on something, and the entire section of the floor opened up. Without any hesitation, he jumped down, and the opening slowly began to close behind him.

Mia's heart raced as she observed his actions. Here was her chance, but did she dare follow him? How far down was his destination, and what would happen if she jumped after him? Would she be hurt, injured? This wasn't real; she was just watching a very realistic movie. But certain sensations were still there—heat, smell, touch.

Yet falling down on the sidewalk the last time hadn't hurt at all. And the opening in the floor was closing more with each second. To hell with it, Mia decided. She was already risking her life by being here—what's a potential injury in a virtual world?

Taking one deep breath, she jumped.

At first, there was only darkness and the stomach-churning sensation of falling, and then the hard floor was beneath her feet, and Mia landed on it easily, like a cat. Gasping for air, hardly daring to believe that she had made it, Mia felt her legs and knees with her hands. Everything seemed to be fine, and Mia's breathing began to return to normal. She had survived the jump in one piece, and now she just needed to figure out where she was.

The room where she had landed was small and nondescript, but there was a door. The K had to have gone through there. Carefully opening it, Mia peeked inside.

Beyond the door lay a large room, occupied by several Ks, including the one Mia had been following. Her heart skipped a beat. She had never seen so many aliens gathered in one place, and it was a striking sight.

There were five males and two females, all tall and beautiful in their own way. Their clothes were clearly intended for hot weather, with the males wearing shorts and various styles of sleeveless shirts and the females dressed in light, floaty dresses that only covered their breasts and hips, leaving most of their golden skin exposed. Despite their attire, Mia doubted they were there to enjoy the ocean breeze. They looked tense and worried, their gestures sharp and almost violent as they argued about something in the Krinar language. In general, they reminded Mia of a pride of lions, prowling around the room with that animalistic grace peculiar to their species.

Finally, one of them looked at his wrist, where a little device seemed to be attached. Barking out what sounded like a command, he pressed some button and a holographic image appeared in the middle of the room. The rest of the Ks gathered around, and Mia moved closer, trying to see what they were looking at. To her surprise, it was a human man, possibly someone in the military, judging by the uniform he wore.

"We're all safe," said the black-haired K in a perfectly accented American English. "All of us left the Center at various points this morning and last night. Are you ready on your end, General?"

General? Mia felt icy terror spreading through her veins. These had to be the Keiths—and they were working with the human forces that John had mentioned. And since she was observing them this way, their identities were no longer secret. Korum knew exactly who they were and what they were up to. Nearly hyperventilating in panic, Mia stared in horror at the scene that she knew could not possibly end well.

The general nodded. "We're ready. Our people are stationed at the agreed-upon points outside the Centers. The operation will commence upon your signal."

One of the female Ks, a brown-haired hazel-eyed beauty, approached the image. "And the ones outside? Do you have someone ready to take each of them out?"

"We do," said the general slowly, "but there's one small problem. One of them is missing."

The female's eyes narrowed. "What do you mean, missing? Who?"

"Korum. We haven't been able to locate him this morning."

The Ks hissed in anger, breaking into angry speech in

their own language. The female who spoke gesticulated wildly, trying to convince the black-haired male of something, but he merely shook his head, repeating some phrase over and over. Mia desperately wished she understood what they were saying, but all she could catch was the occasional mention of Korum's name.

Apparently deciding on something, the black-haired K turned to the image again. "General, this is a major problem. Why weren't we notified of this earlier?" His voice was harsh with anger.

"We had the situation under control up until thirty minutes ago. Our two best fighters were on him, tracking him as he left his apartment. And then he walked inside a Starbucks and just disappeared. We never saw him come out, and we searched the entire place top to bottom. I was notified of this development a few minutes ago myself."

"You idiots," the female spat at him. "How many times have we told you how dangerous he is? Why would he disappear like that? Did he spot your fighters?"

The general stared at her with an impassive gaze. "Do you want us to call off the operation?"

The Ks looked at each other, discussing it some more in their language. After about a minute, they seemed to reach a conclusion of some kind. "No," the female said in English, shaking her head, "it's too late for that. If something made him suspicious, then the worst thing to do would be to retreat at this point. We'll have to deal with him later, and hope that not too many lives will be lost in the process."

"Do we have your go-ahead to proceed then?"

"You do," said the black-haired male, and the female nodded.

"Very well," said the general. "Operation Liberty will commence at nine hundred hours, Eastern time."

Mia frantically looked around the room, trying to figure out the time now. An old rusted clock hung on one of the walls. It showed 6:55. If that was correct and she was indeed in Costa Rica, then the attack would take place in less than five minutes, since the Central American country was two hours behind New York.

The image of the general disappeared, and another picture took its place. This one was of a forest, with the familiar greenish-brown circular structures in the background. It was the edge of the colony, Mia realized. The Keiths were going to observe the attack from this underground bunker, where they thought they were safe.

Mia felt her hands beginning to shake. Oh dear God, if only she could warn them . . . But it was too late now. When Mia had walked into Korum's office, it was already well after ten in New York. Had an attack taken place, Mia would have heard about it, would have gotten worried texts from Jessie or an urgent alert from some news source on her phone.

No, the Resistance must have failed. All she could do now was watch helplessly as the disaster unfolded right in front of her eyes.

The Keiths paced around the room, occasionally trading brief comments, but keeping silent for the most part. The holograph showed a calm and peaceful border, with only the occasional flying insect providing some entertainment. Time seemed to have slowed, each second passing by more leisurely than the next. Mia found herself biting her nails, something she hadn't done since high school, and watching the Ks as they grew more and more anxious.

The clock hit seven, and all hell broke loose.

Something shimmered at the edge of the forest, and there was a flash of blue light. The Keiths yelled in triumph, and Mia realized that something had gone their way—perhaps a shield had been breached.

And then there was a blinding light, and the circular structure disappeared, dissolving before her eyes. Another flash of light and another structure was gone. Oh God, realized Mia, the attack was real; it was actually happening. They were taking out the guard posts, breaking through the Center's defenses.

Suddenly, the human forces appeared, rushing toward the border. Dressed in army fatigues, they all seemed to be trained soldiers, and there were many of them— dozens, no, hundreds ... They ran toward the border, everything in their path disappearing in those flashes of bright light.

The holographic image shifted then, zooming out, and Mia could see the magnitude of what was taking place.

Thousands of human troops had massed at the border, most of them armed with human weapons. As the guard posts dissolved, that seemed to serve as a signal of some kind, and the attack began in earnest, the massive wave of human soldiers rolling toward the Center and then spreading out to encircle the perimeter.

She could hear the Resistance broadcasting their demand for the Ks' surrender, announcing that they had the nano-weapon ready to be used.

And in the blink of an eye, everything changed.

As the first wave of soldiers approached the border, there was another flash of blue light and the shimmer was back. The Keiths shouted something, and Mia watched in horror as the people in the front were thrown back by some invisible force, their bodies burned to a crisp.

Her mouth opened in a wordless scream of terror, and then it was suddenly over. A huge wave of red light blasted through the battlefield, and the remaining human troops fell to the ground in unison and didn't move again. Thousands of human soldiers were now nothing more than bodies lying limply on the grass. It was as if a bomb had gone off, but instead of blowing them to bits, it had simply killed them with that bright red light.

Mia couldn't breathe, couldn't tear her eyes away from the destruction taking place. Her chest felt like it would explode from the force of her heart hammering against her ribcage, and hot bile rushed into her throat. It was all her fault; if she hadn't done what she'd done, none of this would be happening. There wouldn't be an attack, and all these people would be home with their families, going about their day instead of dying before her eyes. Thousands of human deaths were now on her conscience.

The Keiths were panicking now, and the room was filled with their shouts and arguments. They were deciding whether to run or to stay here, Mia realized with a sick feeling in her stomach. They had risked everything and lost—and now there would be consequences for their actions. And then the ceiling about their heads shattered, and the Keiths screamed in terror as the bright morning light streamed down, the hut above them apparently destroyed. Mia screamed too, diving for cover even as her brain told her that this wasn't real—that she was not the one in danger. Petrified, she huddled in the corner, hugging her knees against her chest and watching helplessly as other Ks jumped down into the room, dressed in the simple dark grey outfits that she recognized as their military uniforms.

The black-haired male sprang at one of the soldiers, his attack fast and sudden, his motions almost a blur to Mia's eyes—and he was thrown back just as fast, his body jerking uncontrollably as he collapsed on the floor.

Another soldier—their leader, Mia guessed—barked out a command, and the jerking motions stopped. The black-haired Keith was now unconscious. The other Keiths stood still, unwilling to share his fate, their expressions ranging from rage to bitter defeat. Whatever invisible weapons the soldiers possessed were clearly enough to dissuade the Keiths from fighting any further.

It was all over, Mia thought dully. Tears streamed down her face as she watched the soldiers place silvery circles around the Keiths' necks. The K version of handcuffs, perhaps . . . The circles locked into place with a faint click, and there was a sense of finality within that sound—the sound of defeat. The Resistance had lost, their forces utterly decimated and their alien allies captured. Operation Liberty had failed, and thousands of human lives had been lost. There would be no liberation of Earth, not today . . . and probably not ever.

Another K jumped down into the room then, his movements gracefully controlled. Unlike the others, he was dressed in human clothes, a pair of blue jeans and a beige T-shirt. And Mia recognized the familiar slash of dark eyebrows above piercing golden eyes, the sensuous mouth that now looked cruel, set in an uncompromising line in his strikingly beautiful face.

It was Korum. Her enemy, her lover . . . whose kind had just killed thousands of people before her very own eyes.

CHAPTER TWENTY-FOUR

Mia couldn't think, her entire body shaking from shock and fear as she watched Korum prowl toward the Keiths. The expression on his face was unlike anything she had ever seen before, a blend of icy fury and extreme contempt. He spoke to the brown-haired female in Krinar, his voice low and cold, and she flinched, as though he had physically slapped her. The other female interrupted, her tone pleading, and Korum turned his attention to her and said something that silenced her right away. The male Keiths just stared, their looks ranging from fear to defiance. Then Korum turned to the leader of the soldiers and asked him a question. Whatever answer he received made him nod, apparently satisfied.

"I asked him if all the other Centers were secured as well . . . in case you were curious about the translation."

Mia froze, her blood turning to ice. Slowly turning her head to the side, she looked into the gold-flecked eyes of the alien she had just been observing on the other side of the room.

This Korum was wearing the same clothes as his virtual alter ego, but the mocking half-smile on his face was different. So was the fact that he was looking straight at her and speaking in English. Out of the corner of her eye, she could see the drama continuing to unfold in the room, but it no longer mattered. Instead, all she could do was stare at the real-life version of her lover . . . who now undoubtedly knew about her betrayal.

"Fortunately, they were," he continued, his voice deceptively calm. "With the exception of the traitors you see before you, none of the Krinar were harmed. Only a few of our shield posts were destroyed, and they will be easily replaced within the next hour."

Mia could barely hear him above the roar of her heartbeat, his words not registering in the panicked whirl of her thoughts. *He knew.* He knew what she had done, and nothing she said or did would change the outcome. All she could hope for now was to delay the inevitable.

"H-how?" she croaked, her bloodless lips barely moving. Her throat felt strangely dry, and she could taste the saltiness of her own tears gathering in the corners of her mouth.

"How did I know?" Korum asked, approaching her corner and crouching down next to her. Raising his hand, he gently tucked the stray curl behind her ear and brushed his knuckles down the side of her face, his touch burning her frozen skin.

Mia nodded, trembling at his proximity.

"How could I not know, Mia?" he said softly. "Did you honestly think that I wouldn't realize what was taking place under my own roof? That I wouldn't know that the woman I slept with every night was working with my enemies?"

"Wh-what are you saying?" she whispered, her brain working agonizingly slowly. "Y-you knew all along?"

He smiled bitterly. "Of course. From the moment they

approached you and you agreed to spy for them, I knew."

"I don't . . . I don't understand. You knew and you let me do it anyway?"

"It was your choice, Mia. You could've said no. You could've refused them. And even after you agreed—at any point, you could've told me the truth, warned me. Even last night—you could've still told me. But you chose to lie to me, to the very end." His voice was oddly calm and remote, and that bitter expression still twisted his lips.

"But . . . but you knew—" Mia couldn't process that part, couldn't understand what he was telling her.

"I did," he said, reaching out to pick up a lock of her hair. "I knew, and I let things unfold as they will. It wasn't part of my original plan; it wasn't why I was in New York. I wanted to find and capture one of their leaders, to extract the identities of the traitors you saw today. But when you chose to betray me, I knew that a rare opportunity had presented itself—that we could strike a blow to the Resistance from which they would never recover . . . and I could catch the traitors in the process."

He paused, playing with her hair, twisting and untwisting the strand around his fingers. Mia stared at him, hypnotized, feeling like a rabbit caught by a snake.

"And so I played along. I gave you every chance to succeed in your treacherous mission—and you did. You turned out to be resourceful and clever, quite inventive really." His eyes took on a familiar golden gleam. "That night when you stole my designs was . . . memorable, to say the least. I very much enjoyed it."

Mia swallowed, beginning to realize where he was leading. "Y-you planted fake designs," she whispered, a searing agony spreading through her chest.

He nodded, a small triumphant smile curving his lips.

"I did. I gave them just enough rope so they could hang themselves with it. They learned how to disable the shields, but not how to keep them disabled. The weapon they were relying on wouldn't have functioned properly; I had designed it to work under testing conditions but not when it was really deployed. And I let them have a few minor weapons, so they could do some damage and get caught red-handed trying to escape ... like the cowards that they really are. I knew that they would trust you when you brought them the designs—because you had already given them enough real information by that point."

"So you used me," said Mia quietly, feeling like she was suffocating. The pain was indescribable, even though logically she knew she had no right to feel this way.

"It hurts, doesn't it?" he said astutely, a savage smile on his face. "It hurts to be the one used, the one betrayed ... doesn't it?"

"Was any of it real?" asked Mia bitterly. "Or was the whole thing a lie? Did you set it all up, right down to our meeting in the park?"

"Oh, it was real, all right," he said softly, now stroking the edge of her ear. "From the moment I saw you, I knew that I wanted you—more than anyone I've wanted in a very long time. And I grew to care about you, even though I knew it was foolish. With time, I hoped that you would feel the same way about me, that if I showed you how good it could be between us, you would realize what you were doing, the mistake that you were making. And you were close, I know ... Yet you still betrayed me in the end, not caring what happened, whether I would live or die—"

"No!" interrupted Mia, her eyes burning with a fresh set of tears. "That's not true! They promised me ... they promised you'd be all right, that they would give you safe passage back home—"

"Back to Krina?" he asked, his voice dangerously low. "Where I would be out of your life forever? And how would they have ensured that I stayed there?"

Mia could only stare at him. Somehow that thought had never crossed her mind. In the background, virtual Korum left the room, and so did the soldiers with their prisoners in tow.

He gave a short, harsh laugh. "I see. That never occurred to you, did it? That deportation was a temporary solution at best? No, the traitors would've never deported me ... I am too dangerous in their eyes because I have both the desire and the means to return to Earth with reinforcements—and that's the last thing they would want."

Mia felt like she'd been punched in the stomach. She hadn't known ... They'd lied to her. She couldn't have gone through with it, couldn't have done it knowing that he would be killed in the process. She had to convince him of that. "Korum," she said desperately, "I didn't know, I swear—"

He shook his head. "It doesn't matter," he said. "Even if you didn't mean for me to get killed, you still had every intention of exiling me from your life forever, you still betrayed me ... and that's not something I can forgive easily."

"So what now?" asked Mia wearily. She was beginning to feel numb, and she welcomed the sensation, as it took the edge off her terror and pain. "Are you going to kill me?"

He stared at her, his gaze turning a colder yellow. "Kill you? Did you listen to anything I said in the last ten minutes?"

He wasn't going to kill her? The numbness spread, and she could only look at him, unable to feel anything more than a vague sense of relief.

At her lack of reply, he said slowly, "No, Mia. I'm not going to kill you. I've already told you that before. I'm not the unfeeling monster you persist in thinking me to be."

Getting up in one lithe motion, Korum waved his hand, and Mia shut her eyes, seeing the virtual world dissolving around her. When she opened them again, she was sitting on the floor of Korum's office, against the wall, still hugging her knees to her chest.

Bending down, he offered her his hand. Her fingers trembling, Mia placed her hand in his, allowing him to help her up. To her embarrassment, her legs were shaking, and she swayed slightly. Letting out a sigh, he caught her, swinging her up into his arms and carrying her out of the office.

"Where are you taking me?" asked Mia in confusion, disoriented after the recent reality shift. Oh God, surely he wasn't thinking of having sex right now; she didn't think she could bear that kind of intimacy after everything that happened.

"To the kitchen," Korum replied, walking swiftly. Before she could ask him why, they were there, and he was setting her down on one of the chairs. Mia blinked up at him, too drained to attempt to understand his inexplicable behavior.

"When was the last time you had something to eat?" he asked, looking at her with a slight frown on his face.

"Um . . . last night." Mia couldn't fathom where he was going with this.

He nodded, as though she had confirmed something for him. "No wonder you're so shaky," he said reprovingly. "You didn't eat breakfast, and your blood sugar is low." Walking to the refrigerator, he filled a glass with some clear liquid and brought it to her. "Drink this, while I make you something to eat," he ordered, ignoring the incredulous look on Mia's face.

He wanted to feed her right now? Was he serious? Cautiously sniffing the glass, Mia discerned a faintly sweet coconut scent. What the hell, she decided, if he wanted her dead, she sincerely doubted he would use poison to kill her. Taking a sip, she realized that her nose hadn't lied; Korum had indeed given her fresh coconut water to drink. It was exactly what her body was craving right now, a perfect blend of carbohydrates and electrolytes. The frozen numbness that had been encasing her like armor began to crack, and tears welled up in Mia's eyes again. Why was he acting like this now, after everything that she had done to him?

Finishing her drink, she watched him move about the kitchen, making her an avocado-tomato sandwich. Now that the main adrenaline rush was over, she was starting to think again, her brain beginning to function at some fraction of its normal ability. The truth about their relationship had been revealed. This entire time she'd thought that she was spying on him for the benefit of all humanity, but he had really been using her to crush the Resistance once and for all. All those lives today had been lost because of her . . . No, she couldn't focus on that now, or she would shatter into a million pieces.

She concentrated on the puzzle of Korum's intentions instead. He wasn't going to kill her, he'd said. But would he punish her in some other way? She couldn't imagine that he would want her around after the way she had betrayed him. Their farce of a relationship was over. He had won: Earth would remain firmly under Krinar control. And Mia had outlived her usefulness. He didn't need an unwitting double agent anymore—

"Here, eat this," the object of her musings said, placing the sandwich in front of her and sitting down across the table. "And then we'll talk."

"Thank you," Mia said politely and obediently bit into the sandwich. Her stomach growled, and she was suddenly starving, her lumberjack appetite making its appearance despite the trauma of this morning's events. In less than a minute, she had devoured the sandwich and looked up, slightly embarrassed by her greediness. The smile on his face was a genuine one this time, and she remembered that he liked that about her—the healthy appetite she possessed despite her small size.

"So what now?" Mia repeated her earlier question, and Korum's smile faded. He regarded her with an inscrutable gaze, and Mia shifted in her seat, growing increasingly nervous.

"So now," Korum said quietly, "you will come with me while I help clean up this mess."

Mia felt all blood drain from her face. "Come with you where?" Surely he couldn't mean—

A small smile appeared on his lips. "To the same place you went while snooping this morning: Lenkarda, our settlement in Costa Rica."

All of a sudden, there wasn't enough air in the room for Mia to breathe properly, and the sandwich felt like a rock inside her stomach. What was he saying? He couldn't still want her, not after everything . . .

"Why?" she managed to squeeze out, staring at him in horrified disbelief.

"Because, Mia, I want you with me, and I can't stay in

New York any longer," he said calmly, with an unreadable expression on his face. "I've been away far too long. There are things that require my attention—not the least of which is what to do with the traitors."

Mia shook her head, trying to get rid of the mental fog that seemed to be slowing her thinking. "B-but why do you want me with you?" she stammered. "You were just using me—"

"I was using *you* because you chose to betray *me*—don't ever forget that, darling," he said in a dangerously silky tone. "I've wanted you from the very beginning, and nothing you've done changes that fact. You're mine, and you'll remain with me for as long as I want you. Do you understand that?"

There was a dull roaring in her ears. "No," she whispered, her words barely audible. "No. I'm not going anywhere. I won't be a slave ... I refuse, do you hear me?" Her voice had risen in volume with each sentence until she was almost yelling at him, the red mist of fury taking over her vision and getting rid of any remnants of caution.

"A slave?" he asked with a puzzled frown on his face. And then his forehead smoothed out as he apparently realized what she was talking about. "Ah, yes, I almost forgot that you've been laboring under a misconception this whole time. You're referring to being my charl, aren't you?"

"I will not be your charl!" Mia snarled, her hands clenching into fists under the table.

"You will be anything I wish you to be, my darling," he said softly, a mocking smile curving his lips. "However, your friends in the Resistance have misinformed you—either inadvertently or on purpose—about the real meaning of charl."

Her temper cooling slightly, Mia stared at him. "What do you mean? Are you telling me that you *don't* keep humans in your Centers as your . . . pleasure slaves?" She spit out the last words with disgust.

He shook his head, with that same sardonic look on his face. "No, Mia. A charl is a human companion—a human mate, if you will. It's a unique term that we use to describe a special bond between a human and a Krinar. Being a charl is a privilege, an honor—not whatever it is that you've been imagining."

"A privilege to be with you against my will?" asked Mia bitterly. "To be forced to go where I don't want to go—unable to see my family, my friends?"

"Don't lie to me, Mia," he said quietly. "Or to yourself. Being with me is hardly a chore for you. Do you think I don't know why you've been crying this week? You need me . . . just as much as I need you. What we have together is rare and special—even though you've done your best to tear us apart. If I were young and foolish, I would let my hurt and anger get the best of me . . . and leave you, full of bitterness at your betrayal. But I've been around long enough to understand that when you find a good thing, you hold on to it; you don't throw it away on a whim."

"Really? You hold on to it even if the other person doesn't want you?" said Mia sarcastically, infuriated by his arrogant assumption that he knew all about her feelings. Maybe she *had* fallen for him; maybe she'd even thought she loved him—but that was before she knew how he'd used her, before she witnessed the deaths of thousands of human soldiers as a result of what he'd done. He might be able to get over his hurt and anger, but Mia couldn't be so magnanimous right now.

"Oh, you want me," Korum said softly. "That much I

know for a fact. Would you like me to prove it?"

And before she could come up with a retort, he was next to her, swinging her up into his arms and bringing her toward him for a deep kiss, his tongue pushing into the recesses of her mouth. Infuriated, Mia tried to remain impassive, to temper her response, but her body didn't know, didn't care that he was about to ruin her life. It only knew the pleasure of his touch, and Mia found herself melting against him, her hands clinging to his shoulders instead of pushing him away. A familiar wave of heat swept through her, and she felt a surge of moisture between her legs, her body eagerly preparing itself for his possession.

Still holding her in his arms, he walked somewhere, and Mia was too far gone to care where. They ended up in the living room, and he lowered her onto the couch, still kissing her with those deep, penetrating kisses that never failed to make her crazy. She heard the zipper of her jeans getting unfastened, and then he was tugging them off her legs along with her sneakers, leaving her lower body clad only in a pair of white lacy panties. His thumb found the sensitive nub between her legs, and he pressed on it through the underwear, circling it in a way that made her insides tighten, and Mia moaned helplessly, arching toward him, wanting more of the magic that she had only experienced in his arms.

He let go of her then, taking a step back to remove his own clothes, stripping off the T-shirt with one smooth motion and then swiftly taking off his jeans and underwear, leaving himself fully naked. Mia stared at him with unabashed lust, taking in the powerful muscles covered with that beautiful bronzed skin, the smattering of dark hair on his chest, and the hairy trail on his lower abdomen leading down to a large, fully aroused cock, with the heavy balls swinging underneath.

He didn't let her enjoy the view for long, grasping her shirt to pull it over her head and unclasping her bra. A second later, her panties were pulled off her legs and joined the heap of clothes lying on the floor. He paused for a second, raking her naked body with a burning gaze, and then he bent over her, his hot mouth closing over her left breast, sucking on it. Mia moaned, feeling the pull of his mouth deep within her belly, and he sucked on the other breast, his tongue flicking over her nipple in a way that made her desperately wish his head was two feet lower. As though reading her mind, he touched her wet folds with his hand, one finger pushing into her opening, pressing on the ultra-sensitive spot inside her pussy, and Mia gasped from the intensity of the sensation, her body throbbing on the verge of release. Without removing his finger, he brought his mouth down toward her sex, his tongue finding its way inside her folds to tease the area directly around her clit. At the same time, his finger moved slightly within her, starting to find a rhythm, and Mia's entire body tensed as the tingles of pre-orgasmic sensation began to radiate from her lower regions outward. His tongue flicked at her nub, first lightly and then with increasing pressure, and Mia screamed under the almost cruel lash of pleasure, her inner muscles clamping down on his finger and then pulsating with the aftershocks of the release.

Withdrawing his finger, he flipped her over, pulling her toward the edge of the couch. Lifting her briefly, he placed her so that she was bent over the plush couch arm, face down and her feet on the floor. Covering her with his body, he began to push inside her, his cock penetrating her inch by slow inch. Mia was soft and wet from the orgasm, and her body accepted his gradual entrance, the tender inner tissues stretching and expanding to accommodate the intrusion. As he pushed forward, he kissed the side of her neck, and she shivered, the tension starting to build again. Her sex spasmed around his cock, and he groaned in response, sheathing himself fully within her. Mia inhaled sharply from the feel of his shaft buried to the hilt; he was impossibly hard and thick, and she felt like she was burning from the heat of him inside her, over her, all around her.

And then he began to move, his thrusts pressing her deeper into the arm of the couch. Every muscle in her body tensed, and she cried out, each stroke intensifying the agonizing pleasure, until her world narrowed to nothing more than the cock moving back and forth within her body and she existed purely for the sensations, stripped down to the raw and elemental parts of her animal nature. She could hear the rhythmic cries in the distance and knew that they had to be her own, and then the massive climax swept through her, her inner muscles rippling around him and her entire body trembling from the shock of the orgasmic wave. And, with a hoarse shout, he was coming too, his hips grinding into her as his cock pulsed inside her with his own contractions.

When it was all over, he withdrew from her, leaving her lying there naked, still bent over the sofa arm. Without his large body covering her, Mia suddenly felt cold—and the realization of what had just happened added to the icy knot growing inside her. Standing up on quivering legs, Mia bent down to pick up her clothes, refusing to look at him and trying to ignore the wetness sliding down her leg. With the heat of passion over, her anger returned, magnified by the shame of her unwanted response to him.

"Mia," he said softly, and out of the corner of her eye,

she saw him standing there, completely unconcerned about his nakedness. She turned away, putting on her bra, and using her shirt to wipe off the traces of the sex session before putting on her underwear. Pulling on her jeans, she felt slightly better, but the cold fury inside remained. Without even thinking about it, she walked over to the little purse she'd left sitting on the couch earlier this morning. Reaching inside, she pulled out the little device Leslie had given her and pointed it in his direction.

"I'm leaving," she said with icy calm. A stranger seemed to have taken over her body, and the normal Mia couldn't help but marvel at her daring, even though she knew that her odds of success were nil.

At the sight of the weapon, the golden glow in Korum's eyes cooled.

"That's a dangerous toy you have there," he said quietly, staring at her with an unreadable expression on his face.

Mia nodded coolly. "Don't force me to use it."

"So you walk out of here, and then what?" he asked with mild curiosity. "There's nowhere you can go where I won't find you."

Mia hadn't thought that far; in fact, there'd been no thinking involved in her actions at all. It was too late now, though, so she just shrugged and said bravely, "I'll cross that bridge when I get there."

"Are you going to go on the run? Change your identity?" he continued, an amused note appearing in his voice. "None of that would work, you know."

"Because of the tracking stuff you put in me without my knowledge or consent?" she asked bitterly.

Korum just looked at her, neither admitting nor denying it. "There's only one way you could be free of me," he said slowly.

Mia stared at him in frustration, not understanding where he was leading. Now that the initial wave of fury had passed, the full stupidity of her actions dawned on her. He was right; even if she managed to walk out of his penthouse—a big if, given the laser-quick reflexes she was up against—he would catch her before she could go more than a few blocks. By pointing that weapon at him, she had only succeeded in angering him, and she felt a tendril of fear at the thought.

"And what way is that?" she asked, deciding to stall for time.

"You could shoot me," he said seriously. "And then all your problems would be solved."

Horrified, Mia gaped at him. The idea of actually pressing the button and watching him dissolve before her eyes, like those shield posts at the colony, was unthinkable. She'd never had any intention of actually using the weapon. All she'd wanted was to regain some measure of control, to feel like she was in charge of her own life. She'd wanted to threaten him, to make him bow to her will, to make him feel the way she felt when he took away her freedom of choice. She'd never wanted to hurt him, much less kill him.

"Go ahead, Mia," he said softly. His powerful naked body was relaxed, as though they were having a regular conversation—as though he didn't have a deadly weapon pointed at him. "Go ahead and shoot."

Her fingers trembled, her palms slick with sweat, and she felt her eyes burning with stupid, unwelcome tears. "Please," she said, not caring anymore that she sounded like she was begging. "Please don't make me do it. I just want to leave . . . to go home. Please just let me walk out of here—"

"Just press the button, Mia. And then you can go

wherever you want."

Mia felt hot and cold, her stomach twisting with nausea. The tiny device in her hand was suddenly unbearably heavy, and her arm shook with the effort of holding it pointed at him. The tears spilled over, running down her cheeks, and she lowered the weapon, sinking down to the floor, her trembling legs unable to hold her any longer. Burying her face in her hands, she cried, bitter at her own cowardice, her own idiocy. She couldn't hurt him, couldn't kill him; she would have sooner cut off her own limb. How could she feel this way about him even now? What was wrong with her that she had fallen in love with someone who wasn't even human . . . an alien whose kind had just murdered thousands of people?

In the depths of her despair, she felt him wrap his arms around her, lifting her from the floor and onto his lap on the couch. "Hush, my darling," he whispered, "everything will be all right, I promise. I wouldn't have been able to press that button either—and I'm glad you couldn't." He stroked her hair gently while she cried into his naked shoulder. After a few minutes, her sobs began to quiet. Feeling embarrassed about her outburst, Mia tried to pull away, but he didn't let her, lifting her chin instead to look her in the eye.

"Mia," he said softly, "I'm not taking you with me to be cruel. After everything that happened, the Resistance—or whatever is left of it—will be looking for you. They don't know the full story, and they'll think you set them up. They'll spare no effort in trying to kill you, and if they figure out how much you mean to me, they'll try to capture you alive to use you against me. I'm sorry, but I have no choice. It's simply not safe for you to be anywhere but in Lenkarda right now."

Mia stared at him, her vision still blurred by tears. She

hadn't thought about that, but it was true. As far as the Resistance was concerned, she was a traitor to all of humankind. They would definitely blame her for the huge loss of life she'd just witnessed. A terrifying thought occurred to her. "What about my family?" she asked, everything inside her turning to ice at the possibility that the freedom fighters might try to hurt those she loved.

"Your family had nothing to do with it, and I doubt the fighters would be vengeful enough to needlessly harm fellow humans. But your kind can be very unpredictable, so I will make sure that several of our best guardians are stationed near your family, to keep an eye out for them."

Mia opened her mouth to ask, but he forestalled her. "And no, that wouldn't be enough to ensure *your* safety. There are still a few key Resistance leaders unaccounted for, and they're armed with some Krinar weapons. I expect them to go into hiding and leave your family alone, but they may be willing to risk everything to get to *you*. So until they're apprehended, you will be safest in Lenkarda. And if you have to venture out, it will be with me by your side."

How convenient for him, Mia thought bitterly, he could now keep her prisoner with good justification. Of course, the Resistance would want to kill her—and they would be right to do so. She was responsible for all those deaths today . . .

"How many people were killed this morning?" asked Mia, feeling like she wanted to die herself.

Korum shrugged slightly. "I don't know if the medics got to the ones who were burned fast enough to save them. Some of them might have died from their encounter with the shield."

"What about all the other ones, the ones who were hit with that red light?" asked Mia, her heart beginning to pound in wild hope.

"They were knocked unconscious—and so were the ones who attacked our other Centers. They deserved to die, of course, but we decided to let your governments deal with them. It'll be interesting to see what their punishment will be for violating the Coexistence Treaty and endangering your entire species in the process."

The relief that Mia felt was indescribable. The painful grip in her chest seemed to ease, letting her breathe freely for the first time since she'd witnessed the attack.

And then Korum added, "Of course, we're not going to leave it to chance. All those fighters now have surveillance devices embedded in their bodies, so we'll know everything they do and everywhere they go. They've been effectively neutralized as a threat to us, and we can now use them to catch the rest—those that were not near our Centers today."

So he had succeeded in his mission of squashing the Resistance movement. Given the number of fighters lying on the field, Ks would now have thousands of walking, talking surveillance mechanisms all over the globe. It was quite clever really; why bother killing a human when you could use him instead? Pure Korum deviousness at work.

She must've looked upset because he said, "Mia, stop worrying about this. The Resistance is over. It was a foolish movement to begin with. Just think about it. So they don't like us being here and changing a few things. Is that really a good reason to risk so many lives? You have to admit, we're nothing like the alien invaders of your movies. We have no desire to enslave humans, or to take away your planet. If that had been our agenda, we would've already done it. We settled here as peacefully as possible, living in our Centers with minimal interference in human affairs. That's far better than what your

Europeans had done to the American natives."

Still sitting on his lap, Mia looked away. If Korum was telling her the truth and John had lied about the meaning of charl, then the entire Resistance movement was misguided at best—and criminally irresponsible at worst.

"And do you honestly think it would've been a good thing for you to have those seven traitors as your rulers? Because, believe me, that's what they would've been. They wanted power, and they didn't care who got hurt as a result of their actions. Do you really think they would've been content to live quietly among humans, obeying your every law and selflessly sharing Krinar knowledge?"

Now that Korum put it that way, Mia could see the implausibility of what John had originally told her. Maybe the Resistance leaders had thought they could somehow control the Keiths once the other Ks had left—but that could've easily been a dangerous assumption to make. Mia mentally kicked herself. Why hadn't she probed further into the Keiths' motivations? But no, she'd blindly gone with what John was telling her, too caught up in her own personal drama to fully think about anything else.

Korum sighed, and she felt the movement of his chest. "Look, it won't be so bad being in Lenkarda, believe me. Aren't you the least bit curious to see how we live?"

Mia looked up at him again, feeling completely drained. "Korum, I just can't... I can't simply leave everything and everyone—"

"What if I take you to see your family in a couple of weeks as we originally discussed?" he asked softly. "Would that make you feel better?"

"We'd go to Florida?" asked Mia in surprise.

He nodded. "You could spend a few days with them

before we have to go back."

She smiled, the pressure in her chest easing further. "That would be wonderful," she said quietly.

He smiled back and gently brushed a curl off her face. "And hopefully, by the end of the summer, we'll catch the rest of the Resistance fighters—so if you still want to come back to New York then, we'll return here and you can finish your last year of school."

Mia blinked at him, hardly daring to believe her ears. "You'll bring me back here?"

"I will . . . if you still want to return by then." Getting up, he placed her gently on her feet. "Now put on a shirt and some shoes while I get dressed. It's time to go."

* * *

Korum allowed her to take her purse with its entire contents, the weapon excluded, and nothing else. When she protested that she needed her computer and her clothes, he laughed. "I promise you, there's plenty of everything where we're going," he explained with a smile.

"What about my passport?" she asked, and then realized that it was a stupid question. She might be heading to a foreign country, but she sincerely doubted she would be going through airport security. Somehow, Korum had managed to travel there this morning and then come back to New York—all within a span of a couple of hours. No, thought Mia, they likely wouldn't be traveling by airplane.

Her suppositions turned out to be correct.

He led her into his office, holding her hand as if afraid she would bolt. Walking toward the back of the room, he held his other hand in front of the wall and it slid open, revealing stairs that likely led to the rooftop.

"Come," Korum said, and she followed him with hesitation, her pulse racing at the thought of where she was going. It was too late to turn back now—not that he would have let her—and Mia felt a heady mixture of excitement and fear rushing through her veins as she walked up the stairs.

They exited onto the rooftop, and Mia looked around. She wasn't sure what she was expecting to see—perhaps some alien aircraft sitting there. But there was nothing. The roof was empty, with the exception of some evergreen shrubs growing in neat rows around the perimeter. The rain had mostly stopped, but it was still wet and humid outside, and Mia could practically feel her curls frizzing up from the moisture in the air.

"What are we doing here?" she asked in surprise. "Is someone coming to get us?"

Korum shook his head and smiled. "No, we're going by ourselves."

"How?" asked Mia, burning with curiosity.

"You'll see in a second. Don't be afraid, okay?" He squeezed her palm reassuringly.

Mia nodded, and Korum let go of her hand, taking a step forward. Extending his arm, he made a gesture, as though pointing at the empty space in front of him. All of a sudden, Mia could hear a low humming. The sound was unlike anything Mia had heard before—too quiet and even to be the buzzing of insects.

"What is that?" she asked warily, wondering if Korum intended to teleport them somewhere. Mia had no idea what the limitations of K technology were, but she did know that Krinar physics had to have gone far beyond Einstein's theories; otherwise, the Ks wouldn't have been able to travel faster than the speed of light. Who knew what else they could do?

Korum turned toward her, his eyes glittering with some unknown emotion. "It's the sound of the nanomachines that I just released. They're building us our ride." And Mia realized that he was excited, pleased to be going home.

Something began to shimmer in front of them. Goosebumps appeared on Mia's arms as she stared in fascination at the strange sight. The shimmering intensified, as if a bucket of glitter had been thrown in front of them—and then the walls of the aircraft began to form in front of her eyes.

Barely holding back a gasp, Mia watched as the structure assembled itself, seemingly out of nothingness. The walls slowly solidified, thickening layer by layer, and then a small pod-like aircraft stood in front of them. It appeared to be made out of some unusual ivory material, with no visible windows or doors, and was smaller than a helicopter.

Mia exhaled sharply, releasing a breath she had been holding for the last thirty seconds.

"It's called advanced rapid fabrication technology," Korum said, smiling at the look of utter astonishment on her face. "It's one of our most useful inventions. Come with me." And taking her hand again, he led her toward the newly assembled structure.

As they approached, the wall of the pod simply disintegrated, creating an entrance for them. Mia blinked in shock, but followed Korum inside the aircraft. Once they were in, the wall re-solidified, and the entrance disappeared again.

The inside of the pod did not look like any aircraft she could have ever imagined. The walls, the floor, and the ceiling were transparent—she could see the ivory color of her surroundings, but she could also see the world outside. It was as though they were inside a giant glass bubble, even though Mia knew that the structure was not see-through from the outside. There were no buttons or controls of any kind, nothing to suggest that the pod had any kind of complex electronics. And instead of seats, there were two white oval planks floating in the air.

"Have a seat," Korum said, gesturing toward one of the planks.

"On that?" Mia had known that Krinar technology was far more advanced, of course, and she had expected to encounter some unbelievable things. But this . . . this was like stepping into some fairy realm where the normal laws of physics didn't seem to apply—and she hadn't even left New York yet.

He laughed, apparently amused by her distrust. "On that. You won't fall, I promise."

Warily, still clutching his hand, Mia perched gingerly on the plank. It moved beneath her, and she gasped as it conformed to the shape of her butt, suddenly turning into the most comfortable chair she had ever occupied. There was a back now too, and Mia found herself leaning into it, her tense muscles relaxing, soothed by the strangely cozy sensation.

Grinning, Korum sat down on a similar plank next to her, and Mia stared in amazement as the white material shifted around his body, fitting itself to his shape. She was still holding his hand with a death grip, Mia realized with some embarrassment, and she let go, trying to act as nonchalantly as possible when confronted with technology that seemed exactly like magic.

Korum nodded approvingly and waved his hand slightly.

Softly, without making a sound, the pod lifted off the ground, rising swiftly into the air. With a sinking sensation in her stomach, Mia looked down at the see-through floor, watching New York City shrinking rapidly beneath them as they gained altitude. Surprisingly, she didn't feel nauseated or pushed into her seat as one might expect during such a swift ascent; it was as though she was sitting in a chair at home, instead of rocketing straight up.

"Why don't I feel like we're flying at all?" she asked curiously, looking up from the floor where she could now see only clouds.

"The ship is equipped with a mild anti-gravitational field," Korum explained. "It's designed to make us comfortable by keeping the gravitational force at the same level as you'd experience normally on this planet; otherwise, accelerating like that would be very unpleasant for me—and probably deadly for you."

And then she could see clouds whizzing underneath them as the pod traveled at an incredible speed, taking her to a place that few humans could even imagine, much less visit in person. Never in a million years could Mia have thought that a simple walk in the park could lead to this, that she would be sitting in an alien ship headed for the main Krinar colony . . . that she would feel like this about the beautiful extraterrestrial who was sitting beside her.

A couple of minutes later, they seemed to have reached their destination, and the ship began its descent.

"Welcome home, darling," Korum said softly as the green landscape of Lenkarda appeared beneath their feet, and the ship landed as quietly as it had taken off.

Mia's new life had begun.

FROM THE AUTHOR

Thank you for reading *Close Liaisons*, the first book in the Krinar Chronicles series! I hope you enjoyed it. If you did, please mention it to your friends and social media connections. I would also be hugely grateful if you helped other readers discover the book by leaving a review on Amazon, Goodreads, or other sites.

Mia & Korum's story continues in *Close Obsession* and concludes in *Close Remembrance*. Both books are currently available. There will also be other novels with different characters set in the Krinar world, as well as books in contemporary settings. Please visit my website at www.annazaires.com and sign up for my newsletter to be notified when new books become available.

ABOUT THE AUTHOR

Anna Zaires fell in love with books at the age of five, when her grandmother taught her to read. She wrote her first story shortly thereafter. Since then, she has always lived partially in a fantasy world where the only limits were those of her imagination. Currently residing in Florida, Anna is happily married to Dima Zales and closely collaborates with him in the writing of the Krinar Chronicles.

To learn more, please visit www.annazaires.com.

CPSIA information can be obtained at www.ICGtesting.com
Printed in the USA
LVOW04s1511030415

433204LV00014B/305/P